Praise for *A Brutal Chill in*

"With *A Brutal Chill in August*, Alan ... his terrific fictionalized accounts of the Ripper's victims—always compelling, and always expertly evoking nineteenth century London. Gripping, suspenseful—written with sensitivity and heart."

—Simon Clark, author of *Night of the Triffids*

"*A Brutal Chill in August,* one of a series wherein Alan Clark masterfully recreates the sorry lives of the Ripper's victims, is awash in atmospheric detail of those dark days in 19th century London. Exhaustively researched, Clark brings to life the plight of London's poor, and the extremes to which they must go in order to merely survive...or succumb as victims to disease, abuse, alcoholism, or worse. A great read."

—Elizabeth Engstrom, author of *Lizzie Borden*

"*A Brutal Chill in August* does a fantastic job of taking you on a mental time-travel jaunt. Full immersion, all too vivid and real. [...] Alan M. Clark is as masterful a writer as he is an artist; sure to blow you away. [...] Historical fiction done right. I cannot love it enough."

—Christine Morgan, *The Horror Fiction Review*

A Brutal Chill
in August

Other Books by Alan M. Clark

The Paint in My Blood
Siren Promised (co-written with Jeremy Robert Johnson)
Pain & Other Petty Plots to Keep You in Stitches
The Blood of Father Time, Book 1, The New Cut (co-authored with Stephen C. Merritt and Lorelei Shannon)
The Blood of Father Time, Book 2, The Mystic Clan's Grand Plot (co-authored with Stephen C. Merritt and Lorelei Shannon)
D.D. Murphry, Secret Policeman (co-written with Elizabeth Massie)
Boneyard Babies
Of Thimble and Threat: The Life of a Ripper Victim
A Parliament of Crows
The Door That Faced West
Say Anything But Your Prayers
The Surgeon's Mate: A Dismemoir

A Brutal Chill
in August

A NOVEL OF POLLY NICHOLS
THE FIRST VICTIM OF JACK THE RIPPER

Alan M. Clark

WORD HORDE
PETALUMA, CA

First Edition

ISBN 978-1-939905-25-3

A Word Horde Book

For all the murder victims forgotten
in the excitement over the assholes who kill.

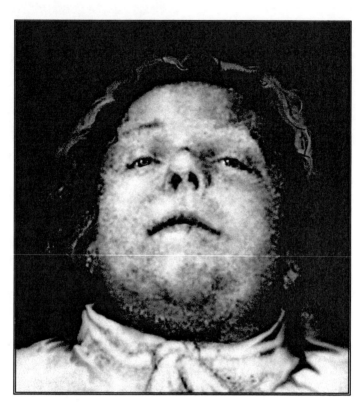

In an effort to bring life to an image of Mary Ann "Polly" Nichols, the author digitally manipulated a mortuary photo of the woman to arrive at this portrait.

Author's Note

A Chill in London

This is a work of fiction inspired by the life of Mary Ann "Polly" Nichols, a woman believed to be the first victim of Jack the Ripper. For purposes of storytelling, I have not adhered strictly to her history and I have changed the names of the principal characters subtly. I have assigned to my main character emotional characteristics and reactions that seem consistent with her life and circumstances. This novel is not primarily about Jack the Ripper, but is instead about Mrs. Nichols's survival within the increasingly difficult and dangerous social and economic environment of London, England between the years of her birth, 1845, and that of her death, 1888.

The summer of 1888 had been a chilly one. In suburbs of London, snowfall had been reported in the small hours of the morning on July 11. Since the cataclysmic eruption of the Indonesian volcano, Krakatoa, which had thrown fine ash high into the atmosphere five years earlier, the climate in the northern hemisphere had been significantly cooler.

In London, a cold-blooded killer would soon begin the work for which he'd be known. What we don't know is how selective Jack the Ripper was in choosing his victims, whether he acted spontaneously or was attracted to prey with certain traits. The five canonical victims were women. They were impoverished. Each of them had engaged in prostitution. Most were in their forties. Perhaps all were alcoholics. All of these traits were to be found in his first victim, Mary Ann "Polly" Nichols.

On the night of her death, August 30/31, a Thursday night and a Friday morning, the temperature in London hovered around 50 degrees Fahrenheit. The social chill in the city that followed would be much worse, as the police were powerless to stop the killer and the murders continued into the autumn with at least four more victims.

To understand the extraordinary furor in London over the Ripper killings, one must know something about the frequency and variety of death that already occurred within the Whitechapel area of the time. The murder rate was quite low. Disease took most lives at a younger age than today. The rate of industry-related deaths (violent accidents or chemically induced) was quite high, as was the suicide rate and the infant mortality rate (at least 30%, but probably closer to 50% died before the age of 5). The average human being had an expected life span of around forty years. Many prostitutes were brutalized and much violent crime occurred during the years between 1887 to 1889, yet few who died were seen to be murders. Perhaps this is attributable to the desire of authorities to keep quiet about the crime rate during a time of swift economic change and social upheaval. Whatever the case, the violence characteristic of the Ripper killings, with multiple stabbings and apparent sexual degradation of the victims suggesting piquerism on the part of the killer, certainly surprised the citizens of London.

The city's East End was filled with the poor, many of them immigrants. Most suffered under a class system that maintained a sharp division between the haves and have-nots. Due to the resentment this naturally caused, the idea that the killer might be a gentleman slumming in Whitechapel and killing for pleasure was not unbelievable to many in the lower class. Within the upper classes, many believed the lower classes were spoiling for a rebellion, and saw the murders as just another indication of the moral corruption of the denizens of the East End.

Fear on the streets resulting from the Ripper murders became so powerful that groups among all classes began to fight against it. Although many weren't in agreement over the causes of or solution to the outrage, the conversation or argument that followed helped bring attention to the sad conditions in which people lived within the city's East End. Their anger became a hot response to the chill in London in the summer of 1888, one that ignited a fire that slowly brought change to the city.

As we continually face questions about the worth of those with little versus those with much, the banked coals of that fire ignited in London in 1888 still smolder.

Likely, Mrs. Nichols would have been surprised to learn of the history that flowed from the moment of her death. Like many throughout history, she had a simple life, but not one without controversies and drama. As with all of our stories, simple or complex, rich or poor, it's the emotional content and context that counts.

—Alan M. Clark
Eugene, Oregon

1
Tell Me a Dreadful

London, August 31, 1858, during the Great Stink

Polly knew the presence of the jar of gin troubled Bernice Godwin.

"Won't we become drunk?" Bernice asked. The outer corners of her eyes angled downward, giving her a look too serious for a child.

Sarah Brown had complained about that look before. At present, she sat watching Bernice with contempt in her green eyes. Polly knew Sarah disliked Bernice because the Godwin girl had bowed legs and suffered frequent nose bleeds.

Martha Combs shrugged. "We all have gin when the air and water go bad."

Bernice slowly shook her head. "*In* our *water*. Even then, I don't like it."

You'd better learn to like it, Polly thought, remembering the misery her brother, Fredrick, experienced as cholera took his life a few years earlier.

Carrying the stench of the river Thames, a bitter haze in the hot autumn air swept by the girls and moved up the narrow lane between the leaning buildings toward the setting sun. For the past two months, during what was commonly called the Great Stink, Gunpowder Alley had belonged to Polly and her three friends since adults didn't willingly endure the smell out-doors for long. In the late afternoon, the girls sat on the rotting crates and half-barrels normally occupied by hard-drinking men. They talked, played games, and shared what they could, like the gin.

Martha hid the jar of strong drink under the hem of her skirt as people walked by, yet the adults who used the alley on the way to their night shifts hurried past, intent on their own business, not the girls. Polly and Bernice knew most of them as neighbors in the lodging house behind them. All but Mr. Edgar completely ignored the girls. As he went by, he paused beside them. "You want to get in out of the stink before you catch your death," he said, and quickly moved on.

Even fragile Bernice rolled her eyes at that. Her uncle, Benjamin Sand, worked the sewers as a tosher. His two sons had recently joined the ranks of countless mudlarks, who scavenged along the banks of the river. They earned their crust working amidst the worst of the smell. "Would he have us shut up indoors in this heat?" she scoffed.

"Not me," Polly said. "I'm with you." For much of July, when the extraordinarily high reek coming from the Thames was at its worst, she'd stayed indoors. Fear of the various diseases borne on bad smells had fed the city-wide uproar over the Great Stink. Those who could, had fled London, at least temporarily. Parliament had shut down. While those of a higher station had the luxury of avoiding exposure, the lower classes took their chances in order to keep their livelihoods. Although much of Polly's work was done indoors, she had become so lonely, hot, and miserable through July that enduring the odor for a bit of freedom didn't seem so bad in August, especially as the stink had lessened somewhat.

"Bernice," Sarah said, sneering, "you don't have to have

any of the gin. Leaves more for the rest of us." As Bernice looked downcast, Sarah turned to Martha. "How did you get so much?"

Martha shrugged, pushed the red hair out of her round face, and pulled the jar out from under the hem of her skirt. "Last night, when Da sent me to the Black Dog with his bottle to fetch his drink, I poured off half of the pint into the jar. Filled his bottle back up with water, I did. He calls the publican a macer for giving me watered-down drink, but he never suspects me. I've done it twice before for my brother. Today, it's for us. We're celebrating Polly's birthday."

"That were five days ago," Polly said.

"So, we're late," Martha said. "Let this be your *new* birthday."

"Yes. Why not? Papa and Eddie didn't remember me on the twenty-sixth. My new birthday is August thirty-first."

"In honor of your birthday," Martha said, holding the jar up in a toast. She took a sip of the filched gin, made a face, and passed the jar. Polly accepted the drink eagerly since she hadn't had anything to eat since early morning. Her father had promised to bring home potatoes. Although Fridays were usually a short day for him, had he come home on time, she would not be with her friends, but busy fixing supper. She'd done her piece work, fur pulling, for the last ten hours. Polly relished the break in the monotony of doing what she considered her mother's work. She had few fond memories of Caroline. With her death, Polly had left school and her friends there to begin a life of toil.

Polly raised the jar to her lips, held her breath, and swallowed quickly to avoid tasting the horrible liquid. Unadulterated and fiery, the gin forced a painful cough from her. She quickly offered the jar to Bernice. Predictably the girl shook her head. Polly passed the gin to Sarah.

Polly's Papa wasn't the drunk Martha's Da was, nor as gullible. He and her brother, Eddie, locksmiths by trade, worked a barrow with a foldout workbench on the street most of each day. If she did her chores and her piece work, her father didn't bother to keep up with her activities. In what precious free time the young girl had, she did as she pleased.

"Bernice lost the game last time, so she has to go first," Martha said, "and then it's my turn."

Bernice smiled nervously, nodded, and swallowed hard. Sarah mocked her. Clearly, Bernice didn't like the game, but as clearly, she wanted the other girls to like her. The late light caught her face as she narrowed her pale blue eyes with a defiant look, glancing left and right along the alley before beginning. "The Bonehill Ghost has been at it again. He violates at least one girl a night—" She paused, looked at Sarah, and added, "—always the selfish ones."

Sarah huffed.

"He grabs them in his metal claws," Bernice continued, "and makes them look him in the face. The girls fall insensible at the sight of his fiery eyes." Finished, she looked down, apparently disinterested in the reaction her words had on the others.

Polly took Bernice's words as fact because such stories about the Bonehill Ghost were common. The idea that he went after selfish girls was the only part of her statement new to Polly.

Sarah's expression suggested she thought little of Bernice's offering. Even so, she grinned and that made Martha grin. They had spoken of the Bonehill Ghost before. Martha had brought to their gatherings stories about the demon from her mother, who had been friends with Mary Evans, one of his early victims. "His name was Mr. Macklin," Martha had said. "He was an Irish rummy who jumped off the Blackfriars Bridge, and was buried in hallowed ground at Bunhill Fields.

Because he took his own life, he cannot rest. He's half ghost, half demon, doing the Devil's work, stealing souls. He goes about his work with a tippler's glee. The glow of Mr. Macklin's eyes is the devil's brand. They are red because they're bloodshot from too much drink. A bottle of gin that never empties, no matter how much he takes from it, hangs from a chain round his neck. His rummy breath is so potent, he can set it ablaze, and breathe blue flame. He's not fixed firm to the ground, but bounds about, leaping over houses at great speed to catch his prey."

Polly had thought the Bonehill Ghost sounded much like Spring-Heeled Jack of South London folklore. He had the same ability to jump high, the metal claws, and flaming blue breath. Such menacing spectres added a frightful element to the considerable mystery and danger of a London night.

Dusk descended and shadows crept up on the girls. Telling such tales at that hour, they knew they tempted fate, yet that was part of the game they called "Tell me a dreadful."

Martha's and Sarah's grins loomed skeletal in the dimming light. *Their faces are enough to scare away death itself,* Polly thought. Since the Grim Reaper had crept close enough to steal family from each of the girls, perhaps defiance of death was what the game was all about. The contest started with the recounting of something dreadful. Then each of the other girls in turn had to add to the tale with a fact, a lie, or a guess. They drew liberally from local folklore in an effort to frighten. The first to flee for the safety of home became the loser, the winner the one who provoked the response.

Facts rarely surprised Polly, and she believed she could spot a lie. The folklore fell somewhere in between, punching holes in the wall between the prosaic world in which she lived and worked in daylight and the supernatural possibilities of the night. Polly found the glimpses through the holes exciting. She'd never lost the game. Occasionally, she'd won.

"Do you know what *'violate'* means?" Sarah asked.

"Of course I do," Bernice said. "You only ask because you want me to explain it so you'll know."

Sarah scoffed but dropped her challenge, a hint of worry in her features.

"My turn," Martha said. She took a sip of the gin, coughed and wiped her watering eyes. "They say some of the girls who met up with Mr. Macklin got such a bad case of the vapors they've gone glocky and will never be right in the head again." She looked around to assess the effect of her words.

Sarah responded with a shrug. Polly agreed that Martha's addition, although no doubt true, was a weak play. Polly had heard of such severe cases. Diseases abounded in the dank, smelly gutters and gullies of the city and got into people through their noses. She couldn't imagine, though, how the vapors might be dispensed from the eyes of the Bonehill Ghost. As she prepared for her turn, she remembered something about his breath.

She nodded sagely as if to confirm the truth of Martha's words, an important play before elaborating with falsehood upon an opponent's offering. "Throughout the city," Polly said, "whether he's seen or not, Mr. Macklin causes the worst cases of the vapors. The blue flame he blows on those poor girls isn't just his rummy breath. By day, he leaps back and forth over the Thames, filling his chest with the foul air above the water. His burning breath carries with it the poisons of the river." Then she thought of something that gave her a shiver.

"Oh, but like the blue of flame in daylight," she said, "you cannot see Mr. Macklin in bright light."

Martha glanced at Polly with mischief in her eyes, and

nodded toward Bernice. The girl had bowed her head, perhaps in prayer.

Sarah fortified herself with another sip of gin before her turn. "One of the poor girls," she said, looking rather pleased with herself, "one named Bernice, by chance, can no longer speak, and does nothing but stare into the distance and drool *all day*."

Bernice gasped and looked up upon hearing her name. Martha and Sarah gazed at the girl in the half-light, their grins straining toward grimaces. Bernice's eyes had grown so large, they seemed to glow in the gloom.

Polly got a ghostly chill, even though she believed Sarah's offering a lie. *Good play.* Using an opponent's name, and the unknown in Sarah's statement—both brilliant. *What is the poor victim, Bernice, staring at all day? Something stuck in her mind, her memory—the moment she met Mr. Macklin!* Polly stifled a giggle.

She found herself glancing around to see if anyone or anything approached along the alley. Although she feared an attack from supernatural forces, she told herself she watched for ruffians who patrolled the back lanes, looking for the weak to prey upon. The stench of the two privies that stood within a fenced court at the eastern end of the lodging house was all that assailed the girls. When the gin came back around, Polly took a larger swallow to fortify herself, and passed the jar to Sarah Brown.

"It's your turn," Sarah said, poking Bernice with an elbow.

"Don't," the girl said, shoving Sarah's shoulder. "I'll take my time."

Bernice remained quiet for a moment, then pushed the hair out of her eyes and looked up. She took a deep, steadying breath. "It could be the vapors," she said tremulously, "but I think the Bonehill Ghost is like the Wampus Cat of the

Cherokee Indians. My cousin Tom told me about her. He lived in America for a time. She's half woman, half lion, an evil spirit in the forest with glowing red eyes. The Indians fear to find her while hunting. If you look the Wampus Cat in the eye, you'll go mad. The Indians don't care for the mad, so they just waste away." She shuddered at her own tale, and looked embarrassed for having told it.

Pure guesswork, Polly decided. Still, whether Bernice knew the truth of what she'd said or not, Polly thought the tale she told sounded right. Giddy from the gin, she nodded enthusiastically, and grinned her approval to Bernice. The girl offered a brittle smile and Polly stifled another laugh. Sarah sneered.

Taking a sip of gin before her turn, Martha made a sour face. "I think this foul brew was poured from Mr. Macklin's bottle," she said, turning to her left and spitting the liquid out. All but Bernice laughed out loud. "Forgive me," Martha said, "that's the best I've got."

"No," Sarah said, "You must take your turn or you'll lose."

"Yes, it wouldn't be fair, would it?" Martha asked. "Give me a moment." She became quiet for a time. As the moment stretched on and the darkness deepened, Sarah became impatient and poked her. Martha perked up and faced her audience again. "The Bonehill Ghost is stealing the souls of those who look him in the eyes," she said slowly, ominously. "The demon, Mr. Macklin, can take the soul of an infant right out of its mother's womb, and that's why so many criminals are born with no conscience. Although I don't know the tune, I know the words of a song he sings when he's hunting souls:

"The soul of you, the whole of you, that's all what you can preach.
"The soul of you, a hole in you, as what your screams beseech,
"When darkness wants to sort you out, no more or less shall do.
"I take my time, and when I'm done—"

When her voice trailed off, Polly and Sarah spoke in unison: "Finish it!"

"Sorry," Martha said, "but the only ones to hear it sung all the way through are those poor girls who lost their souls and haven't regained their wits."

"Oh, Martha," Polly said, laughing, "that's good!" *A mix of truth and lies,* she thought. Polly assumed Martha had made up the song and had been unable to find within her imagination an appropriate end to it. *Yet the lie she told covering her failure—truly clever.*

Sarah laughed as well. "Yes," she said. "Makes up for all your mag-fibs."

"You think I made that up?" Martha asked.

Bernice nodded vigorously, hopefully.

"How could I think of that so quickly? No, it's truly his song. One winter evening when my mum was young, she dashed inside her home just in time to get away from a dark figure chasing *her.* She'd heard the song riding the chill breeze that pursued her indoors, and then a thump at the window. When she turned to look out, she found the words of the song written in the frost on the window pane. The end of the last line had been wiped clean by a bird that struck the window. The poor creature lay dead on the walk outside. It had broken its own neck to save her. If she'd heard or read that line, she might have gone mad. Mum wrote down the words before the frost melted."

"Why haven't we heard it before?" Sarah asked, scoffing.

"Mum told me the story last night and showed me the words."

Polly decided that she'd been wrong—Martha's explanation had the ring of truth. Despite the warmth of the evening, Polly's small hairs stood on end and she had an urge to shelter indoors against the terrors of the night. She held herself in place, and tried to hide her fright.

Bernice had a worse reaction. Her mouth became a thin, lipless line of worry and her face lost its color. Martha put her arm around her and gave a squeeze.

Before taking her turn, Polly allowed herself and Bernice time to recover. She watched the girl worry at the hem of her skirts and chew her lips. The silence stretched on and the darkness continued to deepen. Polly glanced at the sliver of moon overhead, watched leaves and a piece of paper blown up the alley on a breeze. A mournful horn sounded from the direction of the river.

As Sarah opened her mouth to protest the delay, Polly interrupted. "Whatever the cause," she said slowly, "flaming breath or glowing eyes, the girls aren't going to regain their wits because they are truly already dead. Mr. Macklin isn't just taking their souls; he's scaring the life right out of them. It happens so quick, their bodies don't know yet and keep moving about, like a chicken with its head cut off, but much longer, years sometimes. The families of the poor girls don't know as they sleep each night with the dead in their homes."

Bernice's grimace sagged. Her mouth pinched inward. She began to quake. Her eyes and mouth went wide and she screamed, got to her feet, and ran down the alley to the east.

The three remaining girls laughed and hugged each other.

"I've never seen her so scared," Polly said.

"Did you see her lamps?" Martha asked. "And her mouth looked like she'd sucked on a lime."

"I'd say she pissed herself," Sarah blurted between guffaws.

Realizing that Sarah wanted that to be true, Polly felt sorry for Bernice.

"You've won again, Polly," Martha said. She offered the gin.

"This is for you. Happy birthday."

"Happy birthday," Sarah said.

The jar remained half-full. Polly quaffed the gin all at once, then coughed and choked, smiling at her friends through the pain.

As the laughter trailed away, Martha became serious. "I must go. The match boxes won't make themselves. Da will remind me of that with a whipping if I'm *too* late."

"I told Mum I should help her with mending," Sarah said.

The two girls made their goodbyes and stood. Polly sat back against the lodging house and watched the shadowy shapes of her friends swim a bit in her vision as they hurried away.

2
A Song

Although Polly had been given gin in her water periodically throughout her life, she'd never had so much of the undiluted drink at once. She slumped in a stupor against the hard brick, enjoying a euphoric calm and distance from her cares for a time.

The few people who passed by paid little attention to her. She knew that in the crowded city, filled with unfortunates, few of its citizens would become concerned about the condition of a young girl as long as she appeared alive and whole. Still, she knew the dangers of the streets. As she found herself lacking the coordination to sit up properly, she began to worry that someone might come along and take advantage of her. By the time she decided she should get up and make her way around to the front of the building, she was stumbling drunk.

Looking to the left at the end of the alley, she experienced the confusion of double-vision. Dizzied, she staggered on, and fell to the paving stones twice. Rubbing her knees with her hands the second time, she felt wetness and sought the wall of the building for support. She stumbled again and fell forward, striking brick with her forehead.

Her stomach turned over violently and she vomited. The smell, so biting and acrid, sickened her further. Polly heaved again and again.

Then the Bonehill Ghost came for her. With his glowing eyes, like two lamp flames, he emerged from the darkness. Alcohol fumes overpowered Polly. Remembering Bernice's words about the danger of his gaze, Polly turned away. Her vision swam, even as she tried to escape. He seized her in his iron grip and tried to turn her to face him. With vision skewed, she couldn't tell if she looked in his direction. Against all urges to the contrary, Polly closed her eyes.

Mr. Macklin had Papa's voice, but he sang the song Martha offered to a jangling, sweet yet dreadful tune.

"The soul of you, the whole of you, that's all what you can preach.

"The soul of you, a hole in you, as what your screams beseech,

Polly wailed at the top of her lungs to drown out the song so she wouldn't hear the last line. She thrashed as he dragged her into shadows and beat her backside. When done, he threw her into deeper darkness and left her there to cry. The pain of her beating lessened and her dizziness and retching resumed. She heaved until her abdomen ached and her head throbbed.

Polly regained some control over her vision. She believed she was in her own bed, yet the room was too dark for her to be certain. Much of the pain and nausea had subsided, and she found sleep.

Singing his song, the Bonehill Ghost returned for her in dreams. Trying to wail away his song again, Polly found herself mute.

"The soul of you, the whole of you, that's all what you can preach.

"The soul of you, a hole in you, as what your screams beseech,

"When darkness wants to sort you out, no more or less shall do.

"I take my time, and when I'm done, there's nothing left of you."

With the last line completed, Polly found her feet, and ran blindly. The only light within the blackness came from Mr.

Macklin's eyes. With them closed, he came for her repeatedly, thrusting his jeering face toward hers. Each time, she remained unaware of the closeness of his visage until he opened his eyes. Polly caught brief glimpses of his thin, dark features, the hooked nose, the heavy dark brow, the slack but cruel lips. She'd turn, and flee, screaming. Polly spent the night colliding with hard objects in the utter darkness as she dodged about to avoid him.

She awoke in her bed in the morning, still in her clothes, more weary than she'd ever been. Her father must have found her outside and placed her there. The bed he shared with her brother, in the opposite corner of the room, stood empty. Daylight came through the window. Her backside and legs were bruised and a scab-crusted wound marred her forehead. Despite a severe headache, she rolled over and slept dreamlessly until her father arrived to check on her some time later.

The unlocking of the door roused her from sleep. Her father opened it enough to look in. His haggard face had a hateful look about it, and strangely, a touch of shame. "I saved you from a terrible fate," he said.

She knew that must be true. When she opened her mouth to speak, he shook his head. "No," he said. "I will hear nothing from you. You'll get up, do the laundry, finish two dozen pelts, and cook potatoes for supper. Eddie and I shall be home this evening at eight o'clock. Tomorrow, we go to church."

Papa took his children to church only when he thought one or both had been up to no good. Polly believed in God because her mother had, although Caroline didn't seem to put much stock in the Church of England.

"You don't want to depend on the Vicars to lead you," she'd warned. "Some are not good men. Don't ever let one get you alone."

Polly had asked why, but her mother gave no explanation.

Caroline had required her to memorize numerous prayers. For Polly, they were merely words that belonged to priests. She'd never been curious enough about her religion to learn much about it, yet the belief remained.

With the added insult of her aching head, bruised legs, and unsettled gut, Polly knew that another miserable day lay ahead, yet she felt happy to be home and whole.

She should never have laughed at another's fear of the Bonehill Ghost. She should never have spoken the demon's name while playing a game. Never again would she scoff at the darkness.

Please, O Lord, Polly prayed, *protect me from the terrors of the night.*

As she went about the day's work, she couldn't get Mr. Macklin's sweet and sour tune out of her head. Having run the full song through to its end so many times, Polly decided that Martha had been wrong to suggest the verse would make one mad. Then a frightful thought occurred to her: *Perhaps, I am mad, and don't know it.*

3
Labor

Meeting Martha, Sarah, and Bernice the following Monday in Gunpowder Alley, Polly tried to recite the end of Mr. Macklin's song, but her friends wouldn't have it, and clearly didn't want to believe the tale she told of the demon's visit.

"You had a drunken dream," Martha said, "that's all."

As time passed, Polly began to entertain misgivings concerning the reality of her visit from the Bonehill Ghost, although knowing his entire song, words and jangling tune, seemed to push back on those doubts. Walking home alone after dark on occasion, she'd get a chill feeling that the demon stalked her, her small hairs would stand up, and she would hasten her step.

* * *

In the summer of 1860, Polly was sweeping out their lodgings one afternoon when she discovered a lockbox with a large padlock on it under the bed her father shared with her brother. She wanted to know what the box held, and asked her father when he came home in the evening. He had a troubled look, and she thought he'd become angry with her. She backed away, intending to drop the subject and serve him and Eddie their supper.

"You're not to know about that box," Papa said. His tone held something of anger and fear. He turned to Eddie, who sat at the table in anticipation of the meal. "Neither of you. Do you understand?"

"Yes, Papa," Eddie said. He appeared to be without curiosity. Polly nodded her head for her father and he seemed satisfied.

The mystery tugged at Polly's thoughts for several days.

"What do you know about the lockbox?" she asked Eddie. "Does it hold something of great worth?"

He shrugged. "Something he's been given to open. Someone lost a key, I suppose. Whatever it holds doesn't belong to us."

The next time she looked under Papa's bed, the box was gone. With time, she stopped thinking about it.

* * *

Martha Combs found work in Holborn, finishing shirts, and ceased to spend time with Polly. Sarah Brown did some sort of work for her uncle that she wouldn't talk about. Polly saw increasingly less of Sarah as the months passed.

Polly and Bernice Godwin had worked at home as fur pullers on and off since 1853, and spent much time together. At fourteen years of age, they both wanted to find better work. Bernice had her father's blessing to look for a job.

"You'll stay home, do your piece work, and keep house," Papa had told Polly. Even so, she believed she might persuade him if she found work. With heavy competition for labor, positions rarely became available.

"I've heard the Ryan paper factory needs a rag sorter," Polly told Bernice one day. "Tomorrow, I'll go try to get the position."

Bernice's eyes became large and she shook her head. "The

rags are collected from all over the city. They don't care as some come from the worst places. The vermin, the lice, the disease—you shouldn't want that."

Polly reconsidered.

While they looked into jobs at the Jessup cotton spinning mill, Polly spoke to her brother about the possibility. "Eddie told me the boss there pushes his workers to move fast to meet quotas," she told Bernice, "and the steam-powered machinery snatches a limb or a life at least once a month."

Bernice took a job at the white-lead works for a short time. One day she returned home with a haunted look about her. "I quit. I found out the girl I replaced wasted away and went mad. Then I learned that happens to most of the girls as works there—five already this year."

The rate of accidents, poisoning, and disease, and the stress upon the body of the different types of work available had all become discouraging factors. Polly imagined industry as a hungry giant that preferred to feed on the young and tender, chewing or biting off a limb, crushing a head or chest, setting a poisoned trap to catch the inexperienced off guard, leaving many unfortunates ill, maimed, or dead.

They stuck with the devil they knew: fur pulling. The task involved pulling the loose undercoat from rabbit pelts so that the furs would not shed the down once they were used to line garments. The action created a myriad of tiny broken hair fibers that floated freely in the air. The girls could not avoid breathing the particles into their lungs. The undercoat that didn't float away, they saved in bags to sell for a small sum per pound.

Polly's father and Bernice's mother each paid the deputy of the lodging house, Mrs. Fortuna, a little extra to allow their daughters to perform their labors at home. The girls worked together so they could talk, sing songs, and keep each other company through the hours of toil. They alternated the use of their families' respective rooms with the idea that an open window on the off days would allow some airing out. The strategy seemed to do little good. The casements faced west, and a golden beam of sunlight slanting in through the open sashes in late afternoon always revealed thick motes of the tiny fibers still floating freely within the chambers.

By 1861, most of the inhabitants of the lodging house, those who'd been living there for any length of time, had wheezing, labored breath. When Old Mrs. Fletcher died in a coughing fit, Mrs. Fortuna had had enough. She forbade the girls to do their work within the lodging house.

Polly and Bernice looked for another windless spot to do their work, but couldn't find a good situation.

One evening, as she sat with her father and brother to eat, Polly complained. "Because nobody wants fur pulling where they live or work, the nethers, even for the smallest room, are greater than what you're willing to pay."

Papa swallowed the food in his mouth, set down his fork, and took a deep breath as he turned his dark brown eyes on her. He didn't like to be disturbed while eating. "You're expected to work it out," he said. Papa wiped sweat from his broad brow and pushed dark locks out of his eyes. "I have my work and you have yours. Get it done."

"My work shall never be done," she grumbled.

Papa slapped her. "We work too hard to listen to your whingeing. If you cannot pull fur, you'll have to hawk wares on the street. If you don't, we'll go hungry to pay the nethers on the lodging house, and you'll see whose helping goes first."

He reached with his large hand to snatch some of the buttered bread from her plate. He tore the bread into two portions, gave one to Eddie and the other he placed on his own plate.

Polly glared at him until he raised his hand in threat. She lowered her gaze. The altercation seemed to have little effect on Eddie. He continued to eat in silence, scooping up Polly's bread and making short work of it. Eddie looked and acted much like her father. He wasn't quite as tall, and had their mother's plump nose instead of their father's long, thin one. That didn't give Eddie a much friendlier face.

"Can you get me brush work, Papa?" she asked.

"Mr. Carr has passed away, and his son took the business to South Bermondsey."

Polly wanted to suggest he could find another source for the work, but he'd clearly had a bad day and wasn't in a mood to consider her wishes.

* * *

"What shall we do?" Polly asked Bernice. Their search for a fur-pulling spot seemed to be at an end.

"You won't like my answer."

Polly knew the answer. She'd tried not to believe they had only the one option. "The privies?"

"Yes."

The two young women did their piece work in the privies that stood in the fenced court at the eastern end of the lodging house, where Papa left his barrow when it wasn't in use. Six days a week, they carried into the stalls their rabbit pelts, and the cloth bags in which they placed the undercoat they collected. The privies were close enough to one another that, though the girls each occupied a separate one and the doors were closed, Polly easily heard Bernice's voice coming through the splintery walls. They kept each other company with conversation as they worked.

Polly found the reek discouraging, especially in the morning, yet by midday, she no longer smelled the odor. As she and Bernice made their conversations and singing loud enough to hear one another, all the tenants of the lodging house became aware that the girls did their work inside the privies. Interruption of the labor occurred periodically as the lodgers came and went. Largely, they showed tolerance. They knocked and politely waited for a reply. If a knock came at her door, Polly covered her work, exited, and waited until the lodger had finished before resuming her toil. Few complained about the fibers Polly and Bernice left behind. Mrs. Fortuna turned a blind eye to their activities.

In the spring of 1861, when both of the young women were fifteen years old, Bernice broke the news that she'd found a job at a bag maker.

Polly tried to be happy for her friend. "You'll do well, I'm certain of it. Must be better wages than what we earn at present."

"Yes," Bernice said, nodding sadly and hanging her head.

Without conversation, fur pulling would become all but unbearable. Apparently, Bernice had thought about that.

"I'll ask after a position for you right away," Bernice said. "Perhaps we'll be working side by side again very soon."

"That should be nice."

* * *

As happened, even with good friends, once Polly and Bernice no longer worked together, their rendezvous slowed to a trickle. Polly ceased to see Bernice entirely when she and her mother moved into another lodging house about a mile away. No doubt, the girl had new companions with whom she worked. Polly didn't hold bitterness toward Bernice.

Working most of each day in the lodging house privy stall with no one to talk to, lonely and bored, Polly did battle with herself. A restlessness that demanded satisfaction settled into her bones. Her mind wandered through several scenarios in which she found a companion—sometimes male, sometimes female—with whom to drink. With a certain amount of reckless glee that she found disturbing, she imagined taking up exciting and risky pursuits with her companion. She fancied herself capable of becoming a topnotch pickpocket, a palmer, or a highwayman. Yes, she and her companion might find pistols, and stop coaches along the roads on the outskirts of London. As a dragsman, she would become rich. Several times, she visited a daydream in which she simply became drunk and ran naked through the streets.

Polly knew that if she did any of those things, she would be caught and locked away in prison. When she began to think that perhaps prison would not be so bad, she feared for her sanity. She dreaded her flights of fancy, yet she couldn't stop them.

My wants are a torment, but the boredom pushes my thoughts away from the here and now to seek excitement. This must be how criminals are made.

Her restless discontent with life left her sulking through the long, dull days of work, the lifeless meals in the evenings with her father and brother, and the sleepless hours before dawn when she awoke too early and could not find sleep. She thought a lot about the euphoric feeling and the giddiness she'd had at first when she'd drunk the gin on her thirteenth birthday, and decided that the next time she drank, she'd be careful not to have too much. Polly knew boys in the neighborhood who found a drink from time to time. George Prescott had made eyes at her. She might persuade him to share his gin.

Polly felt particularly disagreeable one day in July of 1861.

"Papa," she cried, "I am *miserable* with my work."

"Everyone is miserable with their work," he said. "Don't be selfish."

His reaction surprised her, and she became silent. The idea that she was selfish troubled her since she had difficulty recognizing the trait within. Polly did her part and resented the suggestion that she didn't. Still, the accusation stung and she didn't know why. She felt as if she'd been carrying a terrible secret and forgotten about it until someone found her out.

"Should you be a good girl," Papa said, "you'll rest in Heaven."

4
Selfish Prayers

August 31, 1861

The notion that she was particularly selfish continued to trouble Polly for some weeks. She didn't want such a terrible trait. Selfish people had few friends and suffered unhappiness. Yet Polly couldn't seem to step back from herself and assess the truth until the day she met up with trouble from an official of her church on her false birthday.

"I'll have to tell your father about this," the man said, "unless you're willing to tell me why you do these things. I should know if you lie."

Polly tried not to show her fear. She believed him to be a churchwarden for St. Bride's Parish. If that were true, he was young for that role. He'd caught her drinking gin with George Prescott and two of his pals behind a tool shed in the churchyard. The three boys had fled. Too drunk to move fast, Polly stumbled. The man had batted the bottle of gin out of her hand and the vessel had fallen and spilled its contents into the dirt.

He took her forcefully by the arm in a powerful grip, and drew her away from the shed. The bright afternoon sky, charged with white haze, blinded Polly as she emerged from the shade.

He led her along the flagstone walk and through a door into

the back of the church. Although her family belonged to the parish and she'd been in the church many times, she'd never seen these rooms. As they moved down a hall, she heard activity in a couple of rooms, but didn't see anyone else. At the end of the hall, they entered a rectory office. The room smelled of polished wood and old men and had furniture made of lathe-turned and hand-carved fine hardwoods. Needlepoint upholstery covered the chair cushions. The desk, also hand-carved, and larger than the bed in which her father and brother slept, stood in front of a tall leaded window with fine drapery.

The man took a simple wooden chair from one corner of the room, placed it before the desk and gestured for her to sit. Polly complied, fighting off her slight intoxication in order to sit upright in the chair. She glanced at the exit several times, trying to decide if she'd get away with making a run for it.

He shut the door.

"I am Mr. Martin Shaw, Churchwarden," he said, standing over her with a stern look. "This is the second time I've caught you profaning Church property."

She'd seen Mr. Shaw in church on a Sunday, sitting in the pews with the middle class parishioners. He had indeed surprised Polly and her friends once before, about two weeks earlier. She and her young men had got away that time.

"As long as I do my work," Polly lied, "my Papa toils too hard to care what I do."

His expression remained unchanged. He was an earnest man, of average height and a thin build. His dark clothes, his long, sober face, framed by the rectangles of side whiskers, spoke of a man who believed the world should be orderly. Although he looked the part, he seemed somewhat awkward in the ornate rectory office. Since he made no effort to move around to sit at the desk, she knew that the grand bureau, indeed, the chamber itself, didn't belong to him. He'd brought her to the office because he believed the room would lend him more authority.

At least he wasn't a vicar. She'd heard stories from friends of what they did to punish girls. Some of them liked doing it to boys as well. Polly walked the other way whenever she saw a priest.

She feared only that Mr. Shaw would tell her father about her activities. If Papa found out, he'd watch her more carefully.

"Why do you do it, a pretty girl like you? How old are you now?"

"Sixteen," Polly said with a bit of defiance. "Today is my birthday and I wanted to celebrate." Of course her true birthday was not the 31st, but the 26th. He didn't have to know that.

"Too young to be drinking. And don't think your young gentlemen friends won't suffer. I know their names."

At least he'd found them before she'd opened her chemise to reveal her breasts—the price she'd bargained with George Prescott for the gin.

Polly considered the first words Mr. Shaw had said to her: "I'll have to tell your father about this, unless you're willing to tell me why you do these things." Would he be true to his word? She had little to lose by telling him something of her life.

"Please, sir, you needn't blame my friends. *I* offered the gin. Young men, being what they are, could not resist."

He nodded his head. "Why do you tempt them so?" he asked.

"They should drink whether I offered it or not," she said. "If I offer it, they drink with *me*."

More lies. Becoming impatient, Mr. Shaw narrowed his eyes.

Polly believed that he asked her to explain her actions in the hope that, as she did so, she'd see the error of her ways. No doubt, he believed that girls drinking with boys led to one thing alone. Those of Mr. Shaw's class concerned themselves with impropriety among the lower class only when the misconduct seemed to threaten their world. She should settle his fears on that score easily.

"You mustn't worry about *that*." She emphasized the last word to express what he couldn't speak to her about openly: Sex. "I would not have allowed them to take advantage of me."

"If the gin didn't leave your judgment wanting." He shook his head slowly.

So, Polly thought, *he chooses to see me as a good girl headed down a dark path because of the drink.*

"I work too hard, sir," she said. "My papa and brother are street locksmiths. They work a barrow in Fleet Street most of each day. I've toiled at home since my mother died nine years ago. My papa brings me work so I don't have to labor in a mill. Still, my work is endless, dull, and lonely, and I want to have fun when I can. I used to make brushes of different sorts. Now, I'm a fur puller."

"What's that?"

Polly looked at him curiously. Who didn't know about fur pulling? Then she realized that a man of his station had no reason to know of such a thing.

"Piece work," she said bitterly. "My papa gets paid per piece for each pelt I finish. I pull the downy undercoat from rabbit pelts used to line garments. He's paid a small sum per pound for the down I collect as well. In the Crimean war, many pelts were needed for coats to keep our soldiers warm."

"That ended five years ago."

"There's still a demand."

"Yes, I have a fur-lined hat." He seemed to think for a moment. "That doesn't sound like hard work."

"The down gets everywhere," she said. "No matter how often I clean, it finds me."

Polly held up her arms and shook them. A cloud of tiny white fluff billowed out from the sleeves of her shift, and Mr. Shaw's eyes went wide.

"It chokes me in my sleep. I become breathless even when walking a short way. It's not as harmful and pays better than many other kinds of piece work. I'm fortunate to have it, and still we barely get by."

"Can you do the work outside?"

"The down will blow away on the slightest breeze."

"Hmm…my hatter charged me next to nothing to add the fur lining," Mr. Shaw said, seemingly to himself.

"We need the income, but the work makes me miserable."

He bowed his head for a moment, then said sadly, "You ought to go to school instead of spending your young life working."

Polly smiled. "Yes, I wished for that. Without my mother…"

She knew she didn't have to continue. He had a sympathetic smile. He was a good man, after all. He meant her no real harm.

"So many have so little," he said. "You don't deserve to grow up like that, and I'm certain that when I tell your father about this, it will not help, yet as Churchwarden, I have a duty."

Polly had to think fast. She had to give him what he wanted; a contrite young woman who trusted God to mete out just punishment.

"Pray with me," she said. Polly quickly took to her knees on the polished hardwood floor.

Mr. Shaw hesitated only a moment before joining her. He cleared his throat before beginning. "When the wicked man turneth away from his wickedness that he hath committed," he said, "and…um…doeth that which is right, he shall save his soul…."

Polly recognized his words as the opening to the Order for the Evening Prayer, something from Ezekiel, if she remembered correctly. He didn't recite the words perfectly. She helped him with the next line, from Psalms, she thought. "I acknowledge my transgressions, and my sin is ever before me...."

Polly opened one eye and glanced at him, and found him glancing back. He looked a bit sheepish, perhaps because a young sinner had shown him up. As a lay official of the Church, Mr. Shaw wasn't required to lead prayer. He nodded in approval, clearly relieved that she'd carried on. Polly closed her eyes as she continued. Her memory of the corporate prayer gave out, and she struggled to fill the gap with an individual expression. "O Lord, please help me to be satisfied as I toil at home. Make my fingers stronger so they don't ache so much after a long day of work. Help me find a husband to provide me with a good life. Please keep illness away. Make Papa a happier man so he should treat me better than he has done."

Polly thought she did well. She opened one eye to see Mr. Shaw's reaction. Again, he glanced at her. He had a troubled look.

"Amen," Polly concluded uneasily.

"Amen," Mr. Shaw said, then cleared his throat. "Is that the manner in which you pray daily?"

"Yes," she said, and he frowned.

Although Polly did believe in prayer, she didn't pray daily. If she didn't get what she wanted, she presumed that God could only hear and respond to so much, and that others more worthy had taken his attention. She and her family went to church rarely. They craved a day of rest from work, and Sunday was usually that day.

"Your prayers are all for you," Mr. Shaw said.

Polly didn't understand why he said that. She tilted her head questioningly.

"You prayed for your fingers to be stronger, for a husband to make you happier, and to be protected from illness. You only asked for your father to be happier so that he should treat you better. Do you always pray only for your own betterment?"

Polly understood, and saw the truth in what he said. She *was* selfish. Her father had been right, yet the problem was much worse than he'd made out. Uncomfortable with the revelation, she was dumbstruck. The intoxication of the gin had fled, and she felt suddenly out of control.

Mr. Shaw clearly saw her distress. He placed a warm hand on her shoulder. "I shouldn't think our Lord responds to selfish prayers," he said quietly.

Polly, lost in thoughts of her past efforts at prayer, staggered to her feet and sat back down in the chair. She thought about when her mother was dying. Her prayers of that time were the first she remembered offering on her own. "Please, O Lord, don't let her die and leave me motherless." She had not been praying for her mother, but for herself.

Polly looked up at Mr. Shaw, and felt naked before him. She had revealed an ugly flaw in her character to an official of the Church. Yet the shame of that notion paled in an instant, replaced with a deep mortification as she realized she'd stood before God her entire life with such a deficiency.

A stinging tear formed in Polly's eye.

No wonder she had such a terrible life. God would not look upon her favorably, had perhaps never smiled upon Polly since her birth. No wonder a demon had been sent to torment her several years earlier.

"I pray only for others," Mr. Shaw said, "never for myself."

Polly half-heard him. How had she come to such a sad state? Was there no way out of misery, then? She sobbed briefly before controlling her voice to ask, "Is there no time when I can pray for myself?"

He touched her cheek and smiled sadly. "Only in the most dire of circumstances. In a situation in which there is imminent danger and there is no time to find help, I should think. I believe He will respond only when we are imperiled and have no other to turn to."

Polly wept openly for a time, unashamed to do so before the Churchwarden.

He shifted from foot to foot, clearly uncomfortable with her reaction. "Pray for your father, and when he is lifted up so you shall be," he said.

As she became calm, he too settled down. "Here is a penitent prayer that helps me," he said. Mr. Shaw pulled a card from an inner pocket of his jacket and handed it to Polly. "Say it with me."

She read aloud from the card as he recited the prayer:

"Almighty God, of great goodness,

"I confess to you with my whole heart

"my failure to uphold your commandments,

"my wrong-doing, my unworthy thoughts and words,

"the harm I have done others,

"and the acts of kindness and proper deeds left undone.

"O God, forgive me, for I have sinned against you;

"and raise me up again;

"through Jesus Christ our Lord.

"Amen."

"Keep the card and ask for forgiveness for your selfish ways often," Mr. Shaw said, "and He will smile upon you."

Polly decided he spoke wisely. He stepped back. She rose unsteadily to her feet and slipped the card into a pocket of her skirt.

"I shall not tell your father about what happened here today, if you will learn to pray for others, and promise not to drink again until you're older."

Polly wiped away her tears and nodded. She looked Mr. Shaw in the eyes. He *was* a good man.

"Yes, I shall—I'll learn how to pray for others," she said. "I can but try."

Mr. Shaw did not seem to notice her omission of the promise not to drink. He moved to the door and opened it for her.

She gave him a grateful smile, then left the office to make her way home.

* * *

After her conversation with Mr. Martin Shaw, Churchwarden, Polly ceased to pray for herself. Instead, she prayed for the well-being of her friends and family, most fervently for her Papa. God did not choose to lift him up, and, consequently, her work load remained the same. Still, she persevered in her prayers, usually following them with the penitent one from the card Mr. Shaw had given her.

When bored, she scolded herself for being selfish.

Please, O Lord help others who labor to find their work fulfilling.

When she had coughing fits, sore hands, and an aching back from sitting for hours hunched over her work, she did her best to ignore the discomfort.

Merciful God, ease the suffering of those who become ill from their labors.

5
Risk

In the early evening of a day in May of 1862, Polly heard her father coming up the stairs of the lodging house to their second floor room. She opened the door for him. He carried something box-shaped, wrapped in a blue woolen blanket, the burden evidently heavy.

"I left my barrow in the lane in front." He groaned as he set the box down beside his bed. "I'll fetch it to the court and be right back. Leave that alone." Papa gestured toward the odd package.

"What does it—"

"Nothing that concerns you." He turned and left.

While Polly spooned potatoes into a bowl in preparation for supper, Eddie came in. Curious about the package, he began tugging at the blanket.

"Leave it be," Polly told him. "Papa doesn't want it disturbed."

By the time she put her spoon down, Eddie had got the blanket off. Seeing the iron box underneath, a thing held together with rivets and metal straps, she forgot about Papa's instruction. A heavy padlock with three keyholes was fitted through a hasp that held the straps in place and the lid of the box closed.

"It's a lockbox," Eddie said. "No, a strongbox."

They heard their father hurrying up the stairs, and Eddie tried to cover the heavy chest up with the blanket again. He had not succeeded before Papa entered the room.

"Get away from that." He turned and glared at Polly. "What did I tell you?"

"I told Eddie what you said."

Papa grumbled, and shoved the box under the bed.

They ate their supper of potatoes and a bit of cold chicken Eddie had brought home with him. Then Polly cleared the table.

"Go out until bedtime," Papa said, "the both of you. Don't return until nine o'clock."

He'd never asked for such a thing before. Polly thought the request a curious thing. Eddie had a confused look. They gazed at their father silently for a moment.

"Go!" he said.

Polly knew better than to question their father when he was in such a commanding mood. She and her brother filed out of the room, down the stairs, and out of the lodging house into the street.

Polly looked silently to Eddie for answers.

"When certain men come to talk to him at the barrow, he sends me away. Papa doesn't want me to know what they're saying, I think. I've watched from a distance."

Intrigued and worried, Polly asked, "Who are they?"

Eddie shrugged. "A tall fellow with black hair and mutton chops. Another with no hair on his head, tattoos instead, but he's hiding them under a hat. He's a big, strong one with a mean look. I think they're family people."

"Criminals?"

Eddie nodded.

The worry had turned to fear, with a chill feeling in her gut. "What do they want?"

He shrugged again. "They look like they're threatening him and he tries to calm them. It happened again at the end of the day. That's why I weren't with him when he come home."

"What more?" Although she asked for it, Polly wasn't certain she wanted to hear more.

"There's lots of trouble along Fleet Street, especially near Farringdon Circus, lots of family people looking for advantage. Most of it comes to nothing. Papa's good with his fists—I've seen him defend the barrow and our purse more than once. Try not to worry."

"What about the box?"

"Something they want opened. As long as the Miltonians—"

"The police?" She had visions of her father arrested, being imprisoned, she and Eddie cast into the streets to fend for themselves.

"Yeah, if they don't catch wind of it, Papa will be all right."

Polly covered her eyes so her brother wouldn't see how upset she'd become.

Eddie took her hands away from her face and looked her in the eye. "You are home *too* much."

She nodded vigorously and grimaced to keep from tearing up.

"A pity," he said, "but I suppose there's nothing for it."

Polly chose to believe he was being sweet to her in his own way. As he turned and walked off, she looked to take courage from his words and found none to be had.

Trying to keep her fears at bay, she wandered up and down the darkened lane until she heard church bells striking the nine o'clock hour.

Polly returned to her family's room to find that Papa had hung up the blue wool blanket that had been wrapped around the strongbox across one corner of the room as a curtain.

"Don't lift the blanket," he said sternly.

"Yes, Papa."

She heard him working on something metal—the lock of the strongbox, she presumed—with metal tools. The light of a lamp behind the blanket reflected off the cracked plaster of the ceiling. By that dim illumination, Polly dressed in her night-clothes and got in bed. She lay awake, unable to sleep for all her worry, listening to the sounds of her father's work.

Eddie came in and received the same warning that she had from Papa. Polly heard him move about for a time, and eventually get into bed.

Then a curious thought occurred to her: *Something exciting has happened. It might turn out bad for all of us, especially Papa, but it isn't dull.* Something *is at risk.*

Polly had craved risk to spice up her life for some time, yet she hadn't got much out of it; gin from neighborhood boys and a look at the trinkets they kept between their legs in exchange for a glance at her dairy. The last time she did that, she was lucky to get away with her virtue intact. She wanted better sorts of risks, ones that might truly pay off in the long run. Yes, looking out for worthwhile risks might make her days a bit brighter.

With that, Polly found herself looking forward to the coming day. She rolled into a more comfortable position in her bed and slept.

* * *

The next day when she awoke, Papa was gone. The strongbox lay open and empty behind the blanket curtain. Eddie arose shortly after Polly.

"Did you hear him go out?" he asked.

"No."

Eddie went to the fenced court beside the lodging house to see if Papa had taken his barrow when he left. If he had, then he'd be in Fleet Street near Farringdon Circus. "He didn't take it," Eddie said when he came back. Papa didn't return for two nights. Polly was beside herself with worry.

The first day of their father's absence, Eddie took the barrow to Fleet Street and worked it on his own. Polly asked her neighbors if they knew what had become of Papa, but nobody did. Unable to fully concentrate on her piece work, Polly barely finished a dozen pelts. When Eddie came home that night, he said he'd heard that Papa was arrested.

"What would he—?" she began, but he cut her off.

"Nobody I spoke with knew anything." He put a hand on her shoulder. "Try not to worry. He's good at looking after himself."

Polly maintained the routine household schedule, serving Eddie breakfast and dinner, and preparing him bread and cheese to take with him while he worked the barrow. Though unsettled by her father's absence, she had a sense that he'd be all right, and she had to admit to herself that with the drama of the mystery, and the idea that he'd done something nefarious, she'd felt more alive than at any other time in her recent past.

* * *

Polly's father came home the afternoon of the third day.

Eddie hadn't returned yet from working the barrow.

When Papa came through the door, Polly dropped the cup she was rinsing in the wash basin, and hurried to his side. "Where have you been?" She bounced from foot to foot, while he set down a bag of his tools and took off his jacket.

"I cannot say," he began.

"Cannot or will not," she asked with a sly smile.

"I am not allowed to talk about it, but if you'll keep it a secret, I'll tell you that I now have a friend at the police court in Lambeth Street. I also owe that friend a great debt of service. That's all I can say for now. One day, I may tell you more." Although his features betrayed little, she thought he seemed rather pleased with himself.

Later, Polly asked Eddie what he knew.

"Very little," he said. "Papa doesn't want us to talk about it."

The box was gone the next day. Papa didn't say what he'd done with it.

Polly chose to believe that her father had taken a risk, committed a crime of some sort, and got away with it because he had a confederate within the police court. Papa might knock her about for discipline, but he'd never truly harmed her. Polly didn't believe he meant to harm anyone. She knew he'd repent whatever sins he committed with his crime, and the Lord would forgive him.

In the following week, Papa fed his children extravagantly. They had mutton four nights in a row. When questioned about the food, he said, "I've saved a little back and thought to see you two happy and healthy after the scare I put in you."

Delighted with his warmth, Polly began to see her father in a new light. She assumed that the crime he'd committed had paid off, yet over the ensuing months, she saw no further evidence of profit from his adventure. Whatever else he'd earned might have gone toward paying off a debt. Even so, her father had risen in her estimation, and she was further inspired to consider new risks.

* * *

Life returned to its dull grind until one afternoon, a few weeks after Polly's eighteenth birthday in 1863. Her brother arrived home early with one of his clients, a young man named Bill Nichols.

"I made new keys for Mr. Nichols," Eddie said to Polly, "but failed to bring them to Fleet Street today."

"A good thing your lodgings are on my way home," Bill said, and then he seemed to think for a moment before concluding, "or I should not have the pleasure of meeting your sister."

Polly smiled.

Heavy and pale, Bill wasn't handsome. His light blue eyes held flecks of brown. They bulged from their sockets a bit. The pores of his nose and cheeks were deep and blackened.

He seemed to notice when Polly looked at the dark stains under his nails and in the creases of his fingers.

"Printer's ink," he said. "I work for Messrs. Pellanddor and Company."

Polly nodded. She knew the company was a printer of stamps and monetary notes, and had offices nearby.

She would have guessed Mr. Nichols's age to be about twenty-five, yet he'd begun to lose his dark brown hair. Although also marred with a few spatters of ink, his garments were of better quality than those her brother and father wore. His black shoes and felt hat also appeared to be a finer grade. A watch chain looped from the fourth button of his waistcoat and disappeared into the pocket, so she presumed he owned a watch. The chain appeared to be silver. The man clearly did well enough for himself.

Polly became embarrassed as he looked about their tiny room. Everything her family owned was old and worn. The room stank of cooked cabbage and boiled trotters. Still, no hint of disdain passed his features.

"Allow me to tell you a joke I heard today," he said abruptly, and both Eddie and Polly showed interest. "Disappointed with the way he treated her, a woman said to her husband, 'You loved me so before we wed.'" Bill gave a winning smile before finishing. "'Yes, I did,' the husband said, 'and now it's your turn to do the loving.'"

All three laughed.

Polly thought Bill showed an interest in her.

Is he one of the risks I've been looking for? Perhaps he'd like to share his life with me.

Deciding that anything would be better than what she currently had, Polly became determined to do whatever possible to catch his eye. When he wasn't looking, she pinched her cheeks to bring out the rosy color. She stood with her hips thrust to one side to offer more curve to her form. She smiled and showed her even teeth. Bill allowed his eyes to linger on her several times, and her hopes rose.

Before taking his leave, Bill turned to Eddie, paid him, and received three shiny brass keys. "You did a good job," he said.

"Thank you, sir," Eddie said. "You know where to find me should you need my services again."

He moved to exit the room, and Polly's hopes fell.

Before passing through the threshold, he turned back, facing her. "I would be most pleased if you would join me this evening for a supper at The Old Bell."

"Yes," Polly said a bit too loudly. She became embarrassed.

"Eight o'clock, then?" Bill asked with a satisfied smile.

"Yes," Polly said more evenly.

Bill tipped his hat, turned, and left.

Eddie poked Polly in the shoulder with an elbow and beamed at her.

"Thank you," she said. Polly grabbed Eddie and kissed him on the cheek.

6
The Dead Lie Quiet & Still

Polly found her piece work more tolerable as she and Bill Nichols courted. Having their time together to look forward to helped the hours of drudgery go by more swiftly. Over the course of the next year, she noted that he was good with money. That seemed promising to one who had been poor her whole life. Bill Nichols saved up to take Polly on outings and to buy her gifts of clothing, a pendant watch, and a green agate cameo brooch depicting an angel in flight. He liked fine food and took Polly to eat extravagantly at a couple of the finer taverns.

Although Polly would have welcomed sexual advances from Bill, he didn't make any. She told herself that was a sign of his respect for her. He asked her what sort of outings she might like, presented her choices, and seemed to genuinely want to hear her opinions.

Wherever they went, Polly clung to him for fear that he might get away. She considered her clinging an expression of affection, and her enthusiasm for his company a sure sign of love. As he allowed her to draw close, hope grew in her that he did indeed want to share his life with her. Polly decided that her future wasn't set, after all, and that the daily drudgery she'd known all her life would soon fall away when he proposed marriage.

"You and Bill are quite the pair these days," Eddie said to her one evening as she dressed in preparation for another outing with her beau.

"I've never wanted so much to be with anyone before," Polly said. She spun around, allowing her new skirts to billow out. "Bill Nichols has opened up the world for me. We'll have a good life together should he choose me. I have the hope that he will."

Eddie's smile reflected her own happiness.

That night, after watching a performance of popular music at the Royal Standard Music Hall, Bill backed her up against the exterior wall of the building while the crowd exiting the theatre flowed around them. His face gleamed with sweat and his clothing, dampened by rain before the show, smelled of mildew, but she readily kissed his smiling face.

He pulled back, looking briefly unsure of himself, and asked, "Will you be my wife?"

Instantly, she decided that accepting his invitation was a risk worth taking. "Yes," Polly cried.

Nearby faces within the crowd quickly turned toward the sound of her voice. She smiled for them, pleased to have an audience in her moment of happiness.

Bill pulled her close and kissed her again.

* * *

Polly and Bill were married in January of 1864. A week later, Bill took her to see her future home. The place was about a mile away from the lodgings Polly shared with her family, south of the Thames in Scoresby Street, just off Blackfriars Road. They entered a blackened red brick building that had once been a large home. The interior, dark and grim, had been minimally prepared for new tenants. Stains on the pitted floorboards had not been removed. Sagging green wallpaper rumpled up a corner over the entrance doorway with the beginnings of water damage showing through. The only interior doorway, which had no doubt once led into other rooms within the old house, had been filled in with brick and mortar. A thin gap appeared between one side of the door frame and the mortar. Polly thought she might shove through the threshold with enough force. She heard the murmur of conversation coming through the crack, perhaps from her future neighbors. Clearly, she and Bill would have just the one room.

He watched her as she moved about. Polly smiled for him a couple of times, trying to conceal her disappointment.

The single window of the chamber was so filthy with soot, the structures across the lane outside appeared as silhouettes against the bright haze of the sky. With the Southeastern Railway running just south of Scoresby Street, the window would never remain clean for long. Polly ran a hand along the window sill and looked at her blackened fingers. The accumulation of soot was a problem throughout London, yet much more so right next to a railway. While Polly presumed she would become used to the noise of the locomotives, she knew that keeping the room clean would be a struggle.

Although she thought she'd hidden her dissatisfaction with the room, Bill must have seen it on her face. "Is it not good enough for a woman such as yourself?" he asked.

Polly saw the edges of outrage in his features. "I've lived in humble rooms all my life. Surely—"

"You know nothing of my finances," he said curtly.

"Do you—" she began, with the intention of asking if he had reason to worry, but he cut her off again.

"Nor is it your place to know." Clearly Bill had become angry.

Polly felt shut out. Did he push her away because he had something to hide or was his response reasonable for a proud man with his affairs in order?

"We'll start out simply," Bill said, "and save until we can afford something grander."

Polly nodded and dropped the subject.

Bill smiled stiffly. "We'll not talk of it again."

Polly realized that she had merely assumed Bill did well financially. *If he will not discuss it,* she thought, *I won't know if we're in trouble until disaster strikes.*

Later, she considered praying to ask God to help her new husband find success and happiness in life. Then she decided that because her own fortunes were bound up with Bill's that the prayer would be too self-serving. Instead, she said the penitent prayer from Mr. Shaw's card.

* * *

With marriage, Polly discovered sex. The experience was more frustrating than it was pleasurable. Awkward in bed, and single-minded in his efforts to find his own sexual release, Bill most often left her frustrated. Shyness prevented her from finding release by her own efforts in his presence within their small room. She was certain he wouldn't react well to such a thing.

Polly didn't want to become pregnant right away, and asked Bill if he would wear a sheath on his penis when they coupled.

"It wouldn't feel right," he said, scoffing. "I don't think I could do it."

"I need time before becoming a mother."

He frowned, clearly unhappy with her statement. "We want children," he said flatly, as if telling her what to think.

Something in his expression told Polly he wouldn't argue the point. She nodded with false enthusiasm, and reluctantly let the subject drop. After sex, she washed her vagina inside and out as thoroughly as possible with the hope that that would help prevent pregnancy.

Polly had nothing with which to compare her sexual experience until she spoke with a neighbor, another young wife named Judith Stanbrough. She was raw-boned, ginger-haired, freckled, and fair. The two women met while pulling dried wash off the lines behind the lodging house. Polly made small talk as she brushed soot from the otherwise clean clothing, folded the garments, and placed them in a basket.

The conversation turned to their experiences as young wives, and Judith brought up frustrations she had in the bedroom. "Swaine, he pushes me around like an animal belongs to him, a dog or a sheep. He can be sweet other times, but not in bed. When he's had his fill, he stops if I'm done or not."

"Yes," Polly said, "when Bill is done, he turns away, and nothing I can do will coax him back. When I told him I should like it to last longer, he gave me a look of disgust."

"Men don't expect women should like it," Judith said. "I've heard it said we *needn't* like it."

"I'm getting so as I don't much," Polly said.

* * *

On a morning when Bill was to be interviewed for a better position at Messrs. Pellanddor and Company, Polly suggested he looked better in his blue jacket and waistcoat rather than the brown he'd prepared to don.

"I'll thank you to keep your opinions to yourself unless asked for," he said with no evident emotion.

Comparing his response to the way he'd acted when they courted, a time when he'd valued her opinions, Polly felt hurt and confused.

Bill's hours at work increased from about fifty a week to at least seventy. Like her father had, Bill found Polly piece work. Thankfully, he brought her brush-making work instead of fur pulling. Polly pushed dull pins through small india-rubber pads. As several hundred pins were required to make a brush of a few inches across, the effort took a toll on her hands. At least the task didn't make breathing more difficult.

With all the hard work, and six months in the new room to become familiar with one another, some of the shine had worn off their marriage. Their outings had ceased. Polly didn't look forward to Bill coming home in the evening. His sense of humor seemed to fade away.

They had been married a little over a year when she became pregnant. Polly feared that even though the child would be hers, she wouldn't automatically have feelings for it. *How can I love one I don't know?*

With the pregnancy, Polly knew her days of freedom were numbered and that gave urgency to a desire for an outing. She proposed several times that an evening at a pub would be a welcome break from their daily grind. Bill rebuffed the suggestions, but she kept asking until he showed irritation.

"When we courted, you enjoyed going for a pint or two," Polly said.

Bill glanced up from his reading, his eyes cold as he briefly watched her set about making the evening meal. "Yes, well, you always make it three or four."

"As have you," she said.

"I can handle it and stop when need be." He returned his eyes to the loose pages in his hands. He clearly didn't like the interruption.

Polly reflected on the joke he'd told upon their first meeting. *You might have been a fortune-teller with a warning.*

Bill had it right, though. She had to admit to herself that once she had a drink, keeping herself from having more required an extraordinary act of will.

* * *

On the 9th of April of 1865, Bill went to visit his sister. Having the beautiful spring day and blue sky to herself, Polly had a wistful desire to visit her old neighborhood and took a walk toward Fleet Street. Her walk began with slight abdominal discomfort that went away as she moved.

Having negotiated an unsteady path along damp wooden boards laid in the mud through a construction area on the southern bank of the Thames, she crossed over the river on the Blackfriars Temporary Bridge. Although crude, the seventy-foot-wide spans of the structure, supported with rough timbers and an iron framework, were impressive. She imagined the new permanent bridge would be much grander still.

Once across the river, she followed an equally muddy and more treacherous path through the area where construction was staged on the north bank, and proceeded up Farringdon Street. At the intersection with St. Bride's Street, she came upon a childhood friend.

"Bernice," Polly said.

The young woman turned to her. She'd grown into an attractive woman, with round cheeks, fine features, and golden hair. She tilted her head slightly to one side, an expression of confusion on her face, then a look of surprise. "Polly! I haven't seen you in over two years. How are you?"

"I'm well. I'm living in Camberwell. I married Bill Nichols."

"We haven't met," Bernice said, "but I hope to meet him soon."

She looked Polly in the eye as she spoke. Bernice seemed to have a good bit more confidence at twenty years of age than she'd had when younger.

Polly noticed that Bernice carried an indigo sack and basket. "Are you on your way to Farringdon Market?"

"Yes, but I have time for a visit. Let's stop at The Boar's Tusk for a couple glasses of bitter."

Once seated with their drinks at the pub, Polly didn't know what to say to her old friend. Thankfully, Bernice made small talk while Polly took in the strangely pleasant old-yeast smell of the place. She struggled to hear her friend over the hubbub of boisterous conversations from the other tables, then the party at the nearest one got up and left and the noise diminished.

Bernice explained that she still lived in the same lodging house and worked for the same bag maker. She pointed out the blue sack she'd brought with her.

"I'm back to making brushes of different sorts," Polly said.

"What have you heard from Martha?" Bernice asked.

"Oh…I'm sad to say I've heard she died of grippe last winter," Polly said, "but I had not seen her for a long time."

"I'm sorry to hear it," Bernice said, taking on a mournful look. "Martha were a gentle soul."

"Speaking of friends from the Fleet Street neighborhood," Polly said, "do you know what's become of Sarah Brown?"

"Yes, I do," Bernice said, with an even sadder expression. She looked down into her drink, then glanced back up. "Let's not start another round of *Tell me a dreadful.*"

Polly didn't understand and frowned.

"Oh, my," Bernice said, clearly embarrassed. "I'm not trying to be funny, I promise you."

"I'm confused," Polly admitted.

Bernice looked at her squarely for a moment, pressed her lips into a thin rosy line. "You don't know," she said, her eyes widening. "I thought everyone knew. A year ago, the poor girl were helping her uncle breed and keep cows in the cellar of a condemned dockside warehouse. At high tide, a swarm of rats came from the sewers through a grate and spooked the live-stock." For a moment, Bernice's expression reflected the fragile girl she'd once been. "Sarah were trampled to death."

Polly noted that despite the many times the Brown girl had belittled the Godwin girl when they were young, Bernice still had sympathy for their old friend, Sarah.

"That would be the work for her uncle she didn't talk about, I should think," Polly said, "perhaps for fear the housing in-spectors might find out."

Bernice nodded.

Both women became quiet for a time, drinking their brown bitter. Polly noted a young man, rather pretty, she thought, sit-ting with his pals across the room, making eyes at her. She gave no reaction, although she thought she'd have fun sitting and drinking with him and his friends. They seemed to be having a good time laughing and making fun of one another.

In the opposite corner, a man sat drinking alone. A ham-mer of some sort rested on the table before him along with his drink. He had dark hair trimmed short, a clean-shaven square jaw, high forehead, and blue eyes with a touch of sad-ness about them. Handsome and muscular, the fellow leaned back, balancing his chair on its hind legs. With his left thumb, he rubbed the smooth glass that surrounded his drink, and looked thoughtful. He glanced at her twice, each time offering a slight, though pleasant smile. She found his quiet presence more compelling than that of the raucous young men. If she were not with Bernice, Polly would risk approaching the quiet man.

Am I so dissatisfied with my husband?

She tore her eyes away from the lone man in the corner and faced her friend. "Do you have a beau?"

"I were married for a short time," Bernice said. "Albert were lost in the fighting with the Māori in New Zealand last year."

So much death. Polly knew she should feel fortunate—having a husband with an ample income, a good home, and a child on the way—yet she didn't. Yes, so much death that Polly didn't want to think about. *Let the dead lie still and quiet, and let me live!*

"How are you getting along?" Bernice asked.

Polly gave her friend a sour look. "My husband, Bill, he were great fun while we courted. He took me on outings; to the pubs, to Hyde Park for music, and to the Alhambra Circus to watch acrobats. We spoke of having much to look forward to in life, and the things we would do together. Bill said that after we married there were the possibility of travel. Within a month of our wedding, he became a stuffy bore. 'You ought to think about how our children will live,' he says. 'We have to save money for the future.'"

Bernice smiled tightly. "You didn't say, but I suspect you're knapped. Is that true?"

The question surprised Polly. At three months, the pregnancy didn't show. "Yes," she said. The prospect of having a child continued to unsettle her. She didn't want to talk about it.

"I were pregnant," Bernice said, looking uncomfortable. "I lost it." She had clearly seen Polly's hard feelings.

"I'm so very sorry," Polly said, reaching across the table and clasping her friend's hands. "I don't mean to seem ungrateful. I pray every day my child will have a happy life. I shall pray for yours as well."

Bernice smiled pleasantly. "You've always been so quick to pray for others' well-being. I've always admired that in you."

I haven't always.

An uncomfortable silence ensued.

Bernice finished her glass of bitter and stood. "So very good to see you, Polly," she said.

Polly stood. "And you," she said.

Bernice took up her sack and basket, turned, and left the pub.

Polly fetched another glass of bitter, and then turned toward the corner where she'd seen the quiet handsome fellow drinking alone. Although she didn't feel completely comfortable with her intention, she'd decided to ask him if she could sit with him.

An empty glass rested on the table. The man and his hammer were gone. Although somewhat relieved, her disappointment demanded satisfaction. She turned toward the raucous young men in the other corner.

* * *

Much later, she would realize she was home. She couldn't remember how she'd got there.

Polly was on the floor, leaning against the wardrobe. Her green striped skirt had a ten-inch tear in the side seam, near the hem. She and her undergarments were wet as if she'd had sexual relations with someone.

Polly thought back to the events at the pub after Bernice had left. She'd had several more glasses of bitter while with the fetching young man and his friends.

"I am Polly," she'd said in introduction.

"And I am Kevin Lace," the young man said. He was indeed pretty for a man, with curly, dark locks and no whiskers. Kevin pointed out his friends and said their names, but she couldn't remember them. "Join us, won't you."

His pals cheered, and one pulled out a chair for her.

Kevin held up a chapbook, his eyes wide, his face beaming. "We've come from the hanging at Newgate and have a ballad to try." The publication was the sort sold for a penny apiece at public executions. The excitement in his dark brown eyes came from something more than drink and laughter with his pals. Polly thought that perhaps the frenzied look came from seeing a man die.

"You should have seen Pritchard swing," one of the friends said, a flaxen-haired fellow with a short beard and a shiny face. He had the same manic look when he spoke of the execution. "Trussed up though he were, he gave it a go, twisting this way and that. I don't think the rope were long enough to break his neck."

"The ballad is by a fellow named Conway," Kevin said, thumbing open the folded broadsheets. "I've always liked Conway's ballads."

Kevin read the part of the chapbook that spoke of Theodore Pritchard's crime. The criminal had murdered his wife and mother-in-law.

A couple of the friends fetched more drinks.

When they returned, Kevin read through the ballad once out loud. "It's to be sung to the tune of 'Farewell My Soldier,'" he said. They began to sing drunkenly.

Polly stopped several times as she started giggling. "Our singing is *sour!*" she said, making faces. "Our timing is *so* poor."

The young men laughed too. With good humor, they kept at it. Kevin flirted with Polly as they sang, and she liked it. She hadn't experienced such excitement in a long time, and she'd missed it. With all four men looking at her, she felt attractive, wanted, perhaps even admired.

A couple of them rounded up more drinks.

They got better at the singing. For a while, Polly belted out the song with all she had, but she became so winded she temporarily lost her senses. She'd had problems with shortness of breath since her time as a fur puller.

Kevin took her out back of the pub for air. He became quite forward, kissing her once she'd regained her breath. She had a vague recollection of thinking she should leave and go home when he placed his hands on her breasts. Then, more wet kisses, and no additional memories of their encounter after that.

Shame blossomed in her mind as she asked herself the pressing question: Did she have sexual relations with Kevin Lace?

Looking for excuses, she wondered if she'd become insensible from too much drink, was sleepwalking, and he'd taken advantage of her.

No, in her exuberant state, though she'd known better, she had welcomed his advances—of that she was sure. Despite the missing pieces of her recollection, Polly knew with a certainty that she'd allowed the man to have his way with her. The shame, coupled with the feeling that she could not trust herself, left her quaking and confused. Perhaps she'd banished the memory to protect herself from what she presently experienced: an aching regret and a nagging fear that if she couldn't control herself, she might do worse in the future. If she could push all remembrance of the afternoon away, she would, but wave upon wave of bitter thoughts kept it all fresh in her mind.

Polly didn't look forward to keeping her secret from Bill, yet that was exactly what she'd have to do. She realized that her desire for risk still drove her and that the need had nearly got her into real trouble. Fortunately, she couldn't become more pregnant. Bill wouldn't have to know about her afternoon.

7
Adventures

While visiting Polly and Bill one evening in the early summer of 1865, Papa spoke of a desire to find a new lodging. "Now as Eddie has gone to Poplar, I'm thinking I could do with a smaller room."

Polly knew that Papa had been unhappy with how much he paid for his lodgings ever since Eddie found work with a smithy and left home to live closer to his job.

Bill must have overheard. Without consulting Polly, he spoke to her father about finding lodging to share. One afternoon, Bill came home to announce that he'd found two rooms in Trafalgar Street, South London. "With your father helping to pay the landlord," he said, "we'll do much better. There's a gated yard where he can keep his barrow, and plenty of crossings nearby with heavy foot traffic."

Polly didn't look forward to having two stern men ordering her about. Thinking about the incident with the strongbox, and how Papa had such hidden ways of making money, she wanted to tell Bill that he'd fallen for a sob story. Fear of her father's wrath and her husband's disapproval of her father's actions kept her from telling the tale. Instead, she said, "You should have asked me before doing that."

Bill slapped her across the mouth.

Holding her split lip and tasting iron, Polly turned away. So Bill would treat her as her father had. Papa had struck her plenty of times in the past, yet that had been in the service of discipline when she was a youngster. Not a child anymore, Polly felt the slap as a betrayal of what bound her to Bill. Resentful, but careful not to show it, she swallowed her pride and looked at her husband.

"What should your answer have been?" he asked coldly.

Although she feared answering him honestly, she did so anyway. "I'd have said, 'No.'"

"And that's why I needn't ask you such things. I must be the practical one and look out for us. Consider that our combined income should offer more stability. Perhaps your papa would be an occasional childminder once our infant has arrived."

Polly did consider the last suggestion. Her father might watch the baby long enough for her to go out for a drink, as long as he didn't know what she was doing.

* * *

The day they moved to Trafalgar Street, Polly had become tired after helping haul two loads of furniture in Papa's barrow through the hard, stone streets to the new rooms. The men sat in chairs in the front room and Polly thought she could do the same. A large stack of household items rested on the only other chair, so she leaned against the wall to relax.

"When will you fix our supper?" Bill asked.

"I ought to rest for a moment," she said.

Bill stood and boxed her left ear.

Polly squatted, cringing against the sharp ache.

Papa jumped to his feet, and Bill backed away.

Bill said something to Polly. She didn't hear his words for the pain and the ringing in her head. She got to her feet and moved quickly to begin work on the evening meal.

Compared to what she'd suffered from her father, Bill's violence was simply cruel. As she worked, Polly avoided looking at her husband.

I don't know him. Was his part in our courtship a deception? If so, to what end?

Her father had shown a willingness to defend her if the violence had continued, but now would not meet her gaze. He'd resumed his conversation with Bill as if nothing had happened.

This is their way, I suppose, yet I don't know how to be what Bill wants me to be. I must have some part that is my own. Polly felt foolish for not understanding.

The pain in her left ear lasted for several days.

* * *

The new home was a step up. Finer than the wooden one they'd quit, the brick building's interior walls were thick enough that conversations weren't easily heard from room to room, from one household to another. Polly had never lived in a building in which she might speak at an even level and expect the neighbors wouldn't overhear her.

They had their own street entrance, a door that opened into the room Polly and Bill shared. Their room held the only window in the dwelling. The fireplace divided the wall that separated the two chambers, its hearth facing the front. Papa received warmth through the backside of the brick firebox or through the door between the rooms. When the door remained closed in cold weather, he complained of the chill. Since he had no window, in warm weather, he opened the door that led to the back of the building, which allowed the smell of the privies in.

Because of the positions of the doors, the window, and the fireplace, the front room was too small to perform as kitchen, bedroom, nursery, and wash room. Although unhappy about it, Papa had to give over part of his room to a table and chairs so they would all have a place to sit and eat, and yet more area to house a wash tub and supplies.

The brick privies out back were the newest Polly had ever seen. Instead of spiders, they attracted small crickets. The first time she used one of the brick privies, she wondered if she'd ever have to enter one to pull fur.

* * *

In 1866, Polly gave birth to a boy she named Edward, after her father. Since her brother was also named for his father, Polly referred to her infant by his middle name, John.

She found that she did indeed have feelings for the boy immediately. Something about the smell of the infant's skin, the downy hair on his head, and the brightness of his blue eyes told her in joyful terms that he was hers. In the same way, she knew that the boy belonged to Bill. Watching him hold his son, touch him gently, and sing him to sleep in the evenings, Polly felt the tenderness as if she were the recipient. She felt close to her husband again.

As she'd expected, the raising of the child took away all her free time. Though quite pleased to spend her days with her infant rather than making brushes, Polly's income suffered and Bill complained.

"I have so much to do caring for our son, little time is left for my work," she said, fearing that he might become angry that she'd explained herself.

Bill pressed his lips together and frowned as if thoughtful, but he didn't look angry. That he had to think about the truth of what she'd said surprised Polly. Finally, he nodded and gave her a slight smile.

Polly's desire for alcohol went unsatisfied for several months. When the need became strong, she'd lie in the bed with John. Feeling the warmth of his little body against her own helped quiet the craving.

Polly left John with Papa on two occasions within the following year so that she could go on an *adventure*—that's how she thought of going alone for drinks at a pub. The first time, her father suffered from grippe and had not gone out with his barrow on that day. She told him she was off to market. Bill had given her the means to buy mutton, potatoes, bread and lard. At the Borough Market in Southwark Street, she bought broxy instead of good mutton, old potatoes and stale bread so she'd have a few pennies left over. If she made a stew from the diseased meat and old potatoes, Bill and Papa wouldn't know the difference.

On her way home from market, she stopped at the Compass Rose pub on the corner of South and East Streets. She sat with a glass of stout, and downed most of the drink all at once. As her eyes adjusted to the dim interior, she saw the quiet, handsome man she'd seen long ago at The Boar's Tusk pub. He sat in the corner about thirty feet away, leaning back in his chair, a drink and his hammer on the table before him. She smiled and he nodded in her direction.

Polly wanted to ask him to join her, but remembering the disaster at The Boar's Tusk put her off the idea.

Another fellow approached and sat opposite her. He smelled of the ships docked along the river. His clothes were threadbare. He had a small head with watery eyes, a swollen nose that dripped, and hair that hung in tangles to his shoulders, shiny with oil.

"I'm Angus," he said. "Are you looking for a man?"

He certainly got straight to it, Polly thought, holding back laughter and keeping a straight face. "I have one of those," she said.

"Must not be much of a man if you're here alone the afternoon of a Tuesday."

Polly didn't respond. She glanced into the corner to get a look at the handsome man, then finished her glass of stout.

"Let me get you another," Angus said.

Pleased with the offer, she nodded. He got up to fetch the drink. While he was gone, Polly watched the handsome man in the corner.

Angus sat back down with two glasses of stout. As he passed one to her, she noticed his blackened hands.

He looked at her sheepishly. "Stained with pitch," he said, and placed his hands out of sight in his lap. "When there's work for me, it's at the dry docks. We're to begin repairs on a ship today, but she broke in two—Ha! I'm no ship breaker—bad luck, that is—so I end up here. Perhaps there'll be work tomorrow."

While nodding politely as if listening, she thought about how she saved a penny drinking the stout provided by Angus instead of buying her own. If she kept what remained of her funds, she'd have a start on her next adventure.

"I must go home when I'm done with this," she said.

"I'll be sad to see you go," he said. He hadn't taken a drink of his stout. His hands were busy under the table. "It's always a delight to watch a pretty woman take her stout."

Curious, Polly leaned back and to one side far enough to get a look beneath the table. He massaged a bulge in the crotch of his trousers. Again, he looked at her sheepishly.

"Angus," the handsome man called out from the corner of the room.

Startled, Angus jarred the table and spilled the drinks. Polly pushed away, as the liquid flowed across the tabletop and dripped onto the floor. She didn't want the smell on her clothing.

"I haven't touched her, Tom," Angus said.

The handsome man, whose name she supposed was Tom, had got to his feet and approached. Tall and strong, he made a striking impression as he stood over them. For a blue-eyed fellow, his skin appeared unusually dark. He wore heavy trousers and a loose linen shirt. "No," he said, "but you'll leave her be, now."

"Yes, Tom." Angus found his feet, adjusted the lump in his trousers and left the pub.

"Let me get you another glass of stout," Tom said.

"Thank you."

He went to speak with the publican, and Polly watched him. His fluid movements were graceful for such a solid fellow. He appeared comfortable within his body, making him all the more beautiful. Polly had never experienced such powerful attraction before.

She got up and moved to the table he had occupied. *I will talk to him, nothing more. Just one drink, and then I'll go home.*

From her new vantage point, she'd lost sight of Tom. Craning her neck to get a better view, she saw the man approaching with a glass.

No, not Tom—the publican. He set the glass on the table in front of her. "Tom gives you this," he said.

"Thank you," she said, and the publican turned back.

The handsome man had slipped away from her again. Polly slumped in her seat and let out a deep breath. Disappointed, she sat and sipped her stout. The brew lay flat on her palate and felt like warm dishwater in her gut.

When she got home, her father was too stopped-up in the head to smell the drink on her. The time was early enough that the smell would have time to dissipate before Bill got home. Both men complained about the stale bread served with supper, but, as she'd predicted, neither of them knew about the poor quality of the ingredients with which she'd made the stew.

* * *

Polly's second adventure of 1866 occurred four months later. Papa had twisted his ankle and couldn't stand all day, laboring at the work bench that unfolded from his barrow. Polly started out to repeat the process she'd gone through before. Instead she bought a glass of gin at the Compass Rose. The liquid smelled like paraffin, but she swallowed the drink anyway and became so stumbling drunk, she had difficulty making her way home.

Papa recognized her condition immediately when she arrived. "You're in a shameful state," he said. "Bill won't have this."

With her father's immediate response, she knew she faced serious trouble. The realization brought fear and nausea. Polly grabbed the basin from the bedside table and vomited hot and bitter into it.

"Well," Papa said, "that's a start."

Polly sat on the edge of her bed and moaned, trying to get the taste out of her mouth, yet unwilling to get up for water.

"Hush, or you'll wake the boy." Papa stared at her and shook his head. "I knew you were a drunkard when you were a girl of twelve and I saved you from the night. I suppose that weren't enough punishment for you."

He meant the night the Bonehill Ghost came for her. *Thirteen,* Polly thought, *I was thirteen.* She hadn't thought of the demon in a couple of years.

"I'll help you this time," Papa said, "but you'd better make a change." He took up the basin and hobbled on his bad foot through his room and out the back door to dump her vomit into a privy vault. Upon his return, he lifted the ewer from the bedside table, and poured water from it to rinse the basin. He tossed the rinse water out the back door. He poured fresh water into the basin and a cup. "Clean yourself up," he said.

Polly washed her face, and rinsed her mouth out. As she did so, her father went through the basket she'd brought home from the market. He looked at her with a frown. "Were this what the market had to offer?"

Again, she'd purchased broxy and old potatoes. "It's all Bill's money could buy," Polly lied. "He doesn't give me much."

Papa looked at her with suspicion. He paid a flat fee into their household accounts for his room and board. "You bought second-rate food so you'd have the means to drink."

Polly hung her head.

"That takes a macer's guile, woman."

Polly hid her face behind her hands.

Papa had become too quiet, and Polly looked at him. He seemed to ponder something.

"The last time I saw him hit you," he said, "it were all I could do to keep from hitting him back. I'll help you now to keep a peaceful home. I won't do it again."

You're the only one who gets to hit me, Polly thought, but kept her mouth shut, since no good would come from angering him while he tried to help her.

"I should fix supper," Polly said.

"You'll rest. I'll fix the stew."

Polly lay down and closed her eyes while he set to work preparing food. Although fearful that Bill would find out about her drunkenness, she found sleep for a short time.

Papa woke her near seven o'clock in the evening. He had a small bottle of gin. "Bill ought to be home soon." He poured a very small amount of gin into a cup for her. He poured a healthy dose into a cup which he kept for himself. "We shall sit and wait for your husband to arrive. When he does, you'll take the sip of gin. I'll offer him a drink as well. I'll tell him as I offered you the drink, and he'll believe the smell on you came from that."

Polly looked to the hearth. She smelled the savory pot of stew which sat steaming on a trivet.

Papa was on to her, yet he tried to help her avoid the consequences of her drunkenness, and she felt grateful. Somehow, Polly knew that greater punishment lay in her future. She would promise herself a change of behavior, but she couldn't imagine a future she would wish to endure without drink.

When the glossy black doorknob turned, Polly had a sickening feeling that the Bonehill Ghost would come through the door.

The soul of you, the whole of you, that's all what you can preach...

Instead, as expected, Bill entered.

Polly quickly drank her gin, and immediately wished for more. Even so, that would be her last drink for a while. How long, she didn't know.

8
Fragile Abstinence

Although Polly had no real hope that her effort would last, she stayed away from alcohol for over a year. She spent her time thinking of her child, keeping house, and doing her piece work.

In April of 1867, Polly's husband borrowed Papa's barrow to haul a printing press that had been manufactured in Holland in 1756. Bill had bought the mechanism from his employer. The press broke the side rails of the barrow, yet he managed to get the thing to his lodging. With the help of Polly and Papa, Bill succeeded in moving the contraption from the conveyance into their home. The press took up a good third of the front room.

"It's broken," he said. "We have a debt to the company for it, a fairly large sum, but we'll make good on it."

He breathed so heavily from his exertion, Polly thought she hadn't heard him correctly.

Bill seemed to see the question in her eyes. "I got it for a good price *because* it's broken. With your father's help, we'll make it right again."

Papa nodded his head. "I've looked it over. I can manufacture and replace the broken parts."

"I'll teach you how to use it," Bill said, "and we'll be on our way to new earnings."

Polly smiled. "No more brushes?"

"That's right, no more brushes."

* * *

A year would pass before Papa had fixed the press. Within that time, a second child, Percy, was born to Polly and Bill. Again, before the child came, Polly had worried she might not love the infant or that her love might shift from John to Percy, leaving the older child out in the cold. With relief, she quickly discovered affection for both.

To help make room, John, at present two years old, slept in his grandfather's room. With the extra work the infant brought, Polly's days began to run together.

Her desire for drink had stalked her since her last sip of gin, distantly at first, but as time had passed, the urge had moved closer. At present, the beast crouched, barely concealed behind the closest hummock of unforeseen circumstance, looking for the right time to pounce; perhaps a moment when emotional hardship tested Polly. Aware that her abstinence was fragile, she imagined the predatory desire watching her from a distance with Mr. Macklin's glowing eyes. She tried to keep a close watch on the beast.

Bill brought home cases of type, tins of ink, bundles of paper, and a dozen or more additional metal and wooden devices that had to be installed on the press for it to perform its function. Polly learned how to create blocks of type to place in frames, or coffins as Bill called them, which were then placed on wooden beds and locked in place on the press. She learned how to ink properly, and then to use the great lever of the press to squeeze paper and type together to get an impression. At first, she didn't have the strength to work the lever with enough force to get consistent results on paper.

"Do no better than that," Bill said, "and I'll have to work nights as well as days to make a go of it."

Looking at the expression of disgust on his face, she wondered if he tried to discourage her. *Shaming will not make me stronger.* "I shall gain the strength," she said calmly.

"See as you do."

With persistence, she became proficient with the press. Bill brought home jobs for her to do, simple single sheet jobs at first, then more elaborate orders that required several broadsheets to be folded together, sewn, and cut to form a small book.

Polly became fascinated with the process and the machinery. She spent her days tending her children, and trying different configurations of the mechanisms to improve her results. Within a few months, clients were coming to the lodging in Trafalgar Street to receive their orders directly from Polly and pay her. She earned more than she ever had with piece work.

Bill kept up with all the transactions at first, yet with his mind on the work he did for his employer, he began to forget to make entries in the bookkeeping.

"I can keep the books for the printing," Polly told him. "You have enough to worry about." With all the responsibilities she had with housekeeping, the two children, and working the press, she didn't know why she'd made the offer, but she had a suspicion and decided not to look at her misgivings too closely.

Bill looked at her skeptically.

"I learned my maths when I were a girl in school," she said.

Her father overheard. "She's always done the ciphering for me when I've had need of it."

"Show me," Bill said.

They sat at the table in Papa's room, and Polly demonstrated her abilities with numbers. To see the surprise in her husband's eyes left her simultaneously annoyed and satisfied.

Bill came to trust her to keep the accounts for the printing. He also put her in charge of getting the ink and paper she needed and keeping a record of the costs. Within a few months, Polly was skimming off a penny here and there to go on *small adventures*, as she liked to think of them; she'd stop at a pub for half an hour and have one drink. During the second adventure of that sort, she saw her old neighbor from the Scoresby Street address, Judith Stanbrough, at the Compass Rose pub.

"If you see Bill, don't tell him you saw me here," she told the woman as she sat at the table with her. Judith appeared plumper than in the past. If anything, she had more freckles.

"I won't tell your husband, if you won't tell mine," she said.

They both laughed, Judith loudly. Polly looked around for fear they'd attracted the attention of people at other tables. No one watched.

"Do you still live in Scoresby Street?" she asked.

"Yes," Judith said. "I come this far so my husband needn't hear of my drinking. My Swaine, he's a teetotaler. He works for a butcher, stays over Mondays and Fridays near the Portobello Road Market to help with cattle auctions. I take the time to have a drink." She smiled crookedly. "Last I saw of you were the day I helped you home from The Boar's Tusk. You were full of the lush."

Polly felt her mouth drop open as she tried to recollect.

Judith laughed. "You don't remember!"

Polly shook her head. Full memory of the afternoon she'd spent singing with Kevin Lace and his pals still eluded her.

"I found you with that pretty boy between the privies out back. He'd reached under your skirts and were about to have more. I saw what you weren't with us."

Shame gripped Polly.

"I shouted and he scampered away, the coward."

Ah, he didn't have his way with me! Despite relief in knowing the truth, Polly remained ashamed that Judith knew what she'd done.

"I saw you home that day."

Polly lowered her head, and took a drink of her stout.

"No need to feel bad," Judith said, gently touching Polly's left hand. "I've got that way too. Life is hard, and we have need to get away from it sometimes."

Grateful to have a sympathetic friend, Polly looked up, smiled, and clasped Judith's hand. Knowing that another young wife also liked to drink, and for similar reasons, she didn't feel so lonely and dishonorable.

"You were knapped, I think."

"Yes, I have two children now, John and Percy, so I don't have much time. I ought to finish this and go."

Judith rubbed her tummy. "And, now, I have one on the way. Soon, I'll not have time either. Perhaps we can help each other. I could keep yours when you want to have a drink, and, in return, you could do the same for me."

Polly found the offer unsettling, but had to think about why. She felt comfortable with the idea of small adventures because the time she allotted to them and the funds she committed each outing were both limited. Even if she gave herself more time, fear kept her from taking more than the occasional penny from the printing accounts, so her drinking was regulated to one glass of bitter or stout, and nothing stronger, per adventure. The freedom Judith's offer entailed seemed dangerous, yet Polly didn't want to close the door on it.

"That might be a good thing," she said. She finished her stout and stood.

"If you want to talk about it," Judith said, "I'll be here Monday afternoons—at least for a while—I'm two months along already."

"Thank you," Polly said.

9
Something in Common

I n mid-summer of 1868, Polly received an order for a chapbook about the life and crime of a condemned criminal,
Thomas Wells, who would hang at Newgate Prison in August. Following the hanging of the Fenian murderer, Michael
Barrett, in May, executions had ceased to be public events. She
had assumed that would put the writers of gallows ballads out
of business.

Looking over the materials her husband had brought her
for the job, a hand-written manuscript and a small woodcut
block for the front page illustration, she noted with discomfort
the author's name: Conway. The day she'd spent singing the
man's ballad about Theodore Pritchard with Kevin Lace and
his friends wasn't a good memory.

Over the next few days, as she went about the work of setting type, printing, folding, sewing and cutting two hundred of
the books, Lace's voice rang in her head, singing the song over
and over. Thinking about the loss of memory and control she'd
experienced that day at The Boar's Tusk was an uncomfortable
reminder of her problem with alcohol, and brought on a nau-
seating shame. She finished the job on her third day of working
on the chapbooks, but the unsettling recollections continued.
In an effort to feel better, she opened a small set of watercol-

or paints and brushes her father had given her for Christmas ten years earlier, fetched a cup of water, and hand-colored one copy of the woodcut illustration, a picture of one man shooting another in the face. Polly thought she'd done a good job, although, once dried, the front page puckered slightly.

She continued dreading the moment when the author would come to pick up his order. To keep from thinking about that, she began adding color to more copies of the picture.

Her husband got home late. Polly, the children, and her father had already eaten by the time Bill arrived. Papa and the boys were in his room. She had colored half the run of chapbooks, and they sat staggered on a shelf by the open window to dry.

"What have you done?" Bill shouted when he saw the colored chapbooks. "You've spoiled the lot of them."

She cowered away from his angry eyes.

He grabbed Polly's arms and spun her around roughly. "He'll not pay for that!"

Polly scrambled backwards. He punched her in the face and she fell, striking her head against the lever of the press. He moved forward and kicked her. She blocked his foot with her thigh. "No," she cried, reaching up with her hands to ward off more blows as he struck out at her face again.

Bill grabbed her left wrist and twisted. As she screamed with the pain, she heard little John, Percy, or both, begin to cry.

Papa hurried from his room. "You can't treat her like that as long as I'm here," he said.

Bill swung on Papa, but the elder man dodged the blow and raised his own fists. Polly's husband knew of her father's reputation among the costers as a good pugilist. He seemed to see the danger he'd brought upon himself, and lifted both hands in a gesture of surrender. Papa backed off. Bill sat back on the bed and hung his head. Polly slowly got up from the floor, grateful for Papa's help.

"Mr. Conway won't pay for the chapbooks, Polly," Bill said quietly. "But *you* shall," he added ominously.

Polly realized what a horrible mistake she'd made. Of course, the customer had not asked for color and might therefore refuse the order. What had she been thinking? To fill an order properly, one gave a customer the required goods and service; no more, no less.

"We'll just see about that when he comes for them tomorrow," Papa said, his eyes still warning Bill off.

Polly soothed her sore cheek with gentle fingers. "Tomorrow, at noon."

"I thought the color a charming touch," Papa said.

Bill scoffed. "You don't know the printing business. Now, get out of our room."

Papa passed through the door into his room. Polly heard him calming the children.

"You shall spend every moment between now and noon tomorrow if necessary printing and binding enough of the chapbooks to make up for those ruined."

"May I serve your supper?" Polly asked, averting her eyes.

"Yes," he said. "Then to work, straight away."

Polly prepared him a plate and returned to the grind of printing more of the chapbooks, toiling late into the night.

Both John and Percy slept with Papa. Bill slept, but got up around midnight and began helping her with the sewing and cutting of the books. "You'd better hope the customer is satisfied," he grumbled.

They worked in silence for another three hours, finishing the task.

* * *

Polly awoke as Bill got up at eight o'clock in the morning. Papa had already left with his barrow and the two boys still slept.

"I shall be late if I don't hurry," Bill said. He dressed, grabbed a crust of bread, and left.

Polly got up, ate, roused her boys from sleep and fed them. She tried to put her room back in order after the tumult of violence and labor from the previous night. She feared the inevitable moment when a knock on her door signaled the arrival of Mr. Conway. She had stacked the colored chapbooks and hidden them under another stack of paper on a shelf of supplies in the corner so that he would not see them. Some of the chapbooks pressed late in the night were inferior to those done more carefully earlier in the day. She began to anticipate an angry reaction, perhaps even a refusal to pay for the product.

When finally that knock came, Polly felt a jolt as if her body might leap out of her skin. She gathered herself together, took several deep breaths and moved slowly to answer the call. Upon opening the door, she found a woman with auburn hair, hazel eyes, and a heart-shaped face.

"I am Mr. Conway's wife," she said. "I've come for the chapbooks he ordered."

So relieved that she didn't face another angry man, Polly leaned heavily against the door frame and held her hands to her chest.

"Are you feeling ill?" Mrs. Conway asked.

"No," Polly said, "I didn't sleep well." She stepped aside and gestured for the woman to enter. "I am Mrs. Nichols. Polly."

"Please call me Katie."

Polly gestured toward a bundle of chapbooks tied with yellow string.

"Since executions are no longer for the public," Katie said, "I argued against such a large order, but my husband said we needn't change what worked in the past. I've tried to think of a way to attract more attention with the chapbooks."

"My husband is often too proud to listen to my ideas."

Katie smiled knowingly, and Polly knew they had something in common.

Inspired to think that her mistake might become a good thing after all, she said, "Have you thought of color in the woodcut illustration?"

"We can't pay the price," Katie said, shaking her head.

Polly's hopes dimmed.

Still, the colored copies were a loss. If Katie could benefit from them, Polly might as well give them to her for free.

Perhaps if they sell well, Polly thought, *she and her husband will be so happy with the results they'll ask for the color next time and willingly pay for it.*

Polly went to the shelf where she'd hidden the colored chapbooks and removed the stack of paper she'd put on top and set it aside. "I hope you don't mind," she said, "but I tried my hand at adding to the picture." She pulled out a copy and offered the chapbook to Katie. "I completed your order without the color, but should you like, you may take the colorful ones at no charge." She gestured toward the shelf. "I did close to one hundred of them."

Katie looked at the copy handed to her.

Polly noted that the heavy stack of paper she'd placed on top of the stack of colored chapbooks had largely pressed flat the puckers in the illustration.

As Katie's eyes became large, Polly realized too late that if the woman had created the artwork, she might be protective. Despite Katie's friendly manner, Polly thought of Bill's anger, and feared an accusation of impertinence from the woman.

But then Katie smiled brightly. "You made nearly a hundred like this?"

"Yes," Polly said, much relieved. "Should they sell well, perhaps you'll consider color in the future."

"We ought to sell these for tuppence. We can but try." Katie's expression was delighted and hopeful.

She paid for the order. Polly tied the colored copies to the larger bundle of chapbooks and sent Katie on her way.

* * *

When Bill returned that evening, he smiled to hear that Polly had earned her fee for the printing.

"What has become of the copies you colored?" he asked, looking toward the shelf where she'd stored them.

Polly decided he would not like that she'd given them away at no charge. "I sent them away with the dustman today," she lied, glad that Tuesdays were the day the raggedy dustmen made their rounds on Trafalgar Street.

Bill bristled, yet spoke quietly. "You might have used the blank side of the last pages for proofs." He took a deep breath, clearly trying not to revisit his anger from the night before. Likely, he felt remorse for the way he'd acted.

"I'm sorry I didn't think of that," Polly said. "I felt so badly about my mistake, I just wanted them gone."

Bill seemed to accept the explanation. He put a hand on her cheek and kissed her forehead, and, for a moment, Polly felt remorse for lying to him. The feeling quickly passed.

* * *

A week later, an unexpected knock came at Polly's door. She answered the call to find Mrs. Conway standing in the doorway, beaming. "We sold nearly half the colored ones right away. They sold for a penny, ha'penny each." She held out a hand to offer Polly three shillings.

A moment passed before Polly had recovered from her surprise. In that time, her thoughts immediately turned to how and where she'd hide the funds from her husband and her father. Realizing Katie still stood in the threshold, smiling and holding out her hand, Polly took the coins and said, "Thank you. My children are napping or I should invite you in."

"I must return home anyway."

"Please consider the color next time."

"To pay the price is not a risk we can afford with the changes to executions. People gather for the hangings, but they don't stay for long and sales suffer. I shall keep it in mind if things get better. Thank you for taking the risk for us, and trusting me."

"You're quite welcome," Polly said, holding the warm shillings to her breast.

When Katie had gone, Polly hid the three coins under the loose insole in the left boot of her Sunday pair of high-lows. With that much money set aside, she might have a *greater adventure*, if she found the time. She thought of Judith Stanbrough's offer.

10
Scheming

Three months later, in the autumn of 1868, Polly set a plan into motion.

"I must remain home on Tuesday to await a delivery of ink and paper," she told her father on a Sunday, "but the larder is empty. Would you return from the street early tomorrow so I'll have the afternoon to go to market?"

"I'll miss out on at least a shilling's worth of trade," he said.

"I'll speak to Bill about lowering your room and board fee for the week."

Polly's printing consistently produced a good extra income, and that fact wasn't lost on Bill Nichols. That evening, he agreed to lower her father's contribution to the household fund by one shilling for the week. Papa agreed to stay home Monday afternoon to look after John and Percy.

Monday brought a heavy overcast sky that left the city in twilight all day. Before going to market, Polly went to the Compass Rose with the hope of speaking with Judith Stanbrough. As she neared the pub, she worried, and, strangely, hoped that Judith might be too far along in her pregnancy to come so far for a drink.

Polly entered the establishment and made her way into the area where she'd seen Judith before. The green and blue tinted glass windows further dimmed the gray light coming in from outside, making mere silhouettes of the dark wooden furniture and the few desultory figures she saw seated and milling about. The stale tobacco and yeasty odor of the place from untold smokes and spilled drinks over the years, which she usually found somewhat pleasant, currently gave her an impression of decay.

Polly's eyes adjusted to the interior, and she saw Judith sitting with a glass of bitter, reading a book by the light of a small lamp. When the woman looked up, Polly felt she'd become committed to a course that would lead to disaster. Despite her unease, she sat and asked, "How can we help one another?"

Judith set down her book. "Well, I can spell you and you can spell me. I can keep your children, and you can keep mine. Not at the same time, mind you. We want to give one of us at a time the chance to go for a drink. Mondays and Fridays my husband is gone to work the auctions. We each get a day."

"I understand, but where?" Polly didn't like the impatience in her own voice. "If someone were to come home unexpectedly, we'd be caught out."

"My husband will not come home on the days of the auctions," Judith said evenly. "He works long hours and the distance is too great. It matters little if no one is at my home. I'm the one who can move about. We ought to always have the children at your lodging."

Polly thought about that. The woman sounded somehow too reasonable, too confident. Didn't she realize they embarked upon a potentially perilous enterprise?

"We'd need explanations—" Polly began in a tone that sounded as if she argued against going forward with the plan. She stopped and softened her voice before continuing. "Explanations for your child, or you and your child, to be there, if my father or husband were to come home."

"We'll find a way," Judith said calmly. She'd clearly had a drink and couldn't be bothered with worries.

Polly needed the same outlook. "Excuse me for a moment," she said, and went to the publican to fetch a glass of stout. Polly thought through her problem as she waited impatiently for the barkeep to carefully draw her drink. When she'd returned to the table and sat, she said, "If you are seen to be a friend, I should easily say that I took charge of your child because you arrived in need of a childminder so you could run an errand."

"That's right," Judith said. "The same might be true if I were discovered at your lodging with all three children, but we'd lay it a bit different. We should say as I stopped by unexpectedly and you took the opportunity to go out for something needed while I stayed to watch the children. That's what mothers do for one another, after all."

"If we told them we did it weekly—" Polly began.

Judith cut her off. "No, we don't want to give a hint of a plan if we don't have to. No sense allowing them to know how often you're out or they should wonder what you're doing with all the free time."

Polly worried about her capacity to keep lies straight. "I'd need to have something from market as were indeed needed."

"Don't worry, we'll sort it out," Judith said, reaching for Polly's hand. "What day is best for you to be out, Mondays or Fridays?"

"Mondays," Polly said, since her father still came home early on some Fridays.

"You can start by taking me home with you today and introducing me to your family. We must make certain they know we're friends."

Polly wondered briefly if Judith truly was her friend.

"My father is with the boys so I could go to market," she said.

"Finish your stout and then we'll both go."

Polly tried to put away her trepidations about Judith and the plan. The stout helped a bit.

Is the feeling I get from the drinking worth all this? She'd experienced fear when severely drunk in the past, but when lightly intoxicated, she enjoyed a euphoric feeling of separation from her troubles.

Polly rose to her feet. "I'll have another stout to quiet my concerns."

Judith took her hand. "You must learn to have just enough," she said, taking a small sip of her bitter as if demonstrating, "and quit in time to lose the touch and the smell before you rejoin your family."

Polly sat back down, imagining herself capable of what her friend suggested. She had intended to plan with Judith a *greater adventure,* a time of deeper drunkenness for which the three shillings earned from Mrs. Conway would be necessary. What Judith suggested was smarter, safer, and more responsible. Polly had her children to think about, after all.

She finished her stout and rose with Judith to exit the pub and head for the market.

A *greater adventure* would have to wait. How long before Polly's current responsibilities would allow for such a lark, she didn't know. She didn't have to decide right away. Although she had trepidations about her plans with Judith, Polly found the risk exciting.

11
Mistrust

On the day Polly took Judith home with her, Bill had come home early and Papa had left the children with their father and gone out. Polly introduced Judith to Bill as her friend, then didn't think much about not having the opportunity to introduce her to Papa.

On a Monday in the summer of 1869, Polly arrived home to find her father with John, Percy, Judith, and the woman's infant girl, Dorrie.

"I know all the women in the neighborhood. I don't know who this is, staying here with your boys while you're out," he said.

Sitting at the table in Papa's room, holding her infant, Judith remained silent.

"Papa, Judith is my friend," Polly said. Papa might have let the matter go with that, but she knew instantly that her face betrayed her unease, and that he held suspicions about her motives.

"She's pleasant enough," he said, "and her girl is no trouble at all. I find it curious, though, that you haven't spoken to me of her. I saw this woman leaving our abode last Friday, just as I turned into the lane on my way home. She didn't know me, and walked by, carrying her babe, without a word. When I came into our rooms, straight away you asked for my help with John while you put a fresh nappy on Percy, and I forgot about the woman until later. When I did remember her, I thought it odd you never spoke of her. I should think as lonely as it must be for you here, alone so much of the time, you would mention a visitor."

Caught off guard and dumbstruck, Polly laughed hesitantly. To cover her awkward response, she walked to Papa's rickety old bed and lifted Percy. John hid behind Polly's skirts, perhaps a bit frightened to hear the serious tone in his grandfather's voice.

"And now that you've heard my words," Papa said, "you're as gammy as I've ever known you to be."

"I do not deceive!" she said too forcefully.

Papa had acted the same way toward Polly on occasion when she was a child, any time he thought she hid something. His aggressive questioning had always rattled her. Before she'd figure out his tactic, he'd got a few confessions out of her.

Not this time, she decided. "When did women helping each other with the raising of their children become such a curiosity? Judith were our neighbor in Scoresby Street. I've seen her at market and we've made an agreement to help each other on Mondays."

She had forgotten to pretend she'd merely taken advantage of Judith's spontaneous visit. His tactic had spooked her again and he'd got some of the truth.

"And does she live there still?"

"Yes," Polly answered quickly, then realized she'd given away more of the truth when she saw Judith shaking her head. Thankfully, Papa didn't see the woman's silent communication.

He scoffed. "Plenty of women in the neighborhood watch

your children for the hour or two needed to go to the grocer, yet you're telling me you have a weekly arrangement with a woman who must travel nearly two miles to get here. Do you then return the favor, going to her?"

Polly knew that suggesting she'd take both her children such a distance for a childminder wasn't believable. "We haven't worked that out."

"Strange that you haven't mentioned any of this to me before. I shouldn't be surprised to find Bill knows nothing about it either."

When Polly didn't respond with anything more than a glare, he stepped forward to smell her breath.

"Pickled whelks," she said. She'd eaten the sea snails at market to help cover the smell of the stout she drank. Also a product of fermentation, the vinegar used in pickling did wonders to hide the smell of alcohol.

"What did you get at market?" he asked.

"Toke," she said flatly, pulling a loaf of bread from her basket.

"Hmph," Papa grumbled as if he knew his investigation had been thwarted. As he stepped back a loud squeak came from the floorboards and John hugged his mother tightly.

Polly resented Papa's high and mighty manner. She had a mind to bring up his crime involving the strongbox. Although she still knew little about it, he might be embarrassed if she asked him to explain what happened. Fear of his reaction kept her from saying anything.

Polly turned to Judith. "Thank you for looking after my boys. I'm sorry you had to see us at our worst." She walked out of Papa's room, then turned to look back, waiting for Judith to follow.

"Our worst?" her father said. When nobody responded, he shook his head.

Judith was in no hurry. She'd remained calm throughout the conversation.

Papa looked at her and said, "Out."

Judith rose from the table and joined Polly. Papa shut the ill-fitting door between the two rooms.

Polly immediately sagged, and Judith took her roughly by the arm to steady her.

John let go and sat on the floor. He gathered up a wooden doll Papa had made him, and began striking the floor with its head and humming a tune.

Polly and Judith walked out the front door and along Trafalgar Street.

"Are you flat?" Judith asked. She didn't give Polly time to answer. "You must do better. You might just as well have told him all our plans."

Polly winced. She knew she'd pled innocence poorly. The woman's belittling didn't help. "I'll do better next time," she said curtly.

"Let's hope so. Until Friday, then."

Polly watched Judith, carrying her Dorrie, move along the gray lane between the rows of red brick houses toward South Street. Much like the houses along the road, which appeared alike on the outside, she and Judith seemed much the same. Also like the houses, what could be found on the inside was quite different. The complexity of their deception didn't seem to trouble Judith. Polly wondered what made the difference. She also wondered again if Judith considered herself a friend or if the woman merely used her.

As Polly made her way back to her room, the gray dustmen, in their buckled down clothes and fantail hats, drove by in the same direction. She usually found the way they set their "dust ho" song to the rhythm of the clomp of their horse's hooves clever and amusing. At present, though, above all else, she heard the grating of the iron-rimmed cart wheels cutting through the roadway mire to the paving stones beneath. The whole seemed an ugly tune to which the flies following the conveyance danced. Polly watched clods of horse manure tumble over the high sides of the overburdened cart bed and land in the road. Somehow, the sight, sound, and stench reflected how she felt.

12
With Time

For over a year, in the evening of each Monday, Polly's father got in close enough to smell her breath. "You like the pickled whelks, don't you?" he'd said to her more than once, a smirk on his face.

She tried not to react.

Although unhappy to find herself pregnant again, Polly's vexation turned to delight when the child she bore in 1870 was female. She named the girl Alice. The last two months of her pregnancy, Polly and Judith ceased to take their Mondays and Fridays for drinking. They agreed to resume the schedule again two months following the child's birth.

The time off from drinking didn't go well for Polly. With three children, the housekeeping, and the printing, she had more work than ever, and desperately sought a break from it. One month after Alice's birth, Polly couldn't wait any longer, and wrote to Judith, asking her to come as soon as possible. Shortly thereafter, the two women returned to their schedule.

Having gone without drink for a time, Polly had a frightening desire to cut herself loose from constraints and become truly sodden, yet she succeeded in controlling her drinking enough during her Monday outings to avoid exposing her indulgence.

* * *

One Monday afternoon at the Compass Rose, Polly saw the handsome fellow named Tom enter and speak to the publican. Assuming that once he'd fetched a drink for himself, he'd walk toward the corner where she'd seen him sit before, she planned to invite him to join her.

She watched him receive a bottle of gin from the publican, then turn and exit the pub without ever having looked in her direction. Polly wanted to get up and go after him, but knew she'd feel foolish. What did she have to say to the fellow? He probably wouldn't remember her.

Twice more in the next couple of years, she saw Tom. Each time, she longed to approach him, to get to know him, to touch him, and with each encounter, the idea seemed more ridiculous. On the occasions she found a moment of solitude in which to pleasure herself, the desire came from thinking of Tom, his muscular form, his graceful, sure movements, the slight sadness in his thoughtful eyes.

* * *

In the spring of 1871, Papa ceased to smell Polly's breath in the evening. "So long as you don't eat too many of those 'whelks,'" he said, "I have no quarrel with you."

Polly decided that he meant he accepted her drinking if she didn't take the habit too far.

Because he hadn't said anything about his suspicions to her husband, Bill remained ignorant of Papa's misgivings about his daughter.

Despite the increased time and care Polly gave to her

children, she continued to earn an income from printing. Some relief came in 1872 when John started attending Saint Mary Magdalen National Infants School. At six years of age, he enjoyed making his way to and from school, walking with friends, though he did not like the "Infants" designation of his school.

"The debt for the printing press has been fully paid," Bill told Polly in the winter of 1874.

Though considerably cooler than in their days of courting, her relationship with her husband seemed steady and unchanging. The sex still frustrated Polly. Bill would not be denied sex, but he saw no need for her satisfaction in the endeavor. She'd asked him to make an adjustment in his method to increase her pleasure on several occasions.

"If you should make it last a bit longer, I will be most grateful," she'd said once.

"If you want me to treat you like a tart," he said, "you'll have to suffer all that a tart does. I don't think you want that."

His statement made little sense, but seemed an ominous warning. She did wonder what he might know about what a tart suffered. Polly didn't bring up the subject again, and the tension in bed thereafter let up.

Polly felt secure in her marriage, if unsatisfied.

She felt no need to pray for herself or others.

The Bonehill Ghost had become a distant memory.

13
A Tempting Choice

On Monday morning, December 20 of 1875, Polly hid away the tinplate toys she'd bought for the children's Christmas stockings—a steamship for John, a train for Percy, a horse-drawn carriage for Alice. As she imagined the children's faces when they received their gifts, a knock came at her door. She answered the knock to find Judith had arrived early. Dorrie wasn't with her. The cold and windy air outside tried to push its way in. Judith didn't respond when invited to come in, so Polly stepped out and pulled the door shut.

"At first I couldn't decide," the woman said, "but I have, at present. Dorrie will begin school in the new year. She's with her grandmother now and during the holidays. No longer shall I come on Mondays and Fridays."

Perhaps Polly should have seen the day coming, since Percy was the same age as Dorrie, and he had already begun at the infants school. Polly had happily let go of her daytime duties of minding Percy, especially since the discovery she was pregnant again. She hadn't told Bill or Papa about the pregnancy. Although she loved her children, she didn't look forward to having yet another so soon.

Her surprise left her struggling unsuccessfully to think of a way to change Judith's mind. Finally, Polly said simply, "I'm not prepared for the change." Straining against the chill breeze, she knew she looked as if she might cry. "Could we do it just a bit longer until I can make other plans?"

Judith appeared unmoved. "No, I shall not have a child to keep during much of the week and shan't need your help. I have plans for Christmas to think about today."

Indeed, she wasn't a *good* friend.

Polly hung her head wearily. "You're lucky you don't have the quick womb I have."

"Are you knapped *again?*" Judith asked with a frown.

"Yes."

"It's not my luck," Judith said. She grimaced slightly, then asked, "Haven't you asked Bill to wear a sheath on his manhood?"

"He won't."

"Swaine does, and when that fails, I know how to end a pregnancy. There's a woman can help you."

"The Church tells us that's murder."

"Yes, well, a life unloved and spent in poverty," Judith said, coldly, "what's that?"

Polly had no answer. Judith started to turn away.

"Please," Polly said, "I must have a drink today."

"And that's the difference between us," Judith said. Shaking her head, she turned and walked away.

Polly stepped back inside, and slammed the door, shutting out the biting cold.

The woman's abrupt manner aside, her suggestion about abortion made Polly uncomfortable because of the tempting option the procedure presented. She considered abortion wrong, and believed that if she took the option, she'd be guilty of murder. Apparently, Judith had chosen just such murders in the past.

Still, Polly believed the life in her womb would be better off if it never saw the world. With each child she'd had, her ability to provide for them, the time she had to share with them, her capacity for affection, and, yes, she admitted to herself, even to love them, had diminished.

What had Judith said? "A life unloved and spent in poverty."

Perhaps if God knew how Polly felt, He would help. Yet, the Lord should know already what she held in her heart, even if the feelings were a jumble. Polly wanted the best for the three children she had, and if that meant she shouldn't have another mouth to feed, another heart to soothe and love, then possibly He should take the infant in the midst of her pregnancy. The idea that she might have a miscarriage gave her a small hope which she knew must be dismissed, but which she clung to for fear that if she didn't, God might not know her preference. The conflict within her turned to nausea. Although most likely mere morning sickness, the discomfort bore with it a chilling uneasiness.

She didn't have time for such distraction, and tried not to think about the matter further. Her schedule for the afternoon required her to print a broadsheet that advertised a boxing match. She had the materials, including a nicely done wood-cut of men preparing to punch each other while others in the background cheered. She needed to take care of Alice first. As she occupied herself, stoking the fire, cleaning the dishes and the pot used to prepare the meal from the night before, nausea and disquiet continued to hound Polly. Her hands trembled and her heart periodically hammered in her chest.

Finally, she promised herself that she'd find a moment to say a prayer for the infant in her womb and one for Judith. That did little to calm her.

She hurriedly fed Alice a midday meal of bread and butter,

then placed her in the bed, wrapped in a faded red wool blanket, hoping the girl would take a nap. Before beginning work on her broadsheet, Polly found her moment for prayer. Alice had become quiet, and a calm came into the room, but not into Polly. The conflict in her heart had turned to an unaccountable foreboding. She voiced the words before she'd had a chance to think them through.

"Please O Lord, take this child now before it's too late." Polly regretted her plea immediately. While trying to persuade herself that God understood that she meant for the child not to suffer, she knew her true motive to be self-serving. After years of carefully avoiding any mention of herself in prayer, she'd found a new way to demonstrate her selfishness to God. She quickly said the penitent prayer from Mr. Shaw's well-worn card, but she didn't feel any better.

Polly couldn't do her work. Feeling naked before the eyes of the Lord, she paced. When Alice began to stir, Polly knew she disturbed the child's slumber. She had to get away.

Stepping outside, she had the intention of pacing the lane's granite footway outside her door. Having traveled half a block up Trafalgar Street, she decided she should keep going. She imagined walking the two or more miles to the docks, and stowing aboard a ship headed to some land where people believed in a different god, one who would not know her so well.

Then, she remembered she'd left the front door open. She broke out in a sweat. Her heart moved uncomfortably as she thought of a stranger entering her room while Alice slept. She imagined John and Percy coming home from school to find nobody home, their confusion and sadness when they found out their mother had abandoned them, and so close to Christmas!

Polly turned and walked back the way she'd come.

Although the shame had become so large inside her that she saw little else, she knew that her children needed her.

* * *

Bill came home from work around noon. His foot had been hurting him for over a week after an accident at the offices of Messrs. Pellanddor and Company. He'd explained on the day of the mishap that a case of letter—a heavy wooden box full of metal type—had fallen from a rack onto his foot.

He hobbled crookedly as he came in, using a cane he'd borrowed from a workmate. "I'm no good at work the way I am," he told Polly. "Richardson sent me home. Says he's tired of my curses. I must rest up and go back no sooner than the new year. I think a bone is broken and I should be much longer, though."

He leaned against the wardrobe, removed his jacket, and unbuttoned his checked waistcoat.

"Alice, make room for your father," Polly said. "Soon, you must get up and help me impose pages."

"Yes, mum." The girl smiled sleepily, and moved over to one side in the bed.

Polly helped her husband lie down. She pulled the shoe off his good foot, then proceeded to more carefully remove the other. He kept his lips tightly closed throughout the process.

"Have you eaten?" she asked.

"Yes," he said with a strain in his voice. "I can wait 'til supper."

Polly had missed some of her Monday excursions in the past, when Bill or her father had been ill and not worked for a day or more. On those occasions, with Judith's help, Polly had always been able to look forward to a time when she'd have a day to herself again. At present, she didn't know when she'd have another chance to have a drink. Her hands began to tremble as she thought about the problem.

"I'll need a drink for the pain," Bill said. "Go around to the Compass Rose and fetch a pint of gin."

Polly concealed her excitement.

He pulled his purse from a pocket of his trousers and fished out a shilling. "I expect tuppence back."

Polly took the silver coin. She might not have time to go for a single drink, but she could get a bottle of gin to have on hand at home for herself. Surely, a circumstance would arise in which she might have some secretly.

"Alice, don't bother your father while I'm gone. He's not feeling well."

"Yes, Mum."

Polly turned away, opened the wardrobe, and used her body to conceal her efforts as she retrieved a shilling from under the loose lining of the left boot of her Sunday high-lows. Pulling on her shawl and bonnet, she left, carrying a basket to hold her purchase. On her way up Trafalgar Street toward South Street, against the bitterly cold wind, she decided that if she ran the whole way, there and back, she'd stay warmer and have the time to drink a glass of stout when she got there. No, Bill might smell the alcohol when she got back.

Even so, she walked briskly. She smiled uneasily at the women she passed, but looked away from each man.

At the Compass Rose, she bought two pints of gin, placed them in her basket, and headed for home, again walking briskly. Polly hadn't had anything stronger than stout for many years, and looked forward to getting the gin home and finding a chance to take a deep draft.

Bill might see that she had two bottles if she wasn't careful.

The basket held a couple pieces of coarse linen. She arranged the bottles so that each rested under its own piece of cloth. That also kept them from clinking together. When she got back, hopefully Bill and Alice would be asleep in bed. If not, she'd hurry to the larder, a set of shelves within a cabinet built into the wall to the left of the fireplace, set the basket down, and reach inside to take one bottle out. If they were asleep, she'd retrieve the second bottle and hide it away before awakening Bill.

But where?

14

Obsession

Bill was awake when she returned home. Next to him, Alice still napped.

Polly offered a bottle of gin to her husband. He drank half the pint before lying back down on the bed. The remainder of the bottle, Polly hid with the tinplate toys in the back of the wardrobe. Bill might not need any more gin. If he forgot about it, the rest would be Polly's.

Once he'd begun to snore, she pulled the second pint from the basket, stepped into Papa's room, pulled the cork from the bottle, and had a gulp of the gin. Although Bill would not smell the drink on her after the lush he'd had, she risked her father noticing when he came home. John and Percy would be home soon, as well.

Putting the cork back in place, Polly returned to her room, having decided to hide the bottle behind the wardrobe. No, Bill could see her when she tried to retrieve the gin if she left it there. She thought to put the bottle in Papa's room, but decided he knew his living quarters well enough that he'd notice anything amiss and easily find the gin. The eave above the door that led out back had a few broken boards. Perhaps she could hide the gin behind them. If the landlord came to fix the eave unexpectedly, though, he'd discover her bottle. He might well take the gin for himself. Worse, he could ask Bill or Papa about it.

The drink in her belly had created a warm spot that grew. Soon the warmth would enter her head and her worries would flee. She wanted to find a hiding place before that happened.

The privies! She thought that the bricks that lined the floors of the facilities measured a bit larger than the bottle she needed to hide. She grabbed a spoon, stepped out back, and entered the closest privy. Down on her knees, she pried up one of the bricks from the corner beside the door, and found the earth underneath tightly packed. Despite the distance from the seat, the soil smelled of old urine, and she briefly feared the odor might carry with it cholera or other diseases. Undeterred, Polly used the spoon to scoop out enough earth to create a space the bottle would fit into even when the brick was returned to its spot. Settling the bottle into the space, she put the brick back to see if it sat flush with the others. The hole required more digging. She tested two more times before the preparation looked right. Before placing the gin into the hole for storage, she tipped the bottle upside down, making certain the cork sealed well. Polly placed the gin in her excavation, returned the brick to its spot, and worked the soil on top so that the floor didn't look as if it had been disturbed.

Returning to her rooms, she found Alice up and around. Polly resumed her work on the boxing broadsheet. She gave to Alice the printed pages of a chapbook job to fold.

John and Percy came home, and Polly instructed them to sew the edges of the chapbook pages.

Papa arrived two hours later. Somehow, he knew she'd been drinking.

"Yes, I had a nip after Bill took his fill," she said, "but it wasn't much." She showed him the bottle. "He took half of it."

"He's not a drinking man," Papa said. "He'll be asleep for a while, then."

Polly prepared supper and sat with her father and the children to eat. Thoughts of the bottle in the privy distracted her. She worried that one of her neighbors would find it. She worried that the cork would leak; that either the bottle would lose its contents or that the urine of careless visitors to the facility would somehow get into her gin.

The children occupied themselves through the evening with their grandfather, playing simple card games. By lamplight after dark, Polly completed the order of broadsheets for the boxing match. When she'd finished, Papa was asleep in his room with the boys, and Alice slept in bed next to her father. Although he had not completely awakened, Bill had grumbled and shifted a few times on the lumpy mattress. She knew that when he awoke, he'd be hungry.

Polly stripped and put on her nightclothes. She lay down next to Bill and tried to sleep. The gin still haunted her. She imagined exhuming the bottle and having a drink. Once she'd played through the scenario in her head, she couldn't get rid of the idea, and so she seriously thought it through. Her father was accustomed to having her pass through his room on the way to the privy at night, and easily slept through the sounds of her tread upon the noisy floor. Even so, she feared that as soon as she tried to get to the gin, he'd sit bolt upright in his bed and ask what she was doing. No, he would take no notice of her. She'd go to the privy, dig up the bottle, have her dram, and no one would be the wiser. By the time they all awoke in the morning, the powerful smell would be off her. Polly tried to put the plan out of her head and go back to sleep, but couldn't.

Finally, she rose, lit a lamp, and pushed her feet into her

boots. As she made her way toward the back door, her heart leapt with each pop and squeak of the floorboards. She moved quickly, got to the door leading out the back, and opened it. Stepping through, she discovered bitter cold and frost clinging to everything outside. The full moon rode wisps of cloud, high in the clear sky. She scampered to the privy. The door opened easily.

Polly entered, set the lamp on the seat, pulled up the hem of her nightclothes, and knelt with her bare knees on the cold, hard floor. She found the brick frozen in place. Having forgotten her spoon, she clawed at the floor. Her breath plumed so heavily about her head, she had difficulty seeing. She scraped the skin off her finger tips before the brick finally gave a little. While her fingers stung, she worked at it. After a time, she got the brick loose.

The gin lay undisturbed. The glass that held the potent liquid gleamed like a jewel in the soft orange light. Polly lifted the bottle and pulled the cork. She leaned back against the gritty brick wall of the privy, put the mouth of the cold glass to her lips, and sucked hungrily. Half the contents were gone before she lowered the bottle to the brick floor.

Ignoring the icy chill, Polly closed her eyes and gave the alcohol time to wash over her in soothing waves of intoxication. As she savored the sensation, she lost awareness of the passage of time. Entering a state in which nothing troubled her, she relaxed and decided that if she were discovered that instant, whatever the consequences, she would not care.

She hadn't had so much gin since she was a girl. The alcohol had a powerful effect. As her intoxication deepened, she had a desire to throw caution to the wind and drink the rest of the bottle. Polly searched with her hands until she felt the cold glass. The bottle rested on its side next to her. Raising the vessel into the light, she saw that most of the gin had drained out.

Realizing she didn't have a good dose for later, the troubling loss quickly became a tragedy in her mind. As a moan escaped her throat, the door to the privy opened. In her haste she'd forgotten to latch it.

Bill stood in the doorway, supporting himself with the cane. "What are you doing down there? Are you hurt?"

"I—I—" she began, although she had no good answer. Despite her earlier sense that she would not care if she were caught, Polly cowered in fear.

Bill lifted her by the arm. The bottle fell from her lap upon the brick floor with a hollow clink.

Bill inhaled deeply. "You drank my gin?"

"No!" Polly said.

"Don't lie to me." Bill dragged her out of the privy as she clawed at the wooden threshold to get away. He threw her down and struck at her with his cane. Polly dodged out of the way and tried to rise. He swung again, and hit her shoulder, knocking her onto her right side. She held her tongue to keep from awakening the neighbors. He landed a solid blow to her ribs that forced a cry out of Polly.

"Quiet," he said, and struck her in the face. "This is between you and me."

As Polly got her feet under her, he brought the cane in low, using both hands to plunge the staff into her gut, and knock the wind from her in a great bellow. She fell backwards, striking her head on the cold, hard ground. Her skull seemed to ring like a bell and a taste of iron filled her nose and mouth.

She lay on her side, unable to move for a time, watching as the door to their rooms opened and Papa came out. He looked at her briefly, then spun on her husband and struck him in the face. Bill went down and Papa followed him. He crouched over Bill and struck him in the head repeatedly. Billowing vapor shot out of Papa's mouth and nose with every angry breath.

As neighbors began to emerge from their rooms to watch, the back lane filled up with people.

Then, Cynthia Dievendorf, who lived two doors down, was cradling Polly's head.

Gerald Guinn, who lived next door in the opposite direction, tried to pull Papa off Bill. Once her father allowed himself to be hauled away, Polly's husband seemed a dark, lifeless lump, except for the light, rolling mist of his breath in the cold air. His blood ran black in the moonlight, giving off a lazy vapor of its own.

She knew nothing more until she saw warm daylight coming through the front window of her room. She lay in her own bed. Polly ached all over and didn't want to face the world. She saw no sign of Bill. Cynthia sat in a chair that had been moved from Papa's room to a position beside Polly's bed. Alice sat in Cynthia's lap.

Before they noticed her wakefulness, Polly closed her eyes and willed herself back to sleep.

15
While She Was Out

The Bonehill Ghost chased Polly for several days and nights through the empty streets of London. With the sun barely visible through the London particular, which hung heavily in the air everywhere, she had a vague sense of the passage of time. Unlike the incident in her childhood, when the demon had chased her with no goal but torment, she knew that this time he'd come to take something from her.

Polly called out for help as she ran. She saw no one and nobody answered. The sound told the demon exactly where to find her. As she tried to find her way home, he repeatedly thrust his devil face at her from out of the choking haze. Sometimes, she heard the slosh of the demon's bottle, the rattle of its chain around his neck, and his rapid steps behind her. Other times, silently and with his powerful smell masked by the fog, he surprised her, leaping out of hiding with a chortling laugh and a flash of blue flame. To avoid madness, Polly turned away before her gaze and mind fixed on his red, glowing eyes. Mile upon mile of dank, abandoned thoroughfares, mired in horse dung and running with raw sewage, passed beneath her feet. Brooding brick buildings and rotten wooden houses with darkened windows loomed on either side, some leaning so far out over the street, she feared they would fall on her as she passed.

Although Mr. Macklin would have what he wanted, giddy with drink, he prolonged the chase for the fun of it. Polly wanted the pursuit to end, yet was too afraid to allow that for the longest time. Her bare feet became raw and bloody, her lungs choked with poisons from gulping the foul air.

Finally, exhausted, she stopped running abruptly. As she stood gasping for clean air and not finding any, Mr. Macklin dashed out of the yellow pea soup mist, his dark features pinched and twisted into a cruel grin. "You have something of mine," he said. He didn't use her father's voice as he'd done on his first visit. Then he looked down at her gut.

Until that moment, she'd assumed he intended to take her soul. Polly realized too late her mistake. He'd come for something else, a thing precious indeed. She had only an instant of horror to react. Polly tried to turn away. He exhaled a blue flame that blinded her, and snatched the tiny child from her belly with rusted metal claws.

"The soul of you, a hole in you, as what your screams beseech," he sang in his jeering Irish voice.

While the agony of iron penetrating her abdomen took away all thought, the plucking of the child from her womb brought an emotional devastation that eclipsed physical pain.

Polly awoke screaming and clutching at herself.

* * *

Cynthia Dievendorf lay across Polly, restraining her. "You're safe," she said repeatedly.

"My baby," Polly cried. She bucked beneath the woman. "He's taken my baby."

Surprisingly strong for such a small woman, Cynthia held Polly against the straw mattress until the fight left her. The woman's oily dark locks hung in Polly's face. Cynthia's features, at first frightening from the strain of exertion, became calmer. Her warm brown eyes gazed into Polly's for a moment. Then, they retreated as the woman pulled away and got off the bed.

Polly's head ached severely. A deep soreness in her muscles suggested she'd lain too long in bed.

She recognized her room. Darkness lay outside the window. The table had been moved from Papa's room to a position beside the bed next to the chair. A lit lamp rested on the tabletop. A book lay open beside it.

"My baby," Polly said again, her voice a croaking whisper. She tore open her night gown to look at her abdomen. Instead of claw marks and rent flesh, no more than a faded greenish-yellow bruise marred the smooth skin of her belly, no doubt from the strike of Bill's cane.

"Lost," Cynthia said. "I'm sorry. You had a miscarriage. You passed her on your second day in bed."

Another girl, Polly thought. A sense of loss overwhelmed her and she wept. Cynthia held Polly's hand.

Bill had no doubt killed the child when he'd struck Polly in the gut. The demon had come after the soul of the little girl, unless his visit had been nothing but a bad dream.

No, that my baby was lost in the nightmare, too, means it was more than a dream.

With her recent prayer gone so horribly wrong, Polly assumed the manner of the loss had been God's answer, one meant to punish her. She'd turned her own husband into an unwitting child killer. When last she'd seen him, he appeared dead. Had she turned Papa into a killer as well?

I am responsible, O Lord. Please do not punish Bill, Papa, or my unborn for my sin. If the Bonehill Ghost has the soul of my little one, reclaim her spirit and comfort her in Heaven. I shall live in misery for what I've done. Amen.

Even as she prayed, she wondered why God would listen to her. Polly wept until her eyes stung from lack of tears. Even then, her sobbing continued.

Cynthia released Polly's hand, stood, and put a kettle by the fire. "Tea will help."

Polly gathered her thoughts and ceased to sob. At the first chance, she'd take Bill's half pint of gin from where she'd hidden it in the back of the wardrobe and throw the bottle into the vault of the privy. She would never drink again. Although abstinence was the logical solution to the bulk of her problems, and she made the commitment without hesitation, she did so with doubts that she would not explore until she felt much better.

Cynthia returned to her seat, and held out a small mirror. Polly reluctantly took it. Cynthia nodded encouragement.

Looking at her reflection, Polly saw no fresh wound on her face. The scar on her forehead—the one she'd got at age thirteen from drunkenly bashing her head against the brick of the lodging house—appeared red and sore, but didn't feel tender when touched. She'd received the wound on the evening of her first encounter with the Bonehill Ghost. Polly wondered if her second encounter with the demon had turned the scar red.

As the water began to boil, Cynthia returned to the fireplace.

"How long have I been here?" Polly asked.

"Seven days. A doctor came. He said if you didn't awaken by Wednesday week, you ought to go to hospital. Today is Wednesday. Your father were preparing to take you in his barrow tonight."

"My children—"

"—are with your husband."

Polly had intended to ask about Bill next.

"I believe he has found a new home for you and the children," Cynthia said. She measured tea into two cups.

So Bill had recovered enough from the beating Papa had given him to be out looking for a new place to live.

"My father?"

"He's here each night—should come home in a few hours."

Papa hasn't been hauled to the drum and locked up.

Would Bill send her away with the children to live somewhere else? If so, where would he live? No doubt he wouldn't want to stay with Papa.

Polly thought of the tinplate toys for the children, hidden away in the back of the wardrobe. "Did the children have Christmas?"

"I don't know. They were away with Mr. Nichols. I believe he is with his sister."

Bill hated his sister, Rebecca. Polly knew he must have truly wanted to escape to seek her help.

Polly choked back shame as she thought of how she'd spoiled Christmas. She didn't want to think about the children's disappointment. If they hadn't received their toys, perhaps she might yet see the surprised delight on their faces. She supposed that depended on how much they knew about what had happened.

"You've been here—" Polly began.

"Since that night," Cynthia said. Crouched on the hearth beyond the foot of the bed, she poured hot water from the steaming kettle into the cups. "I lost my baby boy the day before, and needed to do some good for my own heart."

Polly watched a tear fall from Cynthia's eye and catch the firelight. The woman quickly wiped the droplet away.

"I'm sorry," Polly said. She knew Cynthia's husband was away in the Orient with the Royal Army. "Thank you for staying by me."

Cynthia smiled miserably.

The Lord might not hear me, Polly thought, *but an unselfish prayer couldn't hurt if it came from the heart.*

She thought her words through carefully before beginning.

Loving God, help Cynthia's heart to become whole again. Care for our infants, taken before they had a chance at life. Polly followed that with the penitent prayer.

16
Negotiations & Changes

For the following week of her recovery, rarely was Polly out of the sight of either Cynthia or Papa. She feared Bill would come home anytime and find the half pint of gin in the wardrobe. If he did, there would be no living with him. Polly didn't believe she could create an explanation he'd swallow. Finally, following several days of worry, she found a moment when no one watched her. Polly quickly disposed of the gin down the privy.

Her father had found lodging a half mile away in Maydwell Street. He'd moved most of his possessions to his new room. On the 6th of January, 1876, Polly stood with Papa out front of the rooms in Trafalgar Street on the morning he would leave with the last load in his barrow.

"Bill will come this afternoon to fetch you and the household to your new lodging," he said.

Polly had been away from her husband for two weeks. She feared the moment when she would be reunited with him. "I want to go with you," she said.

He gave her a sympathetic smile. "There isn't room for you and the children. You've cast your lot with Bill. I told him if he strikes you again, he'll have me to answer to. Don't be afraid to tell me about it."

Polly nodded, looked at the paving stones at her feet.

"You have a demon after you," Papa said.

Startled, Polly looked up to catch his eye.

He touched her face. "Don't let him take your soul. Careful with the drink."

Papa had rarely been tender with Polly, and the gesture caught her attention.

Did he mean the Bonehill Ghost or that alcohol was the demon? Since she'd awakened in her bed, with only the bruise on her belly, Polly had entertained some doubts about the reality of her recent dream involving Mr. Macklin. Having seen only the welt didn't mean the demon's attack and theft of her infant's soul wasn't real.

She wanted to know exactly what Papa thought. If he meant Mr. Macklin, she wanted to know how he knew. She would ask, but if he referred to alcohol as the demon, she'd find herself in a dreadful discussion about her drinking. Troubled, yet unwilling to risk opening up the subject, Polly merely smiled sadly and said, "Yes, Papa."

He took up his barrow and moved westward along Trafalgar Street.

Although Polly had difficulty taking the notion seriously, she wondered if alcohol and the demonic Ghost were one and the same? Mr. Macklin was, after all, a drunk.

* * *

Polly had imagined Bill would glare at her and begin a punishing tirade of grievances and demands for change, yet when he arrived in the afternoon, he gave no indication that he wanted to reflect with her upon the hard feelings and violence that had occurred between them. Supporting himself on a different cane, seeming neither angry nor remorseful, Bill hobbled around calmly, inspecting her efforts to pack up their household. She wondered if the cane with which he'd beaten her had been damaged, or if he had decided for her feelings, or his own, not to carry the staff. Possibly, the owner had simply asked for the cane to be returned.

Bill had a few abrasions on his cheeks and a swelling on one side of his jaw. He also had a crooked plum-colored nose. Papa must have broken it.

For all her fear, the worst Polly got from her husband was a sullen indifference, which seemed to evaporate when she looked him in the eye and spoke. "How will we get our things to the new lodging?"

Although Bill seemed relieved that she'd spoken to him, his restless gaze gave her the impression he had difficulty looking at her. "I've hired a wagon," he said. He pulled his watch from his waistcoat pocket. "Please prepare the children. We'll all ride."

* * *

Within the week, the Nichols family was situated in their new lodging. Bill had rented a flat of four rooms on the ground floor in D block of the Peabody buildings in Duke Street. The four-story brick building had been erected as part of an estate built in 1871 with funds donated by American industrialist and philanthropist George Peabody. Numerous blocks of the buildings were going up in several of what had been some of the worst rookeries in London.

Polly felt fortunate to have the opportunity to live in one of the fresh, clean, and spacious flats. The largest room of the four measured sixteen feet by ten feet, and the three smaller ones were each thirteen by ten. Bill paid the superintendent,

Mr. Hess, and a porter, Mr. Silvers, to look the other way when the printing press was moved in. At least until the family grew and needed the space, Polly would have an entire room dedicated to her printing. The boys and Alice shared a bedroom. Since the largest room held the flat's small stove and sets of shelves built into the walls, they located their kitchen and dining area there. The room also served as a parlor. At least part of the room that Polly used for her printing would become Alice's bedroom in due time.

The landing outside the flat's entrance provided a sink and a water closet that the Nichols family shared with their nearest neighbors, the Heryfords, a couple in their middle years with sons that were young men. The roof of the building held laundry facilities and baths.

On January 13, Polly had the chance to give the tinplate toys to her children. Her long-awaited delight blossomed as she watched her children play. John and Percy took their toys to the garden court that the Peabody buildings surrounded. Other boys of the buildings joined them, bringing their own toy miniatures.

"I am Gulliver," John shouted.

"I am Gulliver's twin!" Percy said.

Arm in arm, they stomped around the imaginary town they had built from sticks, rocks and leaves. The other boys made wee, Lilliputian voices, and ran their toys between John's and Percy's feet.

Alice found a friend who was fascinated with the horse and carriage. They spent most of their time playing with the toy indoors. Many tiny courtships occurred in that carriage and one passion-fueled murder and suicide.

Relieved to find the children had no resentment toward her, Polly suspected that since they'd slept on the night of

December 20, 1875, they knew little about what had occurred.

Although he still had a limp, Bill went back to work.

A month after the family took up their new lodging, the superintendent, Mr. Hess, approached Polly while she rinsed clothing in the laundry. "May I hire you to print two hundred of this in Foolscap Folio?" He handed her a printed copy of *The Peabody House Rules* with two new rules added in script at the bottom of the page.

"Yes," Polly said. "How soon?"

"Saturday?"

"That'll be two and a tanner," she said.

"All right, then."

Once he'd gone, she read the list. Certainly, Bill must have received a copy when they'd arrived, yet he'd merely told her what regulations he thought she should follow, rather than offering it to her to read. The list included a rule that forbade opening a shop of any sort within the building. That included, she believed, a printing shop. Another rule stated that the porter and superintendent would be summarily dismissed if they received any sort of gratuity.

Plenty of mothers who lived within the building were willing to share the minding of children. All the tenants had employment. The gate to the garden courtyard which gave access to the building was locked at eleven o'clock at night. Each adult tenant had a key to the gate. The whole arrangement provided a feeling of safety to Polly. For her, the world had become fresh and new again.

* * *

As soon as they'd settled, Polly noticed that Bill seemed to treat her with more respect.

"What do you think?" he asked in late January, during a conversation about whether the boys should attend a school closer to home.

Polly had looked at him blankly for a moment, thinking that somehow he mocked her. "If it means they get to keep their friends," she said after a moment, "they're better off walking a little farther to get to school. But you ought to ask them."

"I'll do that, then."

Polly couldn't have found his response more surprising.

The boys decided to leave Saint Mary Magdalen National School, and attend instead Saint Andrew's School.

One evening in February, fresh home from work at the printers, Bill asked, "Will you start supper soon? I'm famished."

Polly hadn't realized how late the hour had become, and immediately feared his disappointment and his wrath.

"I—I shall…yes, it won't take a moment to begin." She moved quickly to start water boiling on the small stove in the kitchen area.

Bill stopped her gently. "If you're weary, I'll go down to the square and fetch puddings and pies from the vendors instead. The children should be very pleased."

Dumbstruck, Polly looked at the man silently. She didn't recognize him for a brief moment. Realizing that her mouth hung open, she closed it.

Bill chuckled. "Don't you have anything to say?"

Finally, her confusion vanished, and she found her voice. "That'll be lovely, Bill."

When his pleasant behavior persisted into the spring, she began to consider more carefully what motivated him, but at first, she saw no reason for the change.

A possible answer came to her slowly over the summer months. She believed Bill knew about the miscarriage, although they didn't speak of it. She presumed he was aware that he'd been the cause. Bill's change of attitude might be a response to regret for what he'd done, and perhaps that had shaken loose his complacency regarding their marriage. Polly happily accepted that idea as truth because the notion took some of the weight of responsibility off her shoulders.

With her role in the events of December 20, 1875, mitigated, she began to question the punishment she'd imposed upon herself. Was abstinence a fair consequence for her to suffer for her part in the disaster of that terrible night, or had Polly been too hard on herself?

Despite the suffering she had endured and certainly had a hand in bringing about, she wasn't entirely convinced she should blame her drinking. Might Bill have got angry with her for another reason, as he'd done in the past? He'd struck her for questioning his decision to live with her father, for lack of speed in preparing food, and for adding color to material she'd printed. Indeed, he'd struck her not for drinking gin, but for drinking *his* gin when he clearly needed the alcohol for pain. He might make that sort of mistake at any time.

With those notions rattling around in her head, Polly began to think seriously about drinking again.

In September, she discovered she was pregnant.

17
Lonely Hearts

Morning sickness kept Polly from wanting to drink for a time. Then in the autumn, Alice began at Saint Andrew's Infants School, and Polly had time to do what she wanted each day once her housekeeping and printing work were done.

Unlike Judith, Polly preferred not to travel too far to have her dram. Even with the promises she made to herself that she'd drink in moderation, she feared—or perhaps hoped—she'd become so intoxicated that she might have difficulty finding her way home. Polly chose The Hogs pub, where Broadwall met Hatfield Street, a mere three chains away from her building. Since Bill did not spend time in pubs, she thought he wouldn't find her there. Even if he did, she'd persuaded herself that Bill had never been upset with her for drinking. If he found her, as long as she'd done her work and wasn't the worse for drink, he wouldn't become upset.

Judith had been satisfied drinking moderately, but that practice had always been a struggle for Polly. She thought possibly that was the difference between them about which Judith had spoken. Polly needed the feeling that drink gave her and always wanted to be deeper in her cups, while Judith enjoyed mild intoxication, and could take it or leave it, depending upon the needs of her life and responsibilities.

Paul Heryford, the head of the family that lived in the flat next door to that of the Nichols, stepped into The Hogs to pick something up one afternoon in October while Polly sat in the pub having a drink. She did her best to disappear into her seat and ignore him. Two days later, following supper and bedtime for the children, Bill asked, "Were you at The Hogs Tuesday?"

Polly tried to remain calm. "Yes," she said, "I'd finished the handbill for Dr. Fulsome's Liver Cleaner…" She grinned, knowing Bill thought the advertisement funny. Thankfully, his lips curled up in a lopsided smile, and she knew her tactic had disarmed him a bit. "…and the children weren't expected from school for a couple hours, so I had a glass of bitter. How did you know?"

"Paul Heryford saw you there." After a moment, he said, "Don't make a habit of it."

She'd been right. The only anger he'd ever shown concerning her drinking was when he believed she drank his own. Her father got upset with her because he understood and disdained the drive for intoxication within Polly, but Bill didn't know about her craving. She promised herself that she'd drink no more than two glasses of bitter or stout per visit to the pub.

During her next visit, which occurred in November, a fellow approached. A mere silhouette against the far windows, she couldn't identify him until he stood beside her.

Recognizing Tom, she said his name too loudly.

His eyes grew wide and she cringed with embarrassment. Poly didn't want to frighten him away.

What a foolish thought!

"You remember me," he said.

"Why, y-yes," Polly said stumbling over her words. "You

saved me from, uh, *Angus*."

Tom looked thoughtful for a moment. "Oh, yes, at the Compass Rose."

Polly nodded, not trusting herself to speak any more.

Again, he wore heavy trousers and a loose linen shirt. His fat black hammer hung from his belt. She concluded that Tom was a metalsmith of some sort.

"May I sit with you?" he asked.

Still silent, although her unease slowly lifted, she gestured toward the seat across the table from her.

He pulled the hammer from his belt and placed the heavy tool on the table top. Polly wondered why he'd bring such an implement to the pub.

"We haven't truly been introduced. I'm Tom Dews."

"Mrs. Nichols. Polly."

Taking his seat, he set his glass of stout down a bit hard and some of the contents sloshed out onto the worn and pitted table between them.

He must have noticed her looking at the tool. "A fine hammer. Cost me a pretty penny. I never leave it behind."

Polly remained silent. She'd already become comfortable with his presence.

"What are you doing here in the middle of a clear, spring day?"

Polly surprised herself with honesty. "I've need of a drink from time to time. My children are in school and I have a bit of the afternoon to myself."

The surprise faded quickly, and she experienced an odd sense of familiarity with the man. *I know nothing about him!* Yet, she had made love to Tom numerous times within daydreams.

"I have the same need, but must *take* the time to satisfy it. I do so when few of the boisterous lushingtons are about." He gestured around the relatively quiet pub.

Polly understood—she didn't like the idea of becoming loud while drunk because she didn't want to draw attention to herself. Her drinking had for many years been a lonely pastime.

Tom raised his glass in a toast. "To your health, Mrs. Nichols."

Polly raised hers and they both took a drink. They placed their glasses back upon the table empty.

"Allow me to get you another," he said.

"Thank you. The bitter, please."

He took both glasses to the bar and returned with them full.

"And when you don't have time for drink, what are you doing?" Polly asked.

"I work the smithy beside the saw mill, the Salvation Smithy," Tom said. "My apprentice has the forge—thinks I've gone to price coal." He winked.

Polly smiled for him and he grinned. She noted that he had all his front teeth. While Tom became more handsome by the moment, his eyes looked a bit haunted. His attitude spoke of a man who hid his drinking. Perhaps he was as lonely in his drinking as she was in hers. Polly found herself wanting to open up to him. She didn't see any reason not to.

"As long as I'm not the worse for drink, my husband won't mind. He doesn't know how often I come here, though."

"We do what we mus', while our families fume and fuss." He smiled tightly. "My wife left me because of my drinking. She didn't take our girl, Nancy. My young sister, Estell, come from Poplar to live with me. She keeps Nancy while I work. We live in Jane Street, just beyond the sawmill." He pointed toward the southeast.

Polly knew that Jane Street was a two-minute walk away.

"I once owned the Salvation Smithy where I'm now employed. I took the name from the Salvation Army because my business is saving the soles of horses." He smiled. "But I started a fire one day as burned much of my business. Nobody knew I were drunk, and I should have done the same sober. Were an accident. Just unlucky. Had too much debt afterwards and had to sell. That's when my wife left, went back to her family in Birmingham."

Polly found his candor surprising and pleasant. She understood the bad luck that sometimes came with drinking and how family fixed blame unfairly. "The truth is that if Bill knew I came here so often, he'd do me down. He beat me so bad once when I was pregnant, I lost the baby girl. He felt bad for that, I think, but I'm afraid if he finds out, I'll be in for it."

"A man shouldn't do that," Tom said. He had a stern look about him that would have been frightening if Polly hadn't already seen him smile so much. She noticed that he'd also placed fingers on the handle of his hammer.

"You mustn't worry overmuch," Polly said. "My father gave him what for with his fists. Broke his nose." She smiled.

"You lost your girl, though."

"Yes," Polly said sadly. "I have two sons and a daughter, another child on the way." She finished her glass of bitter. "I must go. The children come home from school soon."

"Perchance, I might see you here in the afternoons. I leave the shop to my apprentice about one o'clock on the days when business is light, and come here."

Yes, he is lonely.

Polly also saw that he had an interest in her. Pleasant, handsome, and sympathetic—she couldn't have designed a better man. Yes, he was a drinker, and at times had been a drunk, but then the same could be said of Polly. She could do with feeling less alone in her weakness toward drink.

Although she'd told him about her husband, Tom clearly had hopes she might join him in bed. Polly didn't want to admit to herself that she desired the same thing, yet she did think about the fact that she couldn't become more pregnant.

"The conversation makes the drinking more pleasant," she said, "but perhaps we ought to meet at a pub farther away from my home. I'm in Peabody D-block."

"Lucky you," he said. "Well, there's the Bull in the Pound farther down Broadwall."

"Farther still."

"The Hat and Feathers, then, Gravel Lane."

"Yes," Polly said, smiling. "I'll be there on Thursday afternoon." As she left, he grinned. That told her that he thought she'd committed to go to his bed with him. She supposed he was right.

18
A New Routine

Polly met with Tom Dews twice at the Hat and Feathers Pub, both times on a Thursday in November. The second time, she'd followed him back to his room in Jane Street. His sister and daughter were out at the time.

Tom Dews performed well in bed, but more than that, he showed interest in Polly's enjoyment of sex. Even so, she was less interested in the sex than in his gentle caresses.

Tom's ground-floor lodging in Jane Street didn't amount to much. The single room had two beds, a cupboard, a small wardrobe, a table with a bench, and two chairs. A small fireplace in the eastern wall was used for heating and cooking. Shelves stood out from the walls on either side of the hearth. The north and the west walls each held windows. Curious that little light came through the western-facing one, Polly lifted its blanket curtain to take in the view and saw the stained bricks of the neighboring building mere inches away.

Tom's fourteen-year-old sister, Estell, ran the Dews household as if the dwelling were a palace and she'd had a decade of experience. She regularly washed the clothes for the two beds, and clothing for Tom, two-year-old Nancy, and herself. In addition to cleaning, she made improvements to the room. The southeast corner had damage from a leak. The roof had been repaired. The floorboards beneath were rotten and the walls missing chunks of plaster. The December day when Polly met Estell, the girl was scrubbing the mold off the damaged corner and applying a coat of blue paint, even to the exposed lath. She had laid scavenged boards across the hole in the floor.

"Very good to meet you," Polly said to Estell.

The girl looked her up and down, smiled crookedly and said, "I'll suppose you'll have to do."

"I hope so," Polly said, showing good humor. She looked over Estell's touch-ups on the corner. "Tom is lucky to have your help."

"Yes, he is," Estell said.

Tom raised his brows, and nodded. "Now, off to market," he said, swinging his hammer in mock threat. "You and Nancy go and get that...um...thing we talked about."

Estell grabbed the handle of a small wagon beside the door and rolled the thing out onto the street. Polly hadn't noticed the contraption before, and her curiosity must have shown.

"It's a child's toy wagon," Tom said. He tapped his hammer into his open palm. "I added to it to make a carriage."

Estell situated Nancy in its crude seat, and began pushing it, joining the foot traffic moving east.

She might not think me an intruder if I didn't have a husband.

Polly preferred not to think much about her betrayal of Bill. The wary manner with which the girl treated Polly, though, left her feeling chafed.

I've needed such tenderness as I get from Tom. It will wash away some of the bitterness inside me. I'll be a better wife and mother for it.

Estell will get used to me, and Bill won't find out about Tom.

* * *

On a Tuesday in mid-December, Polly stopped by The Hogs pub for a quick glass of bitter. Bill approached her table as she finished her drink. She didn't see him until she set down her glass. Her startled response got her a stern glare from her husband.

"I brought you work yesterday as you're to get done by Friday," he said, taking her by the arm and drawing her up out of her seat.

"It's only Tuesday," Polly protested, then regretted her words for fear they might provoke him to strike her.

He spoke in low tones, perhaps to avoid embarrassment, as they passed other patrons of the pub and walked to the threshold to the outside. "As slow as you are with the press, you ought not take time in the middle of the day to have a drink."

Of course he would think that. *Women do not work as hard or as well as men,* he'd once said, and she was happy for him to believe that. Polly had found time-saving methods in the use of the press. She'd hidden her efficiency from Bill so she could use the time saved to do as she pleased.

The cold, though bright, hazy day outside The Hogs pub blinded Polly for a moment and her eyes watered. As her vision began to return, she saw a hansom cab standing at the kerb. Bill pressed her against the wall of the pub and looked down at her. Thankfully, he blocked the worst of the light. Bill's head became a mere silhouette against the bitter sky, his features unreadable. He lifted a hand toward her face and she flinched. She got close to pushing him aside and bolting, but his movement slowed, and he carefully wiped a tear from her cheek.

"There's no need to cry," he said. "I forgot the key to the leaf drawer and came home to fetch it. We are using gold leaf in the printing of an invitation. It's quite beautiful. Richardson sent me in a hansom cab."

Although he sounded casual, he still pressed against her to show his power. She told herself to relax, yet felt herself stiffen further.

"When you weren't home, I thought I should find you here. Is this becoming a habit?"

Polly shook her head.

He let out a sigh and stepped back. "I'm sorry I frightened you. Let me take you home." He gestured for her to enter the cab, then turned and spoke to the driver. "Peabody Building, D-block."

Polly had always wanted to ride in a hansom. The interior was clean, the horsehair seat softly cushioned, the view out the front and sides largely unobstructed, but sitting next to Bill, she couldn't enjoy the experience.

"No more drinking in the daytime," he said after they had become comfortable. "If you want to have a drink, have one with me in the evening."

When Polly didn't respond, he frowned and turned away to look out the side window.

The cab moved forward.

Bill didn't drink often. The last time he'd had a drink, he beat her. *Men who drink are more often the ones who beat their wives and family,* Polly thought, *and other men.* More violence occurred in pubs than anywhere else in the city. No, Polly had no desire to drink with Bill Nichols.

19
Pursuit

The third visit Polly made to Tom's room occurred between Christmas, 1876, and the new year.

Before Estell went out with her niece, she looked at Polly skeptically. "You needn't think I don't know what you two are up to."

Polly thought the fourteen-year-old girl pleasant and friendly, and hoped she hadn't got on her bad side.

When the girls had gone, Tom said, "Estell likes you, but worries that, should your husband find us together, he'll make trouble for us all."

He poured a small amount of gin into a glass and handed it to Polly. He then took up a glass of his own.

Polly took a sip. "I worry too," she said, yet she didn't often contemplate the terrible scenario he'd suggested. Polly concerned herself with the details of her deception. If she kept those in order, the larger aspects would work themselves out. She thought the time to be about one o'clock in the afternoon. The lesson times for each of her children differed and varied a bit through the week. Polly required them to stay together, to see each other home. They always arrived shortly after five o'clock, Mondays, Tuesdays, Thursdays and Fridays. If Polly finished her gin within the next hour, the smell would be off her when the children got home. Her husband came home around half past seven each evening.

"We have been careful," Tom said. "We shall be careful, but I'll understand should you want to break it off."

She noted that Tom didn't treat her like a possession. With their first few meetings, although she'd enjoyed herself, she'd sensed something odd about the man, a peculiar twist to his outlook upon which she couldn't quite put her finger. At present, she realized what had troubled her: He treated her like a friend. That was an unusual relationship for a man and woman, in her opinion, but one that she'd come to value greatly.

Despite her troubles, Polly was happier than at any other time in her life. Tom wasn't such a drunk that he couldn't get along in the world. When she awoke in the mornings, she had her Thursday afternoons with Tom to look forward to, at least for the next few months, until the new baby came.

"I don't want to break it off," Polly said.

* * *

On a Monday in January 1877, Polly chose to go farther down Broadwall to the Bull in the Pound pub to have a glass of stout. On her way home, she saw Bill walking toward her. He clearly saw her, and she knew escape wasn't possible. The smell of stout on her hadn't had a chance to dissipate completely. Hopefully, the cold air would dampen the smell.

"You're home early," she said, trying to sound companionable.

Bill got in close to her and leaned over to smell her breath, then straightened with an angry face. "I have forbidden drinking in the daytime," he shouted.

A woman tossing rubbish out the window of a gutted second-story room across the lane stopped and leaned out to listen. Bill glanced up at her, and quickly returned his eyes to Polly.

She didn't respond, but, then, he hadn't asked a question. Bill backed her up against the wall of the nearest building, an ancient wooden structure that groaned slightly when she bumped into it. Polly kept her eyes down.

Bill spoke in low, growling tones. "Last Thursday I slipped and fell in a great spill of ink. I were miserable in my clothes. Richardson took pity on me and sent me home. Again, you weren't there in the early afternoon, though you had work to do. I hid my spoiled trousers so you wouldn't find them because I didn't want you to know I was looking in on you. I wanted to find out how often you went for a drink."

"I am no shirkster. My work gets done in good time," Polly said, still looking down. "I earn a good income. You have nothing to complain about."

Bill lifted his arm to strike, but she looked up, her gaze fixed steadily on his eyes. He hesitated, glanced to his left to find the woman in the second-story window still watching, and dropped his arm.

"I will do the bookkeeping for your printing from now on," he said. "If you don't have the funds, you can't drink."

Polly wasn't concerned about the bookkeeping. Bill might be good with money. He wasn't clever with math.

He took her roughly by the arm and led her home.

20
A Promise of Lessons

The following Thursday, when Polly arrived at the Dews family room, Estell answered the door. Polly entered and saw Tom sitting at the table, whetting a knife on a flat stone. Estell struggled to dress Nancy.

Polly sat next to Tom and turned to the older girl. "Do you miss Poplar?" she asked.

"No," Estell said flatly.

"You don't miss family there?"

"Tom and this little one are all I have."

Nancy whined, her arm folded wrong inside a sweater sleeve.

"If you give up the fight," Estell said impatiently, "you won't get hurt." She looked up at Polly. "She hates wool because it's scratchy."

"How did you get on in Poplar before you came to live with Tom?" Polly asked.

"Get on?" Tom said. "Ha! She thought she were a flue faker."

Polly glared at him.

"I pretended I were a boy," Estell said proudly. "Got on with a master chimneysweep right after Mum died."

Tom looked up from his work. "She didn't last a month. Got stuck in a flue and had to lose some clothes to get out. When he saw she were a girl, he let her go."

"The job wasn't too hard, mind you," Estell said. "Bad luck, is all."

"Did you go to school?" Polly asked.

Estell shook her head.

"We never had time for that," Tom said.

Again, Polly glared at Tom. "I'm speaking to your sister."

He rolled his eyes, continued with the hissing rhythm of his sharpening.

"I could teach you to read if you don't know how," Polly said.

Estell's eyes grew large. "Truly?" she asked, grinning.

"One hour each time I visit."

Tom huffed.

"It's for her own good, and yours," Polly said.

He smirked and finally nodded his approval. Estell's grin grew larger.

"Now, leave us be," Tom said.

"We'll have your first lesson in an hour when you return," Polly said. She looked to the shelves to find a book and saw none. "It won't be much without books, but we'll make a start."

Still smiling, Tom's sister grabbed a basket, a sack, and the makeshift pram and went out with Nancy. Polly heard Estell's voice as she spoke quietly to her niece, and then the squeaky wheels of the baby carriage on the paving stones, going up the lane.

Tom tested the sharpness of the knife, touching the blade to his fingernail and sliding it sideways. "Nearly done," he said.

Polly's thoughts returned to the troubles with her husband. "Life with Bill ought to be settled and steady if I should allow it," she said, ruminating aloud. She meant that her drinking got in the way of her happiness, yet she didn't want to admit that, even to Tom. "The children are happy at home and in school. They are well-fed and clothed. Our home is better than any I should've hoped for. So why do I risk everything?"

The question got out before she had thought through the possible answers and whether she wanted to share them with Tom.

"I'm not worth it," he said, without looking up. "I wouldn't marry you if you were free. You must make this decision on your own."

Polly liked his answer. She didn't want a different husband. She'd become comfortable with Tom being her friend as well as her lover. He was a sweet man.

But her question had two parts: why did she continue to drink when the habit upset her husband, and why did she risk everything to be with a drunk?

She wouldn't address the primary question about her drinking, even within her own thoughts, but the secondary question had a ready answer. *Because Tom treats me better than Bill ever will, and I'm lonely, as simple as that.*

Tom clearly thought that what he offered wasn't worth her risk. Polly would let him think that. She put her hand to his stubbly face and gave him a kiss. He continued sliding the edge of his knife softly over the whetstone.

"Bill be damned," Polly said. "My children are all I care about at home. If we're discovered, what harm should come to them?"

Tom tested the blade on his fingernail once more, set the knife and the whetstone aside, and turned to her.

"Your husband might sue for divorce," he said. "He could sue me, though my debts should discourage that." Polly frowned, and he smoothed her brow with his hand. "The idea doesn't trouble me," he said. "He could take your children away. You might never see them again."

Tom got up from the table and moved toward his bed.

Polly chewed her lip. Although she had no doubt that Bill would earn enough to keep the children well, she had to wonder if their lives might be somehow incomplete without the love of their mother.

Would they miss me?

The children were growing up. John, currently eleven years old, had expressed a desire to live with his grandfather and begin an apprenticeship. Papa was considering the matter. If not for the pregnancy, Polly could see a time in the future when the children no longer needed her and she might leave Bill.

"Let go your troubles," Tom said. He had taken off his clothes. "Come to me." He held out his hand, and when she took it, he pulled her close and undressed her.

The clean bedclothes felt good against her naked flesh. Tom felt good too. When he touched her—the way he touched her—Polly's chronic loneliness always fled.

* * *

On a Thursday in March, as usual, Polly left Tom's room to get home about half an hour before the children would return from school. She found Bill waiting for her. He smelled her breath, but the odor of the gin she drank had had a chance to dissipate.

"Where have you been?" he demanded.

Polly didn't want to lie, so she ignored him. She moved to the stove to start a fire to cook supper.

Bill grabbed her by the arm and turned her. He backed her into the corner of the room.

"You'll tell me what you've been up to."

Although Polly kept her eyes on his face, she didn't respond.

His features twisted with frustration and he raised his hand to strike her.

"Go on," she scoffed, thrusting her swollen abdomen at him, "*hit* me."

Her gumption obviously surprised Bill.

"It won't help," she said, "but you'll feel better, just like *the last time* you *beat* me."

His angry face sagged a little.

"You *did* feel better afterward," she asked, "*didn't* you?"

He dropped his arm and stepped back, his eyes and mouth wide.

So, his shame over the miscarriage would be her ally.

"I didn't know you were knapped last time," he said.

"Well, that makes *all* the difference, *doesn't* it," Polly said viciously, knowing she went too far.

The rage returned to his voice. "You *cannot* talk to me that way." She thought he would finally strike her. Still, he continued to back away. Frustration turned his pudgy features into those of a petulant boy. He tried to rally his face to express anger again, yet his eyes remained defeated. "You will *not* drink again. If you do, I *shall* beat you. I'll be more careful, but I *will* beat you. I have the right to teach you a lesson."

Bill pushed past her and exited their rooms, slamming the door behind him.

Polly fought to keep herself from laughing. Considering that her husband was a troubled man, she thought her glee unbecoming. Although she seemed to have won a victory over his worst inclinations, she knew the matter was far from settled.

She said a prayer for Bill Nichols, followed by the penitent prayer.

21
A Need for Worry

Polly took books, paper, and pencils to the Dews family lodging to help her teach Estell to read and write. Clearly impatient as he waited through the first lesson, Tom paced quietly. Even so, he didn't show an ill-temper.

"Thank you, Polly," Estell said.

Tom smiled. "My little sister, turned bookish. Look at your happy lamps."

Bashful, Estell punched him lightly in the chest.

While the girls got ready to go out, Polly spoke to Tom quietly so the others couldn't hear her. "Bill has caught me out three times now. He has forbidden me to drink. I cannot go to pubs any longer."

"He doesn't know how to find you *here*," Tom said. "You'll have your drink here."

For fear that he might take his fine hammer to her husband, Polly didn't tell Tom about Bill's threats of violence.

Before leaving for market with Nancy, Estell placed her hand on Polly's pregnant belly. "Your child has got big. Don't let Tom poke a hole in her."

Tom swatted at Estell, but she dodged out of the way. "You shall *not* talk like that!"

"Why not?" Estell said.

Polly liked the girl's pluck. She smiled, realizing that Estell had referred to her infant as female. She probably looked forward to having another little girl around.

"Young ladies ought not speak of such things," Tom said, eyes wide with outrage.

Polly made a calming gesture toward him, while Estell stood with her hands on her hips.

"Oh, that's a rule, *is* it?" the girl said. "Well, if you needn't follow the rules, why should I?" She saw Polly smiling and grinned. "I know what you two are about. I like Polly, and want her baby to be safe."

Tom covered his face with a hand, groaned, and turned away.

"I shouldn't worry," Polly said. "We won't hurt her."

"Somebody has to worry," Estell said, too reasonably. She took Nancy by the hand, grabbed her basket and sack, and left the room.

Yes, the child on the way was a matter Polly hadn't fully sorted. If Bill found out about her adultery and divorced her, he might require her to turn her unborn over to him after the birth. She wouldn't want the child to grow up without a mother, and yet, she thought resentfully, the infant would prolong the years she must remain with Bill. Perhaps she would be better off if he took the child and divorced her. She had considered making certain Bill discovered her adultery. The potential consequences for her choices and actions seemed to grow increasingly complicated and difficult to consider.

How could the happiest time in her life also be the most distressing?

Knowing the infant had no responsibility for her feelings, she said a prayer for her baby, followed by the penitent prayer.

For the well-being of her unborn, she must keep Tom a secret, but that didn't mean she'd give him up.

22
The Girl's Decision

At the beginning of May 1877, Polly saw Paul Heryford among the foot traffic moving along Jane Street when she exited Tom's room. Mr. Heryford touched his cap and nodded a greeting toward her. Thankfully, Tom had not seen Polly to the door. She waved to Mr. Heryford and smiled with the hope that he'd think little about the encounter. Even so, she waited on tenterhooks through the following week, expecting a confrontation with Bill at any moment.

"I must stay away for a time," Polly told Tom the following Thursday. Unwilling to enter his room when invited in, she stood uneasily on the doorstep, glancing up and down the lane as she spoke. "I am sick much of the time and cannot have a drink with you."

He nodded uncertainly. "We don't have to drink."

She held her round, bulging belly. "Lately, when we dap it up, it hurts. We should give it a rest until after the baby comes."

"We can still be together," Tom said somewhat pitifully.

"Our neighbor, Paul Heryford, saw me leave here last week. I'm afraid he might say something to Bill about it."

"Has your husband said anything?"

"No, but it's best I stay away for a time."

"If he hits you, I'll nobble him good." He made a frightful

face as he struck his left hand with his right as if his fist were a hammer.

Polly feared that he would go to prison if he harmed Bill. She shook her head vigorously. "No, he hasn't done anything like that." She touched Tom's hands gently. "I will come back in July, not before."

Although he had a sad look, Tom said nothing.

"I'm sorry," Polly said. "I'll miss you until then." She turned away and began walking. A glance back showed him watching her. She smiled, waved, and continued on.

* * *

Bill had been cold to Polly since their last altercation, but he gave no indication that Paul Heryford had said anything about his sighting of Polly on Jane Street. Over the next month, since she had ceased to go out, his icy demeanor thawed, and an uneasy truce prevailed in the Nichols household.

Polly bore a girl in June 1877 that she named Eliza. Two weeks after the birth, Polly had not seen her lover for more than a month. On a Thursday in early July, she put her baby girl in a sling and walked with her to Jane Street in the hope of seeing Tom.

Estell answered her knock. "Come in, come in," she said, beaming for the infant.

Polly entered and immediately took a seat to rest on the bench beside the table. She hadn't been sleeping well, having to get up so often in the night to take care of Eliza.

Nancy sat on the floor mouthing a crust of bread.

"My little niece," Estell said, reaching to touch Eliza's cheek, "where have you been?"

Does she think Eliza is Tom's? Polly wondered. The question must have been obvious on her face.

"I know she's not truly my niece," Estell said. "You're married to *another man*," she added in a scornful tone.

Nancy shook her head with a comical scowl.

Polly frowned.

"It doesn't trouble me," Estell said, making a face that contradicted her words. She pulled up a chair and sat.

Polly reached to take her hand, but Estell wouldn't allow it.

Nancy got up and sat on the floor next to Polly, leaning against her leg. She had a stuporous look about her, as if she hadn't been eating or sleeping well.

"May I hold her?" Estell asked.

Polly lifted Eliza into Estell's arms. "How do you know the baby is a girl?"

"I just *know*."

"Her name is Eliza," Polly said.

"Hello, Eliza." Estell touched the infant's head and gently twirled the flaxen, downy locks at the crown upon her finger.

"Is Tom about?" Polly asked.

"Not today," Estell said. "He's working at the smithy. He didn't work for a time, drank up our money and there weren't much left for food. I told him he had to go back to work."

"I see you have toke, so you *have* eaten today?"

"Yes. He gave me a penny and I bought old bread."

"Was Tom ill?" Polly knew she'd asked a foolish question. Drinking too much wasn't the same as having an illness.

"No," Estell said, "just *lonely*."

While saddened to hear he'd been unhappy, Polly was pleased to imagine why. "He didn't find someone else, did he?"

"He should have done. I told him so. He doesn't listen to me."

"He went back to work when you told him to," Polly said.

"He were hungry too."

"You aren't happy with me, are you?"

Estell didn't answer for a time. She handed Eliza back to Polly and sat back in the chair and worried at the cuffs of her worn linsey shift. "Tom missed you," she said finally. "He were worthless with drink for weeks."

"I told him when I'd come back."

"Yes, but he can't count on you the way you do him. He fears you might not come back one day."

"He said that?"

"He didn't quite say the words." She pressed her lips into a thin line. "He were wretched-drunk and muttering. I knew as what he meant."

"I've hurt him."

"In a way, yes," Estell said. Tears brimmed in her eyes. "It's not your fault. He'll say as you're not his doesn't trouble him, but it's not true."

The young woman's distress upset Polly. "He said he wouldn't marry me even if I were free."

Estell wiped her eyes before the tears fell.

"Tom's scared to try again. He pretends it doesn't matter his wife—that witch, Ester—left him, but he didn't expect it and the loss hurts. He felt it again when you went away, even though you said you'd come back. It's the not knowing, not trusting, I suppose."

Polly thought Estell astute for such a young one. What was she, perhaps fifteen years old at present? *A young woman, now.* Polly envied Estell's ability to keep another's concerns in mind. Thinking, rather than feeling, seemed to drive Polly's own efforts to be considerate of others.

Although she didn't like the question that occurred to her, she voiced it anyway. "Shall I go and not come back?"

Estell became thoughtful for a long moment, and Polly wished she could withdraw the question. She felt a tightness around her heart at the thought of not seeing Tom again. She needed him, his affection, his companionship. Why should she care what Estell thought?

Damned selfishness. Polly had discovered she'd hurt someone, yet all she could do was think of herself.

No, I must think of Tom and his family. For reasons unclear, she did care what Estell thought. *I'll leave the decision to her.*

The young woman looked at Polly in silence. Waiting for the answer, Polly became uncomfortable in her seat. Her eyes stung, she blinked repeatedly, and her mouth went dry. Finally, when she could take the wait no longer, she opened her mouth to speak and was interrupted.

"Who, then, would give me my lessons?" Estell asked.

Polly felt a flush of relief that took the strength from her. Eliza slipped from her grasp. Estell sat up quickly, and reached to help Polly catch the infant.

The young woman seemed to pull back tears as she smiled uncertainly. "I'll put her in the bed for a while if you'll teach me."

Polly smiled and nodded. She handed the infant to Estell, and began to assemble the materials for their lesson.

23
Reprisal

During their first tryst following Eliza's birth, Tom asked Polly, "What if I'm the one gets you knapped now?"

"If I'm to bear another child," she said, "I'm just as happy to have yours." After a moment, she added, "No, I'd be more pleased."

Tom never spoke of his reaction to Polly's temporary absence. They picked up where they'd left off with two exceptions: The new infant took up most of her time and when Tom offered her a drink, she turned him down.

Two months after Eliza's birth, Polly hadn't had a drink in so long, she experienced little desire. Bill had not found the smell of alcohol on her for three months, which had allayed much of his suspicion. Tom didn't seem to care if Polly drank. Thankfully, much of the strife in her life had diminished with the absence of alcohol. Although she considered making a new abstinence pledge, the thought of her disappointment and shame when breaking earlier promises discouraged her.

In January 1878, when Eliza was six months old, Estell began taking her along on the Thursday afternoon expeditions to market. Tom had altered the seat of the baby carriage to accommodate an extra passenger. A length of rope, cushioned by a small blanket, helped to secure them for the ride. Then,

Polly and Tom could bed one another in the afternoon without interruptions.

Not much changed at home. John went to live with his grandfather and begin his apprenticeship. Bill and Polly settled into their routines.

* * *

In April of 1878, Tom saw Polly to the door when she left his room in the afternoon of a Thursday. As she walked away, carrying Eliza, she saw Paul Heryford moving up the lane in the opposite direction. Again, he nodded a greeting and touched his cap. Polly smiled and kept moving. She could only hope her luck held. Perhaps he hadn't seen Tom. If he had, hopefully, he wouldn't speak of the matter to Bill.

* * *

Around half past seven in the evening, Polly heard Bill's voice outside the door to their flat. Fearing that he spoke with Paul Heryford, she became determined to act as if nothing were amiss. She had prepared a potato and fish stew. Percy and Alice sat at the table. Eliza occupied a recently acquired high chair. They all waited for their father before beginning their supper.

Bill walked in calmly enough. He took off his jacket and hung the garment on a hook beside the door.

"Good evening," Polly said.

He didn't respond to her, but turned to Percy and Alice. "Go outside for a little while before supper," he said. "I must have a talk with your mum."

Polly's stomach seemed to drop and her heart beat a faster rhythm.

The two children got up, and went out.

As soon as the door shut behind them, Bill turned toward Polly with a dreadful scowl. "Mr. Heryford saw you twice going into a room on Jane Street. The second time, he saw you speaking with a man there. Explain this to me!"

Rattled, Polly struggled to find a voice and a manner that Bill would find believable. "I-I have a girl who watches Eliza so I can go farther to market. Those on this side of the river don't have the prices to be had at Farringdon Market. The women I may leave Eliza with here haven't the time for me to be gone so long."

"The first time he saw you there was before Eliza was born."

"Just before, perhaps," Polly said. "I knew I needed someone I could trust. I were looking in on her to see how she lived before leaving my child with her."

"Why have I not heard of this girl before? What is her name?" His fists balled and his face turned red.

Polly tried to think fast, to cover all the possibilities with the new lie. She'd seen Estell sunning Nancy and playing with her in the Peabody buildings' courtyard garden. "She's a girl, Estell, I met and spoke to her *here* in the courtyard garden. She brings her charge, her brother's child. I give her ha'penny an hour."

Bill seemed to relax, and Polly moved toward him, to take his hand as a gesture of affection.

He looked up, a rage on his face, and struck, boxing her left ear. Pain, everywhere at once, dropped Polly to the floor. Bill kicked her in the gut, knocking the breath from her. She coughed and then gulped for air. She looked up at him, and he smiled.

"You're lying, I know it," he spat. "You're a bloody coward. You hid behind an unborn before, but you're not knapped now, and you'll have a lesson, you will."

Eliza began to cry. The sounds seemed distant as Polly heard only with her right ear.

Bill leaned down and hauled her up.

"No," Polly cried. She tried to strike at him with her fists, but his arms and elbows got in her way. He clutched the collar of her chemise with his left hand while striking her in the face with his right hand. Polly felt two front teeth give way under the assault. She screamed with the pain.

Her chemise tore, and Bill's grip slipped. Polly stopped struggling, became deadweight, and slid to the floor. He followed, continuing to strike her in the face as she tried to curl into a ball. Once she'd tucked her face between her shoulders, he pummeled the side and back of her head with his fists.

Finally, the punches ceased. She heard him, breathing hard, rise and step back.

Weeping, Polly tried to crawl toward the corner of the room. Her clawing hands slipped in smears and puddles of her blood, saliva, and tears on the hardwood floor.

She glanced up to see Bill standing over her. "You shall *not* keep secrets from me," he said, pulling back his foot. She tried to move quickly, but his leg moved faster, and his dirty shoe crashed against the side of her head.

24
Unexpected Allies

Polly awoke unable to focus her eyes. She lay in bed with her torn clothing on. Daylight came through the window, illuminating nothing but stillness within the flat. She listened for a long time before making a sound, and heard only the ever-present hubbub of the city outside. Normally a murmur, the sounds coming in from outside, those of hooves, shoe leather, and the wheels of various conveyances wearing against paving stones, as well as the occasional voices of man and beast, were quieter still. Polly turned her head this way and that, and realized she couldn't hear with her left ear.

She decided that Bill and the children must be out. She presumed her husband had put her in the bed.

Polly felt two holes in the gums of her lower jaw and something under her tongue. She spit it out into her hand, but couldn't see the object. Her face was tender and swollen in several places and she suffered a terrible headache. She assumed she had at least one black eye.

Polly would not be able to see Tom until she'd healed up or he might take his hammer to Bill and suffer the consequences. As she lay worrying about all the possible details of her lies to Bill and the ones she'd have to tell Tom, her vision began to improve. Eventually, she focused on the tooth in her hand. Even if she healed up before she saw her lover, Polly didn't know how she might explain the loss of teeth.

She couldn't face all her concerns at present. She had to get up and move or she thought she might turn over and sleep forever. Polly struggled into a fresh chemise, pushing it down over her bloodied skirt, and then walked into the front room. She heard Eliza's voice, crying. The sound came from the Heryfords' flat.

Reluctantly, she stepped out onto the landing and knocked on their door.

Paul Heryford answered. Seeing Polly, he gasped. His mouth remained open as he backed away. Susan Heryford came to the door. Seeing Polly, the woman hurried forward. "Come in and sit," she said.

Both the Heryfords helped Polly to move to a table and chairs. They settled her into one, then took chairs of their own.

Mr. Heryford struggled to find his voice. "I-I…um…uh… had no idea he…"

"I'm so sorry," Susan said. She looked sternly at her husband. "This is what *your* meddling has got." Her accent said she was Scottish.

"Eliza," Polly said, the name coming out mush.

"She's fine," Susan said. "I've put her in Brian's bed since he's gone weeding and hoeing with his brother in the north."

Polly noted that Eliza's crying had stopped.

Paul said something too quietly.

"Pardon me," Polly said, "I'm not hearing with my left ear."

"I said, let me get you something to drink, Mrs. Nichols." Paul went into another room and returned with a bottle of whiskey and a glass. He poured a large helping and offered the drink to Polly.

The whiskey stung her mouth, especially at the gums, but she downed the amber liquid all at once.

Susan fetched a basin and flannel and spent some time cleaning Polly's face. Paul watched, a wretchedness in his eyes. As dramatic as the Heryfords' reactions had been to her appearance, she dreaded looking into a mirror.

"I'm so sorry," Paul said.

"As well you should be," Susan said. Finished with the cleaning, she turned to Polly. "You shall get in the bed with your bairn. Your husband won't have either of you until you're better."

Polly gratefully allowed herself to be led into a bedroom where she saw Eliza sleeping. Susan helped her to lie down, bunching the bedclothes to help protect Eliza. Polly felt safe.

Once the Heryfords had gone, Polly found the least painful position for her head, torso and limbs. She placed a hand on the back of her infant's warm, smooth head, and went to sleep.

* * *

She awoke to the sound of Eliza fussing. The sky lay gray outside the window. Polly sat up, drew her infant into her lap and gave her a breast. As the child suckled, Polly heard bits of a contentious conversation coming from the next room. Quickly, she realized that Bill and Paul Heryford were arguing, their voices raised.

"The children are with my sister tonight, but will need their mother when they return from school tomorrow," Bill said.

"Tell them to come here tomorrow after school," Paul said.

"Polly must be home to greet them," Bill said impatiently.

"Mr. Nichols, sir," Paul said slowly, disgust in his tone, "the face you have given her would frighten them away."

"She isn't *that* bad," Bill said.

"If you do not leave my door, I shall give you a face to match! How bad would that be?"

Polly heard indistinct grumbling and cursing, and then a door shutting.

The Heryfords couldn't protect her for long. She'd have to return to Bill soon. The thought made her want to drink.

After a time, she put Eliza back into the nest of bunched bedclothes, and got out of bed. Paul and Susan sat in the next room apparently trying to have a quiet evening. He set down his briar pipe and she closed the book she was reading.

"My dear," Susan said. "Are you hungry?"

"No, thank you," Polly said. "I must go to my flat for fresh clothes." She indicated the blood on her skirt.

"Paul," Susan said, "will you go with her to make sure she's safe?"

"Please, don't make a fuss."

"I *will*," Paul said. "Mrs. Nichols, if you'd like to wait until I come back, I should just borrow your key."

"Yes, thank you." Polly pulled the key from the pocket of her skirt and handed it to him.

Paul left the flat. Susan gestured toward his seat, and Polly sat.

"Thank you for taking care of my girl. You are good folks to think of her as you've done."

"I haven't had a small child of my own for many years. I never had a girl." Susan gave a warm and loving smile. "If you have need, you may leave her with me from time to time. Truly, I don't mind."

"Then, if you would, please take care of her tonight while I go see my father." As good as the Heryfords had been to her, Polly hated to lie to the woman. Hopefully Susan would never know that Polly intended to drink that night. "He told me to tell him if Bill should beat me again."

"He's done this before?"

"Yes."

Susan looked at her with such sadness, Polly had to hold back tears. She didn't have time for such emotion. Tonight she would get good and drunk.

"I won't return until tomorrow. If Bill asks, you might tell him I took Eliza with me."

"We won't lie. If he demands to have her, we'll have to allow it."

"I understand."

"While she's with us, we'll take good care of her. Paul told your husband to have Percy and Alice come here when they return from school tomorrow."

Polly had spent little time with the Heryford family. She knew they had two sons and that Paul worked as a clerk at Waterloo Bridge Railway Station. Until that day, though, conversations with them had been limited to small talk, yet Susan remembered the names of the children. The Heryfords were pleasant, good people.

Strange that, living so close together in the same building, we have not become fast friends. Then she realized that what had stood in the way was her need to keep secrets. Presently, she would create another one.

Paul returned. "Mr. Nichols is not in your flat," he said, handing her the key.

"I can't thank you enough."

"Anything I can do to help," he said sheepishly, glancing at his wife.

Polly smiled for the couple and slipped beyond the threshold, shutting the door behind her.

25
A Timely Amendment

Polly retrieved some of the coins she'd hidden among her printing supplies, and went out into the night, walking south to the Compass Rose public house. Although her battered face received plenty of stares, the patrons of the pub left Polly in peace. Finally, she was having her *greater adventure*. Too bad the outing didn't occur under better circumstances. She drank enough gin that she couldn't feel her feet when she stumbled out of the place at closing time around one o'clock in the morning. Few people and little traffic moved along the roads. She made her way down South Street, turned west, and walked past the low, brick building where the family had occupied rooms in Trafalgar Street. She became lost in her memories, some good, some bad, of the years spent there, and when she took stock of her surroundings again, she didn't recognize them. Polly stumbled on into darkness.

* * *

Papa and John awakened her. She lay sprawled on their doorstep, her head leaning against the door jamb. Polly had only been to her father's room in Maydwell Street once before, but somehow her body had remembered how to get there. The open door allowed warm and inviting light from within to reach her. John, a look of shocked concern on his face, tried to help her stand. With Papa's help, they got her to her feet, led her inside to a bed, and lowered her onto a musty straw mattress. John tucked a light blanket around his mother. He and Papa moved to another bed—the one Bill had sent with their son when the boy took up the apprenticeship with his grandfather. Papa pinched out the lamp light and the room became dark. Polly returned to sleep.

* * *

"Wake up, Polly," Papa said repeatedly.

Finally, against a pounding headache, she opened her eyes. Blinding light came through the rag curtain over the room's single window.

"Your drunken ways have finally done you real harm, girl. I hate to see it, but you got what you deserve."

Polly rose up in anger, despite the pain. "You're so high and mighty! *I've* never been arrested. Don't think I forgot about that strongbox you broke into, how worried we all were for your safety. I might be a drunk, but you're a thief, a cracksman!"

Polly thought her words would get her a more satisfying reaction, but Papa merely bowed his head and shook it slowly. She still didn't know the full story of the strongbox, and his silent response said that her assumptions were well off the mark.

"I didn't deserve this," she said pitifully, gesturing toward her face. "Bill beat me."

"*Before* you drank or *after?*"

"Should it matter?"

"If he said you should not—well, he is your husband." Papa

looked as if he had trouble agreeing with his own words.

Polly opened her mouth to show the gaps in her teeth.

Papa drew back, waved his hand in front of his nose. "That is a potent stink, Polly girl," he said. Then, he seemed to focus on her lower jaw. "He did that, did he?"

"Yes, *before* I drank."

Papa's face darkened with a fierce scowl. "I shall pay him a visit tonight."

"No! He would have you jailed this time. Let me sort it out, please."

Papa looked thoughtful, then nodded.

"I must work," he said. "Are you staying or leaving? If you wish to stay, I'll not put the padlock on the door. If you must leave, you'll have to go now. I cannot afford to miss a day of trade. I can make do without John for a while should you need help getting home."

"I must go." She looked around for her eldest. "Where is John?"

"Gone to fetch the barrow. He'll help you when he returns."

"No, I'll make my own way." Polly told herself that for his own sake, John shouldn't see her again before she left. She knew that was, in truth, her pride speaking.

"I should think you'll need the privy," Papa said, pointing toward a rear door.

Polly went out.

"You'll need your strength," he said when she returned from relieving herself. He offered her a healthy slice of bread and cup of water.

"Thank you, Papa."

"You ought leave off with the drinking before that demon kills you."

The Bonehill Ghost is a figment of fevers and bad dreams. She realized she didn't believe in him or prayer any longer. God clearly did as He pleased without considering what mere mortals thought or felt.

Polly gripped her father's hand and squeezed, then left his room to walk the two or more miles home.

* * *

Polly returned to the Heryfords in time to avoid suspicion. The couple had taken in Percy and Alice when the children returned from school. They were out playing when Polly arrived. Coming in some time later, they were frightened to see their mother.

"Will you always look like that?" Alice asked, her voice soft and timid. Polly noted that the hearing in her left ear had returned a little or she might not have heard the girl at all.

She saw that Percy wanted to give a clever response, but he held his tongue, a troubled look on his face as he waited for her answer. Earlier, she had looked in a mirror that Susan provided. Although Polly's face remained swollen and bruised, she'd seen no permanent damage beyond the loss of teeth.

"No, dear," she said. "I'll heal up and look like your mum again."

Alice smiled. Percy kept his troubled look.

While listening for Bill's return, Polly and the children ate an early evening meal with the Heryfords, a joint of lamb with potatoes and peas. Not since she and Bill courted had Polly eaten so well. She wondered with a touch of shame if she'd never quite given her children enough as she watched them wolf down the meal.

"The peas come from a tin," Mr. Heryford said.

The children looked surprised. Since Bill didn't trust tinned

food, the children had never had any. Mrs. Heryford fetched
the empty vessel, removed its sharp lid, and gave it to the children to inspect.

When Bill was heard coming up the stairs, Paul opened the
door. "Please join us," he said. "We've eaten, but saved some
of the joint."

Bill stood indecisively for a moment, then entered with what
appeared great reluctance. His eyes became large when he saw
his family assembled at the table. Percy and Alice seemed unwilling to look at their father.

Bill sat, and Susan served him. He ate in silence while Susan and Paul tried to make small talk with Polly. The children
played on the hardwood floor beside the table with the empty
tin, rolling it back and forth to one another. The Heryfords
asked Polly questions about her printing business. Toward
the end of her description of processes she used in produc-
ing broadsheets and handbills, Bill set down his utensils and
interupted her. "Stop that racket," he told the children. Percy
picked up the can and stood.

Bill turned to Polly. "You'll introduce me to your childminder girl and her brother," he said.

"Give her a chance to heal up," Paul said.

"I don't see as any of this is your business," Bill said coldly.

Alice ducked under the table. Percy gripped the edge of the
table top as if steadying himself to bolt if need be. Susan placed
a reassuring hand on the boy's shoulder.

"Children," Polly said, "go to our flat and play. The door is
unlocked."

"Leave the tin here," Bill said.

Percy set the tin on the table, then he and Alice left the flat.

"We should go home too, Polly," Bill said, standing.

"Please stay the night here," Susan said to her.

Bill's head tilted to one side and his features hardened.

"No, we should go," Polly said, trying to calm him. She got up from the table.

"We fear for your safety," Paul said, getting to his feet. "Susan and I discussed that before you came back this afternoon. You don't have to go with him tonight. You can stay here."

"I don't have to listen to this," Bill said. He turned toward the door.

"You would do well to listen," Susan said. "What we have to say involves legal proceedings."

Bill blustered, his brows knitting furiously and his mouth working to make the cruelest arching scowl, yet a shade of concern trembled in his eyes.

"I learned something of the law today," Susan said. She stood and walked to a cabinet, opened a drawer, and pulled out leaves of paper folded together. "It so happens that Parliament amended the Matrimonial Causes Act earlier this year. If Paul and I provided testimony that you severely beat your wife, you might be convicted of the crime. If that came to pass, Polly would be within her rights to leave you, and you'd be required to provide a monetary maintenance to her for the rest of her life. The new law also allows for her to take the children."

Bill's eyes had become great angry orbs bulging from his red face. "You learned nothing of the kind! You are a wretched, meddling hay—" He glanced at Paul uneasily as the man took a step toward him. Mr. Heryford's face became as hard and determined as any Polly had ever seen.

He's looking for an excuse to strike Bill. While excited to have champions defending her, Polly feared further reprisals for her husband's shaming.

"The company what employs you," Paul said, "was among those the House of Commons tasked with printing and distributing the amendment."

Susan held forth the publication.

Bill approached her slowly, then snatched the pages from her hand and tore them up.

"You might tear the paper, Mr. Nichols," Susan said, maintaining her calm, "but the law remains, and now you cannot claim ignorance of it."

"Now, as your boys are gone," Bill said, sneering, "leading your husband around by the nose isn't good enough? You've got to mind somebody else's business. There's little more despicable than a neighbor who listens through the walls for advantage."

"There's no call for you to mistreat *my* wife too," Paul said. "You are no great specimen, sir. I could easily defend both women."

"I can see you'd like to try."

"Yes, sir, I *would*."

Bill spun on his heels to face his wife. "Come, Polly, we'll go home."

"Take great care in how you treat your wife, Mr. Nichols," Susan said.

Polly didn't want to go with him. She was afraid. But she'd only delay the inevitable if she stayed, and to go seemed the best way to reduce his anger at the moment. He had been shamed and threatened. Although she found that satisfying, she feared that the Heryfords had fed his anger.

Bill took her by the wrist and led her to the door to exit the Heryfords' flat.

"We will be looking out for her," Paul said. "If we believe you've mistreated her further, we'll go to the police."

Bill pushed Polly through the threshold and followed her, slamming the door behind him.

She knew she must become small and nonthreatening. Polly kept her head down and didn't meet Bill's gaze. She would speak only when spoken to. If she made it through the night without another beating, she'd be fortunate.

26
Routine Reestablished

Over the next three weeks, Bill didn't speak to Polly.
Nor did he beat her.
Polly found a copy of the Matrimonial Causes Acts Amendment in a pocket of his trousers.

During the three weeks, he spent extra hours at his job, helping to implement a new die cutting process. When home, he said little to the children, as well. Polly suspected that he was relieved to have an excuse to be away from home.

Thinking about how the Heryfords had treated her, how they had seen only the best in her and responded to that, Polly saw herself as churlish and ungrateful for having lied and fled into drunkenness while allowing them to believe they protected her. Since she had run into fewer problems with Bill when sober, she decided her best course was to abstain from drink, at least until the high emotions of recent life had settled down again.

Morning sickness told her she was pregnant again. She hoped that wasn't true.

If it is, let it be Tom's child.

Since Bill seemed to treat her with perfect indifference, she had plenty of opportunity to slip away to visit her lover. Instead she waited several weeks for her face to heal.

In Polly's fourth week of healing, Bill began to grunt a yes or no to a question. If the communication required more, he allowed nothing but an awkward silence. Then, out of the blue, as if talking to himself, he said things aloud that he obviously wanted her to hear, such as his intention of finding a new home.

For what they could afford, Polly knew he would never find a place to live as fine as what they had in the Peabody building, and that Bill's pride in their home would further discourage him from making a change. She saw him speaking with the superintendent when other tenants were packing up their households to leave, and she assumed he hoped to take rooms within the Peabody buildings farther away from the Heryfords. Nothing came of his efforts.

"I'm pregnant," Polly told Bill one evening, unable to deny the reality of her changing body any longer.

His response to her was the first of any length since the confrontation with the Heryfords. "You shall introduce me to your childminder girl and her brother."

* * *

"You've treated Tom most cruelly," Estell said. "He's not here. He doesn't want to see you."

Polly knew that staying away from her lover with no explanation would be harmful. She had not thought that he and his sister would turn against her. "I need your help."

"No, you don't," Estell said loudly. She tried to shut the door, but Polly had put her boot into the opening.

Eliza stirred in her sling. The rocking on the walk to Jane Street had put her to sleep. Polly hoped she would not awaken.

She spoke quietly, urgently. "Yes, I do. My husband beat me because a neighbor saw me leaving here. I've been healing up since then so Tom won't see what happened to me and become angry enough to harm my husband."

Estell sneered, and Polly clarified her words. "I were afraid Tom would go to prison should he give Bill a dewskitch." Polly opened her mouth to show the gaps in her teeth. "Look here."

The young woman grimaced, and then her features softened some. "He'd have done him a good nobbling, at that."

"I told Bill you're my childminder, what you lived with your brother, and that's why I come here."

"Yes," Estell said impatiently, "all as true."

"He doesn't have to know about Tom and me."

"As for you to worry about. Tom doesn't want to see you anymore."

Polly felt defeated, but then had an idea. She leaned forward and pulled the swaddling from Eliza's face. "She's really growing. Don't you want to hold her?"

"Will you do anything to get what you want?"

"Yes."

Estell seemed to have some grudging respect for her answer, yet remained unmoved. "No, I don't want to see her. You cannot come in. Tom's not here. If you must see him, go to the smithy. You shouldn't like what you'll find."

As Estell tried to crush the foot in the door, Polly had another idea. "How's your reading and writing?"

The painful pressure on her foot let up some. A slight crooked smile took hold of Estell's face.

"I'll give you more lessons if you'll meet Bill and tell him you keep Eliza when I go to Farringdon Market."

"I shan't meet your husband."

"But you do want more lessons," Polly said with confidence. "Should you do as I ask, I'll help you learn more."

Estell seemed to ponder that for a moment, then the door opened.

* * *

Tom came home about half past three o'clock in the afternoon while Polly and Estell were in the midst of their lesson. He didn't seem pleased to see Polly.

"I didn't think I should see you again." he said, taking his hammer out of his belt and placing the tool on the table. "Had you no thought of how I'd worry? I knew better than to come looking for you. But for your husband, I might have done. What became of you?"

"I fell in the courtyard at the Peabody buildings," Polly said, "and struck one of the benches with my mouth."

Tom frowned, his slight anger turned to concern.

"The pain was more than I could bear," Polly continued, trying to remember all the parts of the story she had come up with and refined with Estell's help. "I became feverish and was in bed for several days."

Polly glanced at Estell who nodded encouragement.

"I thought I had a contagion and decided it best not to come here. Within a few days, I lost a tooth and my mouth got worse. A week later, I lost another tooth."

"Show him," Estell said.

Polly demurely opened her mouth to show the gap in her smile.

Tom looked down. He paced back and forth across the floor. Polly couldn't tell if he would swallow the lie.

"Please, say something," she said.

"And all this time," he said, "I thought I had hurt you in some way, though I couldn't think what I'd done." He looked at Polly, and though his affection for her remained in his gaze, the haunted look he sometimes carried had returned.

Polly didn't question the look. She hurried to him and he embraced her.

"I'm sorry you lost your teeth," he said.

"I am too," she said, relieved that he seemed to have taken the lie as truth. "I hope you don't mind too much."

"You're just as lovely as ever."

"That's not the same as saying you're lovely," Estell said. She screwed up her face to mock them.

* * *

Polly took Bill with her to Jane Street at a time when Estell would be there taking care of Nancy while Tom was out. The young woman explained everything to Bill's satisfaction, as she and Polly had planned.

"When may I meet your brother—Tom, is it?"

"Yes, sir," Estell said. "You can see him at the Salvation Smithy until seven o'clock in the evening every day of the week but Sunday. It's just by the sawmill."

"I know where," Bill said. He turned to Polly. "I've got my answer."

"Thank you," Polly said to Estell.

"Yes, Mrs. Nichols. You're very welcome. Anything I can do to help."

Estell had played her part quite well, Polly thought. Still, Bill's curt response to the young woman had her worried he'd seen through their pretense. Having turned off Jane Street onto Broadwall and heading back toward the Peabody buildings, Polly expected them to turn into Meymott Street to head for the Salvation Smithy. Bill continued toward home, and she decided not to question him.

* * *

As the year progressed, Polly's children grew, seemed happy, and did well in school. Her printing business ran a bit slower. She didn't mind the extra time. Estell became a good reader and began to compose written language well. Bill remained largely indifferent to Polly, yet he obviously found her useful since he made no effort to diminish her role in his life. He had ceased to talk about finding a new lodging. If he saw the Heryfords, he turned away from them. Polly found time to speak with Paul and Susan when Bill wasn't around. She would always be grateful to them for what they had done to help her.

Polly and Tom spent as much time as possible together. Although at first he showed no concern that she didn't want to drink, with time he began to press her to join him. When she refused, he seemed troubled, but he wouldn't talk about the matter with her. The further along in her pregnancy she became, the more troubled he seemed to be and the more he drank. That gave her a clue.

"I'll have to be away when the baby comes, as before," she said, "but you know I'll return to you soon as I can."

Tom didn't answer.

"You know I'll come back, don't you?"

"I suppose."

"Don't be foolish, Tom. I have you, the children, and no more."

"Yes," he said, "but what do I have? What if the child is mine, a little brother or sister for Nancy?"

"How will we know?"

"If he should have my likeness."

"Perhaps."

"Yes, perhaps." He sighed. "I have nothing to complain about. I knew what I were doing."

Clearly he didn't trust her, but to explain that she loved him, seemed to Polly an awkward response while he was in such a mood. She let it go.

* * *

As before, a month before the birth, Polly complained about discomfort during sex. They ceased to bed one another. On January 2, 1879, close to the time in which she believed the child was due, she said goodbye to Tom.

"I'll come back in a month," she said.

He gave no indication that he wanted to say anything. Troubled, Polly turned away, and began walking home. Glancing back as she moved along Jane Street, she saw him watching her with a great sadness on his face.

* * *

Henry Nichols was born on January 15, 1879. Although Polly realized she couldn't make a determination until his features developed further, she liked to think he was Tom's.

Susan Heryford became quite helpful with both Eliza and Henry, as long as Bill wasn't expected home.

Two weeks after the birth, she left her two youngest with Susan and walked to Jane Street to see Tom. No one answered. Discouraged, she went on to market to fetch bread, cheese, mutton and potatoes.

Several later attempts to visit the Dews convinced her that they had found a new lodging elsewhere.

Desperate, Polly went to the Salvation Smithy, and spoke to the master blacksmith, a sweat-slicked, blackened man.

"Gone south," he said. "Don't know where."

"He left no word where he'd be?"

"No," he said, turning away.

Polly's heart seemed to sink through the dirt floor at her feet. She turned toward home, a bleakness in her outlook. All that she'd come to look forward to was gone.

27
Exhaustive Search

For several months Polly hoped that once Tom and the girls had settled, word would come letting her know their location. He couldn't read or write, but he might have Estell compose a letter for him. Although she didn't think she'd ever given the Dews her address, if they sent correspondence to Polly Nichols at the Peabody Estates, Duke Street, the message would probably reach her.

By early summer, that small hope had fled. Polly loved her children and counted herself as fortunate to have a home and plenty to eat, but without Tom's touch, his companionship and loving gaze, Polly felt incomplete, as if she had nothing of her very own. She decided she must search South London for the Dews.

At first, Polly left Eliza with Susan Heryford. Carrying young Henry with her in a sling, she made short expeditions on foot to make inquiries at smithies close to home in Southwark. She imagined that when she found Tom, he'd be glad to see his son. Then she noticed that Henry had developed the same brown spots within the blue of his eyes that Bill had, and she could no longer fool herself that the infant belonged to Tom.

She managed her lies to Bill and Mrs. Heryford well, and kept up her responsibilities to her husband, the children, the household, and her printing clients. She made sure to locate along her routes suppliers of printing needs, as well as markets for food, and to avail herself of their goods when needed to save time on her outings and help provide an excuse for her activities. Having had no luck finding the Dews by the autumn of 1879, she began to expand her search of South London, trying to visit all the smithies she could find. Since Henry had begun to take solid food, she left both of her youngest children with Susan for longer hours. As wintry weather came on, she prepared a large fire in the stove early in the morning after Bill left for work on the days she would be gone so that the flat didn't become too cold in her absence. Even so, Bill complained about the chill when he came home in the evenings.

As Polly began to neglect her printing duties in early December, she came up with a plan to put her press temporarily out of service. The large wooden lever, used to apply pressure when printing, had a small crack that she'd noticed ever since the device had first come into her possession. She'd often thought the flaw would become larger and the handle would eventually break in two, yet that hadn't happened. Polly pushed a knife into the crack and twisted as she applied pressure to the lever. She worked at the thin opening for over an hour, her arms and hands becoming sore, sweat trickling down her face and back, until finally, the crack began to expand. Another hour passed before she got the lever to break in two. For good measure, she removed what remained of the lever, and bent the metal fitting on the end where the device was designed to meet the screw of the press.

"I'm certain what Papa can repair it," she told Bill that evening.

"That will take some time," he said with a look of frustration. "I'll speak to those who have orders placed."

"I'll leave the little ones with Estell," Polly lied, "and take the lever to Papa tomorrow."

On her visit to her father, Polly took the time to begin her search through Camberwell.

Because Mrs. Heryford suffered loneliness and needed a sense of purpose, she was easily deceived. Her husband worked at Waterloo Bridge Station for ten hours at a time most days of the week. Her boys were grown and had left home. One had married and lived in Westminster, and the other had found a position as a waiter at an inn in Tottenham. The promise of having little ones to care for seemed to have an attraction that allowed Susan to overlook Polly's increasingly flimsy excuses for going away and having to leave her children behind. With time, Susan even took on the duty of taking in the older children when they came home from school in the early evening if Polly hadn't returned.

The press remained out of commission for a mere two months, and so by spring of 1880, Polly was neglecting her clients and Bill heard their complaints.

"Having to carry around an infant as well as a two-year-old," Polly complained, "has given me such pains in my arms and back that the work is difficult. Please be patient with me while little Henry is so young."

Since she'd given him no reason to believe she'd been drinking for well over a year, and she had never shown herself to be lazy, Bill seemed to believe her. Although cautious about interpreting his moods, she thought a pleasant change had come over him. He smiled more frequently and a spring appeared in his step. Had he received a raise in his salary? If he had, she knew he would keep the news to himself.

Bill knew other small printers to whom he gave the printing jobs that Polly couldn't complete.

She pushed herself to reach as many smithies as possible each day she went out to search. The need to find Tom, having become more powerful than what she had for drink, occupied her thoughts day and night. She mechanically moved though her hours at home while her mind continued to scour South London for her love. Good rest and sleep became rare and increasingly difficult to find. She held down her growing frustration and presented the most happy and smiling face she could to her family.

Although Bill had shown little concern about her behavior, she felt the need to provide explanation for her emotional distance. "I have felt a bit ill of late," she told him.

His face darkened with concern, and she decided that the lie had been a mistake. "Just light-headed, my thought hard to hold onto. I'm certain it will pass soon." Then, she thought of something to add that might easily put him off the trail of the truth. "My monthly turns have ceased again and I might be with child."

Bill nodded with a slight smile, his concern put away.

In truth, her monthly flow had ceased two months earlier, and yet other signs of pregnancy had not followed.

Having to travel farther and farther afield to check locations through the summer months, and continually pushing herself each time to look into *just one more* before going home, Polly began returning too late to fix supper.

Still, with mere suggestions that she might try harder, Bill was slow to anger, and seemed willing to ignore her erratic behavior. Polly thought perhaps he feared that if he gave room for his anger to be expressed he might find himself beating her, and end up arrested by the police. On the occasions when she'd prepared no supper, he went out to gather food from street vendors with little complaint. The children were pleased to eat the food from the street.

Polly had difficulty keeping all her lies to Mrs. Heryford straight. Susan began questioning her about the outings. On an evening in late summer the older woman had finally had enough. Polly had returned from Bermondsey to collect her children about six o'clock in the evening.

"Dear," Susan said, pausing and clasping both Polly's hands as they stood on the landing between their flats, "I love your children and enjoy keeping them, but I have come to the unfortunate conclusion that you aren't honest with me about your reasons to go out and to be out for such long periods. I have shown tolerance because I know you've suffered and need my help. I do wish you would confide in me."

Polly wasn't prepared for the reaction. If she'd had to face anger, she would have been able to respond. The sadness in Susan's eyes said that the woman still thought the best of Polly. The realization that she did not feel the least bit worthy of such goodwill became a pain in her chest that took much of what little strength remained to her. The landing seemed to spin about for a moment, and she reached out to the wall to steady herself.

Susan took her by the arm. "You should come in and sit."

"No," Polly said, "I don't have time. You've been good to me and I've abused your trust. I'm truly sorry for that, yet I'm too weary to speak to you of my problems at present. I'll tell you what has happened soon." Although she didn't think she'd do that, for the time being, the statement might help forestall the matter.

"When you're ready, then," Susan said. She patted Polly's hands affectionately. "Percy and Alice are in the courtyard playing. I told them not to be long."

Polly had not seen the older children when she came in.

With Percy thirteen years old and Alice at age eleven, they were old enough to take care of themselves in the afternoon. She gathered her toddler and infant from the Heryford flat and went to her flat to prepare supper.

Traveling some miles on foot each time she went out to search, several days a week, even at the cost of many of her other responsibilities, Polly wasn't merely physically exhausted, she was wrung out emotionally as well. At some point between starting a pot to boil on the stove and cutting potatoes, she collapsed on the floor.

* * *

"Percy and Alice said they couldn't wake you," Bill said, when she came around much later.

Polly found herself in bed. She saw darkness outside her bedroom window.

"They still fussed over you when I came home," he said, his manner strangely sweet. A flowery fragrance came from his clothing.

"The potatoes?"

"They took the pot off the stove. I fetched meat puddings and we had a feast. They're getting spoiled." He rubbed her arm softly.

Polly didn't want her husband's tenderness, she wanted Tom's. Despite the time—at least a year—that had passed since last she'd seen him, she missed her lover as much as ever. Even so, the thread of hope she'd had of finding Tom had finally broken. Polly knew she'd come to the end of her strength, and that she'd have to abandon the search. The Dews had moved somewhere else, away from South London. Polly would never find them.

She groaned and turned over, away from Bill.

Polly heard his steps as he left the room.

She wanted a drink, but, for the present, she'd sleep.

28
Bed Rest

When Polly awoke, she found a short, plump woman she didn't know sitting beside her bedstead feeding Henry from a small bowl. Eliza sat in a crib beside the door, playing with what looked like a red felt elephant. Polly had never seen the toy or the crib before.

"I am Nurse Flake," the woman said. With a small mouth and nose, fair skin, and large brown eyes, she looked something like a porcelain doll. The beautiful, dark hair on her head was done up in a bun. "Your husband has employed me to watch over you for the week. You are to remain in bed, and I'll do everything for you."

Polly ached all over. The emptiness in her stomach needed filling. She groaned and sat up.

The nurse set the bowl down on the table beside the bed next to a cup of water, then got up from her seat and lowered Henry into the crib. She moved to the cabinet on the other side of the bed, fetched the chamber pot, and placed it on the floor.

Polly stepped from the bed, and squatted over the porcelain vessel to relieve herself.

"Am I ill?" she asked. Her tongue felt thick and dry in her mouth.

"We had a doctor in. He said you suffer from overwork,

178

and prescribed a week of bed rest. You've slept for two days. I should think you'd be hungry."

Although Polly had felt a strong need, little urine fell into the chamber pot. The liquid had a dark yellow appearance and a strong, sour odor. Polly's stomach growled even as she returned to bed. "And thirsty." Her voice came out rough. She reached for the glass of water and the nurse stopped her.

"Let me help," Nurse Flake said. "You'll be unsteady." She lifted the glass and helped hold it, but pulled it away before Polly had her fill. "You mustn't have too much at once."

Polly smelled a familiar odor on the woman. "What is the sweet fragrance?"

"My beau bought me a fine French soap what has a scent— peonies, I think."

Polly remembered that Bill smelled of the peony scent when he'd awakened her. *When was that,* Polly asked herself, *two days ago? Before or after he hired the nurse?*

Nurse Flake set the glass on the bedside table. "Don't try to lift it on your own until you've got a bit of your strength back." She handed Polly a mirror. "I'm sure you'll want to tame your hair. I'll just get some porridge for you." Although she got up and left the room, she continued to speak loudly enough for Polly to hear her. "You're lucky to have such lovely children."

Polly looked in the mirror, and absently straightened her hair. The small scar on her forehead stood out, its shiny oblong shape with the small lip on one side, catching the light. While considering the flaw, something about the nurse troubled Polly's thoughts.

"Are you married?" she asked, trying to make her voice loud enough to reach the next room. The words came out with a bit of croaking, yet evidently were heard.

"Yes, I am, but when we discovered I cannot become

pregnant, Harry left for Australia. He writes to me so I know he still lives or I might have remarried."

During a pause in the nurse's words, Polly heard the clinking of a utensil against a bowl. She wished the woman would hurry back with the food.

"Bill said he hoped I'd like your children, since I'd be spending so much time with them. I'm glad to say that I do."

Is he grooming her to replace me? Polly wondered. She noted that Nurse Flake didn't refer to him as Mr. Nichols.

When she returned, Polly wasted no time asking, "How do you know my husband?"

The quickness and tone of Polly's question seemed to surprise and fluster Nurse Flake. She stopped dead in her tracks, the bowl and spoon held loosely in her hands. Despite the gnawing hunger, Polly wanted to hear the woman's answer right away.

"I-well…I…um…met your husband many years ago…uh… when he stayed with his sister, Rebecca, for a brief time after dropping a crate on his foot."

What Polly most remembered about Bill's injury of that time was the cane he used to help him get around on his damaged foot, the one with which he'd beaten her. Bill stayed with his sister following the thrashing her father had given him.

"His sister and I have been lifelong friends," Nurse Flake said, "and she called on me to take care of him in her home. As I recall, he wasn't married at the time. Are your older children from another marriage?"

"We *were* married at the time," Polly said.

The nurse frowned. "I see."

She drew her chair up beside the bed and awkwardly fed Polly a spoonful at a time of porridge. Polly avoided looking her in the eye. She brooded.

* * *

She didn't care if the woman took her husband's affections. Polly didn't want them, yet she did want some of what came with their marriage. Bill had to provide for her, and couldn't divorce her without evidence of adultery. Apparently, the traces of that were so well hidden, even Polly had been unable to find them after a year of searching.

What bothered her most about Nurse Flake was that the woman had a good way with the children. She treated them as if they were her own. She laughed and played with Percy and Alice when they came in from school. Although they treated her like a friend, when she gave commands, they complied readily. She'd made felt toys for them as well, a yellow lion for Percy, and a white swan for Alice.

The older children couldn't have been pleased with Polly for a long time, especially during the last year. She had been so worn out from her desperate search that she gave them little time or energy. Her presence had been the bare minimum required on most occasions, and at times woefully inadequate. She could not remember the last time one of her children had approached her with eyes filled with delight.

In the evenings, when Bill came home, she listened to him talking in low tones to Nurse Flake. Polly believed she heard tender feelings expressed between them, even though she could not make out their words. Bill slept in the bed next to Polly at night without touching her. The reasonable explanations might have been that he thought she should be left alone while recovering from her exhaustion or that he'd been instructed to do so. Polly thought he'd lost interest in her. The more she considered the idea, the more she hoped that to be true.

Over the days of her confinement to bed, she increasingly felt like a stranger in her own home. When the nurse or any of her family spoke to her, Polly showed little emotion. Her weariness continued, and she drowsed fitfully.

"Polly, dear," Bill said to her, "are you still with us? You seem to have traveled to a distant land." She didn't respond.

* * *

On her sixth day of confinement to bed, she was awakened as Nurse Flake brought her a visitor. Polly hid her excitement upon seeing Estell enter the room carrying a large carpet bag.

"Mrs. Nichols," she said. "Good to see you."

In the year and a half since Polly had last seen her, Estell had grown into a woman.

"I am busy folding nappies," the nurse said, "so I'll leave you two." She turned to Estell. "I've been told not to get Polly excited, but she suffers a melancholia. I should think a lively response from her would be most welcome."

"Yes, nurse," Estell said, dutifully.

"Shall I take your bag for you?" Nurse Flake asked.

"No, thank you. I won't be long."

As soon as the nurse left the room, Polly allowed her eyes to go wide. She opened her arms. Estell sat on the bed and hugged her. When she pulled away, glad tears streamed down the younger woman's face. "Because of you, I have good work," she said proudly. "A position! I'm a clerk for the Sedulential Assurance Company."

Polly had never heard of such a thing, a young woman entrusted with record-keeping. "How?"

"You taught me to read and write. I'm very good at it. The company gave tests for female employees, and I won a position."

"I'm so *very* proud of you." Polly pulled Estell close and hugged her again. When the younger woman pulled away, Polly wasted no time asking, "How's Tom? Where is he?"

Estell's smile turned grim. "My income supports us now. We're in York Street, Walworth. We lost Nancy over the winter, poor girl. She began coughing one day and didn't stop until her little heart did. Tom took it hard. He's not done well since last you saw him."

Where Polly had lived on Trafalgar Street was part of Walworth. Although she'd searched the area—a mere two miles away—evidently, she'd not done a thorough job.

"I'll come right away," Polly said.

"Yes, perhaps that's best," Estell said, her eyes becoming large. "Your nurse speaks freely of things she should not. I'm glad she has done. She said your husband spoke to the doctor, and they decided that if you didn't come out of your melancholia soon, they'd send you to Bedlam."

Estell used the local pronunciation for Bethlem Hospital, the centuries-old madhouse. Polly felt her mouth drop open and her eyes focussed beyond Etsell on the intangible distance where memory lived. In an instant, she saw how Bill might have fancied a form of insanity growing in her for a long time, possibly years. She understood his reasoning as she thought of her secretiveness, her drinking, her indifference to him, and so many evenings lately when he came home to find her exhausted. Within the last year, she'd taken to going to bed early so she didn't have to spend time with him, and also so she'd awaken early the next day and be ready to continue her work or resume her search as quickly as possible. She'd got so that she rarely spoke to him or the children. He probably saw the changes in her as a retreat from the world.

She'd walked past Bethlem Royal Hospital in Lambeth on

several occasions. Perhaps the days were long past when the madhouse had been so defined by the tumult and din of its inmates that the facility fairly rocked on its foundation and the new word "bedlam" was coined. At present, the hospital kept its greens beautiful, and allowed some of its inmates to stroll among the trees while supervised. The current common wisdom held that the patients were well treated, but Polly had heard that the "tours" of the asylum for those who wanted to gawk at the raving lunatics still took place. She had no desire to become a part of the entertainment.

Then again, Bill may know I'm perfectly sane, yet he needs an excuse to be rid of me so he can take up with Nurse Flake. Pretending happiness could spoil their plan.

No, if they don't have the excuse to put me away in the madhouse, they might turn to murder. Polly imagined the nurse bringing her a teaspoon of poison in the guise of medicine.

"I have to get *out!*" Polly said. "I must escape."

"I'll help," Estell said. "Place what you'll need to take with you in my bag. I'll go ask the nurse if she'll allow me to walk you in the courtyard."

"She'll never allow it."

"I can be very persuasive."

While Estell talked to Nurse Flake in the next room, Polly quietly dressed, and assembled a few necessities, including the money she'd skimmed off her printing over the years. She opened the carpet bag to find the interior full of Estell's belongings. Polly was still struggling to get her possessions inside and close it when she heard footsteps coming toward her room. Frantically, she gave another shove and tried to close the bag, yet it remained open, a chemise spilling out, when Estell entered alone. Polly sagged in relief.

Estell nodded to her as she crouched and stuffed the chemise down further and shut the bag. She stood and gestured for Polly to follow.

In the front room, Nurse Flake sat at the table feeding Henry bread softened in milk. Eliza sat on the floor at the nurse's feet tearing open the neck of the elephant with her teeth. Nurse Flake had already repaired the toy once before. "Don't walk fast. If she feels the least bit drained, bring her in immediately. Leave the bag with me for now."

"No, nurse," Estell said, "I am delivering it to a neighbor at the other end of the building. As why I stopped by."

"Well," Nurse Flake said, "I think Polly might make it to the other end if she wants to." She gave an encouraging smile.

Polly thought of Percy and Alice. They wouldn't be home from school for several hours. She wished she could say good-bye to them. She looked at her two youngest. She would miss them, but they would be much happier with Nurse Flake.

Estell gave her an even look, and Polly hid her sadness. She allowed the young woman to take her through the door and out of the Peabody building.

29
Reunion & Departure

When Polly and Estell arrived at the room in York Street, Walworth, Tom was stuporous with drink. He sat at a table against the wall. A glass of gin and his hammer rested on the tabletop before him. Seeing Polly, his haggard face brightened briefly, but then he scowled and he placed a hand on the handle of his hammer. "I don' wan' 'er here," he slurred.

"She's with me," Estell said. "She'll sleep with me. You needn't talk to her if you don't want to."

"I've left Bill and the children," Polly said. "He has a mistress, a nurse who will take good care of them. They don't need me any longer."

His brow lifted with a look of cautious hope. "Come, 'ave a drink, then." He held up a bottle of gin, and leaned his chair back against the wall so that the seat's front legs and his feet lifted off the floor.

"No, thank you," Polly said.

Tom's brow knitted and his eyes darkened. "Then, I don't believe you."

"Believe what you wish, you sodden lout," Estell said. She approached Tom and Polly followed.

"Get out," he shouted, waving his arms. His seat wobbled

on its hind legs, and he steadied himself against the wall with his left hand.

"No," Estell said. She quickly hooked a front leg of his chair with her foot and pulled.

With the sound of wood twisting and cracking, Polly jumped back as Tom and his seat toppled into a heap. He lay on the floor groaning.

Polly gave Estell a hard look.

"Being nice to him does no good when he's like this," the younger woman said.

"Well, you needn't be cruel either." Polly knelt and tried to pull Tom off the remains of the seat. One leg and two of the chair's stretchers had broken loose.

"You ought to fix that chair straight away," Estell said, "or you should have nowhere to sit. Polly and I will be using the other two."

The continued hard feelings surprised Polly. She'd thought Estell loved her brother.

Tom moaned as he rolled off the chair leg to get away from Polly. "She treats me like a wretch, she does."

"That's because you are," Estell said. She held out her arms. "It's my income what pays for all this, such as it is. Should you find work and contribute to our income, you'll have a say in what goes on here—not until."

Listening to the young woman, Polly began to understand and respect her. She'd rarely seen a woman take charge in a household and the sight brought a smile to her lips.

"You're leaving," Tom said, "so what do you care?"

Polly looked at Estell.

"Not for two months."

"I shall never see you 'gain," Tom moaned. "I'll do wha'ever I want."

Polly kept her eyes on the younger woman. Estell clearly became uncomfortable.

"I were going to tell you once you got settled. The company as employs me has opened offices in New York. They want me there to help. They believe I am…well, I'm good at sorting things out." She smiled proudly, then frowned. "I'm sorry."

"You might have told me," Polly said angrily. "You want someone to keep your drunken brother so you won't feel bad about going."

"No!" Estell said. She pressed her mouth into a hard line and looked at the floor. "You love each other. Yes, he needs help and I'll not be able to give it soon. I've taken care of him for a long time."

Tom had rolled onto his stomach and become motionless.

"I didn't mean to trick you," Estell said. "You love him," she added pitifully.

Tom began to snore.

Looking at him, Polly swallowed her anger. "Yes, I do."

* * *

As fall began in late September of 1880, Polly saw her father. She told him about her flight from Bill and about Tom and Estell.

"It's not right you should leave your husband for another man," Papa said with a stern look. Then his expression softened some. "He weren't a good husband, though."

At least he doesn't take Bill's side.

"He came looking for you," Papa said, "but I didn't know where you were." His stern look returned. "You've abandoned your children."

"No, I haven't. Bill and the nurse plotted together to take

them. If I'd stayed they would have done me in. I were certain she'd poison me."

"You saw that?"

"Not clearly, but they wouldn't have put it out in the open, would they? At the very least, Bill would have put me in the madhouse. The nurse said as much."

"So says the sister of your lover."

"She's not the sort to mislead. If I was sent to Bedlam, what good would I have done my children then?"

Papa looked at her for a long time.

"One day, I'll take care of them again," she said, "but for now, Nurse Flake has them. I watched her for nearly a week. She'll do a good job of it, if you want to know the truth. Better than I did, I'm ashamed to say."

"Is that demon still after you?"

"How do you—" Polly cut herself off, then couldn't keep herself from asking, "The Bonehill Ghost?"

Papa narrowed his gaze as he looked her in the eye. "Ah, Mr. Macklin," he said.

Polly nodded. She had the urge to leave immediately and return to Tom.

"I have not thought of him for many years," her father said. "Your grandfather knew him. Mr. Macklin were a drunkard. Met a terrible end. Your grandfather would have told you the Irishman fell off the Blackfriars Bridge because he were besotted. Those who loved him believed so, and he were buried in hallowed ground. Others say drink destroyed him, that he leapt to his death, and it were a mistake to put him in hallowed ground. Misery loves company. They say he serves the devil now, preying upon those who drink too much." Papa raised one eyebrow. "Is he after you?"

Polly glared at her father. He'd never thought the Bonehill

Ghost haunted her. She decided against explaining herself. "I haven't had a drink in well over a year."

Papa kept his eyes on her. Polly tried not to blink. After a lengthy pause, he said, "I have opened a lot of locks for Magistrate Walters over the years. He sits at the Lambeth Street court Mondays, Tuesdays, and Wednesdays. For a beak, he's a decent sort. He'll help us with your separation from your husband."

"What kind of locks?" Polly asked.

"I'm a locksmith," he said indignantly.

"Does he often lock things and throw away the keys?"

"They would be things he doesn't have keys for and can't be opened with a betty, things taken from family people. In his work with the police, he comes across plenty of things as needs a locksmith. That's all I'm saying."

"Family people? You mean criminals."

Papa didn't respond.

Then Polly remembered something about the incident involving the strongbox. "Magistrate Walters is your friend at the Lambeth Street Police Court. You told me about that after your arrest years ago."

Papa's lips drew back in a grim smile. "He saved me from going to prison, saved us all, you and Eddie too."

"What happened?"

"Billy and Rob Bowker, brothers and dragsmen they were, threatened to harm Eddie if I didn't crack that peter. It were the third such lockbox I'd opened for them, each while under the same threat. I knew they'd bring more, and didn't want any part of it. The push in the box was a great sum, hundreds of pounds. I took it to the police at Lambeth Street, told them I wanted to talk to Magistrate Walters about it. He weren't there. They held me two days. The third day I would meet the Bowker brothers in the afternoon to hand over the opened strongbox, and I were worried if I missed the meeting time what they'd hurt Eddie."

Realizing that Papa had no other choice but to help the criminals, Polly felt ashamed of herself for having once believed that he'd eagerly embraced wrongdoing.

"Walters, he came in the morning of the third day, I told him about the Bowkers and their box, and we plotted to capture them. I'd cracked a box for Magistrate Walters once too, did it for nothing because I thought I might need his help one day. Good thing I did. When the Bowkers come back for their box, hidden constables waited for them. The brothers went to prison. I've had a debt of service to the Magistrate since. He's done well by what I've opened for him over the years. He values my service enough to do me a kindness from time to time."

Without her father explaining completely, Polly understood that Magistrate Walters had enriched himself with treasure from the boxes Papa had opened for him over the years, boxes no doubt taken in raids on criminal enterprises.

"You were right when you called me a criminal. I know it's wrongdoing, what I do for him, even though he's with the police court."

"You've done it for your family," Polly said. "No one could fault you for that."

He nodded slowly, perhaps not agreeing with her completely. "If you'll stay the night, we'll try to see him tomorrow. I won't bring up the children with Walters—it would be asking too much, I think." His eyes became hard again. "I expect you to sort that out on your own later."

The next day, they arrived early at the Lambeth Street Police Court, and waited through much of the day before they were brought before Magistrate Walters. In moments, they obtained for Polly an order of legal separation from her husband on the grounds of persistent cruelty and a maintenance order that would require Bill Nichols to pay her one pound, three shillings per month unless he successfully contested the orders within thirty days. In the brief discussion Papa had with the Magistrate, Polly remained silent.

With Polly's help, Papa then wrote to Bill telling him about the legal proceedings and threatening to assemble the witnesses—particularly the neighbors from the Trafalgar Street rooms and the Heryfords—needed to have him convicted of persistent cruelty should he try to contest the orders.

* * *

Tom began to drink less, and found work at a local smithy.

The maintenance started coming in through the post to Papa's address. Though not a generous amount, the funds helped. Polly made a weekly trek to her father's room to get the money. Her first few visits became unpleasant as he asked what she was doing to reclaim her children and she had no good answers. Finally, she had a suggestion that seemed to put an end to his questioning on the subject: "I know Bill won't give them up. To see them, I'd have to get close enough to him that he might do me down again. When he has and you and Tom have taken turns punishing him for it, perhaps I'll be visiting both of you in prison."

Papa lowered his gaze and nodded. She took that to mean that he got her message.

In late November of 1880, Polly and Tom said goodbye to Estell at the docks as she boarded a steamer bound for America. The younger woman had become family and Polly wept to see her go. Even so, she looked forward to having Tom all to herself.

30
Census

side from the maintenance funds from Bill, Polly didn't make any income during the following year, 1881. Tom expected her to keep house, but didn't ask her to find a position of employment or to do piece work. Polly had too much time to think, and little ability to pin down her thoughts. She had never fully recovered from her exhaustion. Her thoughts frequently flew away from the task at hand. Since her monthly flow had ceased to make an appearance over a year ago, and yet she had not become pregnant, Polly knew her time for bearing children had past. Though that pleased her, the idea also contributed to her sense that, at thirty-six years of age, she'd become old before her time.

"Something about my thinking during my escape from Bill troubles me," Polly told Tom as they sat to eat a fish dinner one evening. "I can't decide whether I truly believed the nurse threatened my marriage and my life or if I'd merely needed that to be true to leave my children behind."

"Estell said they plotted to send you to Bedlam."

"Yes, but how can I be certain of that? Perhaps she said that to encourage me to leave."

Tom frowned. "Estell is not given to lying."

Polly nodded. "Most of all, I hate to think my children might believe they aren't lovable, that I did not care for them." Polly bowed her head and covered her face with her hands.

Tom reached across the table to caress her. "I would go with you if you wanted to see them."

"No, Bill mustn't know about you. Should he prove adultery, the maintenance would cease."

"Should you return to him? Would you feel better if you did?"

"No, I would suffer a worse marriage than what I had." Polly knew her husband would never forget what she'd done.

* * *

With Estell's departure, Tom's consumption of alcohol steadily increased until Polly became uncomfortable with the amount he drank each night. After all the contentiousness with her father and Bill concerning her drinking, she didn't think she had any right to criticize. Tom asked her to drink with him and she refused.

She remembered her father talking about Mr. Macklin haunting those who drank too much. Even before that, on her own, she'd thought Papa's statements about a demon chasing her had something to do with alcohol. Although the Bonehill Ghost was linked in her mind with her own alcoholic over-indulgence, and she got a chill every time she thought about it, she told herself she no longer believed in the demon. Still, Polly didn't look too closely at her reasons for abstinence for fear that they might evaporate.

At first, Tom got to work at the Burlington smithy with consistency, but as the year progressed he more frequently tested his employer's patience. If he had not been such a good blacksmith, he would not have lasted at the job as long as he did.

* * *

In December of 1881, Tom had stayed home on a Tuesday to sleep off a bad hangover, despite threats from his employer that he'd be let go. Polly was sweeping the room when a knock came at the door. She answered the call to find a man in a bowler hat, a long mustache, and dark clothes standing on the doorstep.

"Mrs. Nichols?" he asked. "Mrs. Polly Nichols?"

"Yes," she said.

He smiled, said, "Thank you," and walked away.

Nothing about the man or his words made a memorable impression, and though an odd occurrence she didn't think to tell Tom about the incident.

Several days later another man called at their room in the early evening while Polly and Tom were both in. Polly answered the door and Tom stood behind her. The man wore a brown suit, a long topcoat, and felt hat.

"I am a census enumerator from the Office of National Statistics," he said. "Our records for several homes in this neighborhood from the census taken in April were lost. If you please, take this schedule and fill out all the questions and I'll return tomorrow evening to collect it." He handed Polly a sheet of paper.

"Yes, sir," Polly said. "I will."

Once the man had gone and Polly shut the door, Tom said drunkenly, "We shouldn't have to do that."

"We do it so those in Parliament think about us."

"I'm not certain that's a good thing."

As she had in April, Polly noted that the census schedule had been printed by the company that employed Bill Nichols,

Messrs. Pellanddor and Company. Among many other queries, the document asked for the names, ages, occupations, and relationships of all those living within the household.

* * *

The afternoon of the next day, a letter came for Polly from Bill Nichols.

> *My Polly,*
> *I will not waste my time or yours on sentiment or condemnation. Your children will provide that with time.*
> *I am writing to say that the census schedule you returned to my man has proved your undoing, written in your own hand. Since you have been found to be living with a man as a common prostitute, I am no longer legally bound to provide maintenance. You will not see a farthing more from me.*
> *Good riddance, I say,*
> *Bill Nichols*

Polly foresaw future clashes with her children. They would only know their father's side of the story, and have nothing but scorn for her. As saddening as her thoughts were, anger pushed them aside. Polly tore the letter to small pieces.

Later, as she cleaned the pieces up off the floor, she felt foolish for having fallen for Bill's trap.

Without her maintenance to contribute, she and Tom would have to find lesser lodgings. Polly feared that when he found out, he'd drink heavier still. She also worried that she wasn't up to the coming struggle to survive.

31

A Precipitous Decline

Upon hearing the news of the letter and the loss of the maintenance funds, Tom fell into a binge that by mid-January of 1882 had cost him his job.

Polly looked for a position of employment, but found nothing. They sold and pawned what possessions they could, and earned enough to pay for the room for another month. Polly spoke to her father about where to find piece work.

"I've not looked for such in many years," he said. "Go where goods are manufactured and ask what work they might send you home with."

Polly found work finishing shirts for a penny, ha'penny each for the Ellis Shirt Manufacturers in Clandon Street. She finished the collar, cuffs, button holes, hemmed the shirt tail, and applied the buttons to complete a shirt. Each one took her over an hour. She needed to make thirteen shillings a week.

"I work fifteen hours a day," she told Tom, "and you drink it away. You must find work!"

"I'll go out to look every day," he said.

Each afternoon, he left the room for several hours, yet he always returned drunk and without a job. Polly assumed that he either drank the time away or that he looked for work while intoxicated and, of course, got no good results.

"We cannot keep spending what little we have on gin," Polly said.

Promising to spend less on drink, he merely bought the worst available gin at a lower price and drank just as much.

Polly's hands began to shake from fatigue after the first week of finishing shirts. At the end of the third week, with trepidation, she started drinking the horrible gin to steady her hands. The quality of her labor suffered for her slight intoxication and fatigue, and the shirt manufacturer stopped giving her work.

Polly fussed and fumed with worry and pleaded with Tom for a change in his ways. She made demands and gave him ultimatums. He made more empty promises, and continually stepped around her demands. Tom had become an immoveable object. Nothing Polly said or did motivated him to act in his own best interest.

Knowing they could not continue to afford their lodging, she looked for other rooms. "I found two common lodging houses what allow a husband and wife to sleep in the same bed for sixpence per night," she told Tom.

He didn't respond. On the day the landlord came to turn them out into the streets, she thought that, finally, Tom would be forced to act. She'd packed a few of their belongings and loaded them into a carpet bag and the homemade pram once used to carry Eliza and Nancy. On the street, Tom turned from her, and quickly walked away.

Carrying the carpet bag and pulling the pram, Polly tried to keep up. "Burns common lodging is just north on Brandon Street," she called out to him.

Tom turned south beside the Congregational Church on York Street. He fled down the side passage that led to an old graveyard.

Polly abandoned the pram and hurried after Tom, but lost him amidst the broken cogs of tombstones behind the church.

"Tom," she cried, "please, I need you." An old woman and a child, standing before a small marker, and a man hauling a stained sack of something into a tool house watched Polly warily as she made her way through the graveyard. Though she peeked behind every standing stone, she didn't find Tom. Her lover had vanished. Weeping, she made her way back to collect the pram, only to discover that it, too, was gone, along with all her possession but the few articles of clothing she carried in the carpet bag.

Polly went to Papa. He struggled to lift the front of his barrow to head out for the day as she arrived.

"Papa," she said, helping him lift. "Tom and I were turned out into the street. He's left me, and I have no money. Will you take me in?"

He looked at her for a moment. "I'm sorry, Polly girl, but I'm coming off a bout with grippe. Haven't earned a farthing in two weeks. As I'm just getting back on my feet, I haven't enough for us both."

"Isn't John here to help?"

"He has his own barrow now, and found lodgings in Whitechapel. You can go to him or come back in a month when I've had time to earn a little."

Polly shook her head. She couldn't beg from her own child.

"Then you'll have to stay in a four penny hotel," Papa said coldly. "Surely you can do without drink long enough each day to earn that."

Despite his tone, perhaps because of the edge of desperation in it, Polly understood. He didn't need the extra burden while recovering from illness. Papa looked worn down, his eyes sunken and dark, his features pale. He'd become thin and stooped in a way that told her the years weighed on him.

She placed a hand on his rough, whisker-stubbled cheek, and then walked away.

Polly stayed nights at Wiltings common lodging in Emily Street, sleeping in her clothes with strangers, six to a bed. By day, she begged along South Street. Some days, she went hungry in order to have the funds to sleep indoors, safe from the cold winter nights. She had few opportunities for washing, and became increasingly filthy. All the clothing she had, including two extra chemises, one extra skirt, and changes of undergarments which she carried in her carpet bag, had become ragged.

Seeing prostitutes plying themselves outside of pubs, she considered the trade. One evening, she watched a young flaxen-haired woman outside a pub on East Street. Since the young woman wasn't dressed in a particularly alluring manner, she didn't look like a prostitute. Her effort to catch the eye of each man who walked past eventually gave her away, yet she didn't seem so different from Polly. When the woman took a break to smoke her pipe, Polly approached.

The prostitute looked her up and down.

"I'm Polly. If you please, ma'am, I have questions."

"Yes?" the woman said. She wasn't unfriendly.

"What do you earn, and what do you offer?"

"I'm no *Tom*."

Polly thought that somehow the prostitute compared herself to Tom Dews, but then realized she meant that she didn't provide her service to women.

"No, not for me," Polly said. "I want to know what price *I* should ask."

The prostitute raised her eyebrows and nodded. "The going rate is four pence for Miss Laycock."

Just enough to pay doss for one night at Wiltings. She knew that Miss Laycock meant vagina, so she assumed the woman meant full sexual intercourse.

"Dressed like that," the prostitute said, "and smelling as you do, you'll be lucky to get tuppence."

Discouraged, Polly thanked the woman and moved on.

* * *

On a day when her fellow beggars warned that the night would become severely cold, she'd had nothing to eat, and knew she wouldn't find her doss for the evening, Polly weighed the dangers of sleeping rough against the chances of coming to harm from a client paying her for sex.

Surely a woman's first time could not be so terrible or there wouldn't be so many women who stay in prostitution.

Feeling alone and vulnerable, Polly saw herself as the little girl she'd been shortly after her mother died. She realized that a sense of that innocent girl within had never left her, despite all that Polly had done. Though battered and bruised, the girl wore the last shreds of her dignity, and stood in the way of what must be done. Polly shoved the weakened girl aside and took action.

She found a pub with plenty of customers coming and going, and stood outside the establishment beside a group of men who were talking and enjoying themselves. She didn't know how to broach the subject of sex for sale. Hoping her glance would convey the message of her willingness, she tried to catch an eye or two.

Finally, one of the men, a drunken fellow in a checked suit turned to her. "You're a raggedy guttersnipe, you are. Be gone before the lot of us *take* what we want."

She hurried away across the lane to the footway on the other side, carrying the frightened girl within her to safety.

Polly had run out of options, and considered prayer, but since she couldn't pray for herself, the idea seemed laughable.

In the late afternoon, she headed to the Lambeth Workhouse

in Renfrew Road. Polly paced up and down the lane, her stomach aching with hunger pangs, and her weariness demanding a warm place to rest. She tried to persuade herself that all she'd heard over the years of the evils of the institution—the tales of abusive staff, of the food being not fit for man or beast, the enfeebling hard labor, and discipline that included torture for even the smallest offense—were merely tall tales. Although she wasn't successful, she finally entered.

After filling out several forms and an application for relief, she joined a group of six other women. Following a lengthy wait in a small featureless room with benches along the walls, a matron in a black uniform gave them each a card. Polly saw that her own name had been written on the one she'd been given. The matron led them into a large room with a slate floor much like any public bathhouse. The room held ten gray metal troughs with a pipe poised above each one.

"Strip, and bathe," the matron said. "Fold your clothing and place it on the shelf with the card I gave you on top." She gestured toward a shelf at waist height along one wall. She turned a valve and water flowed from the ends of the pipes into the troughs. "Use plenty of soap."

When done with washing, the women, one at a time, were required to stand in a small alcove while the matron doused them with a bitter smelling powder. They were each given a gray uniform, instructed to don it, and the woman in black led them to a high-ceilinged hallway with benches along the walls. Seated on the benches were other women in the same gray uniform.

"Have a seat and wait to see the doctor," the matron said. She asked one of the women in Polly's group to follow her and they passed through a threshold into another room.

Despite the rough fabric of her stiff uniform, Polly was grateful to feel warm, clean, and comfortable for the first time in a long while. Her fears continually tried to surface and take hold of her thoughts, but she pushed them back down.

One by one, the matron took each of the women through the threshold and brought them back. They didn't seem the worse for it. When Polly's turn came, she found on the other side of the threshold an odd-smelling room with gleaming cabinets filled with a strange assortment of instruments, glass containers, and books. A young medical officer stood beside a padded table in the middle of the floor. He was all business as he performed a quick examination of Polly. Then she was returned to the large hallway with the benches and told to take a seat.

Once all the women had seen the medical officer, the matron addressed them again. "If you are offered relief, your clothing will be washed and stored with your personal items until you leave." As she spoke, her eyes came to rest on Polly.

For a moment, Polly thought the matron spoke to her alone. "Thank you," she said. "I'll not be here for long."

The matron glared, and the woman sitting next to Polly stifled a laugh.

What does she know that makes my words humorous?

"While here," the matron continued, looking around at all the women, "you will earn your relief through labor. If you are not offered relief, your clothing and possessions will be returned to you this evening before you leave. Because you currently wear workhouse property, and will want your possessions returned, you must ask for permission to leave the premises. If you have other family members with us, they must leave with you."

"Is permission ever denied?" a young woman asked. Her pale face, haggard with worry, was a mirror of Polly's own concern.

"No," the matron said impatiently, "but the process of release is a lengthy one."

Polly wanted to ask how long the process took, but had not

gathered the words to voice her question before the matron turned and left the room.

When Polly was a child of seven years, she noted that her Aunt Della always appeared troubled. She had a tendency to stare into the distance, even when there wasn't anything to look at, and to become quiet and remote. On one occasion, Polly watched the woman slip into a more frightening state. Aunt Della's eyes glazed over, her arms began to quake, and her fingers to twitch. Polly placed a hand on her aunt's forearm to steady her. The woman cried out as if she'd been harmed. Aunt Della apologized for frightening Polly once she'd calmed down. Later, Polly told her mother, Caroline, about the incident. "My sister was in the workhouse for a time," her mother said. Polly had asked what that was like, and Caroline merely shook her head and said no more about it. That had left too much to Polly's young imagination.

If I stay, I'll know what others have known. The thought produced an uncomfortable rhythm in her breast.

Despite her dread, Polly's experience of the workhouse so far had not been bad. Perhaps things had changed since her aunt had sought relief. Given the chance, the institution itself might convince her that the old stories were tall tales.

I have nothing and nowhere to go. If they accept me, they'll feed me and keep me warm. But at what price?

As the moments stretched on, she tried to decide whether to wait or attempt to flee.

While she waited, she hoped her application would be rejected.

32
The Workhouse

A t the beginning of 1883, Polly had been in the workhouse for nine months. She spent her days at labor, sewing or picking oakum, the latter task the more unpleasant of the two. While seated on a hard bench for hours on end, she unraveled tarry rope that had been cut into one-foot lengths. The monotonous toil left her hands with sore joints, and with tender skin, constantly cracked, and bleeding. She suffered severe back and joint pain until her body settled into the routine, after which she endured with a permanent dull ache in her spine.

Yet the workhouse wasn't as bad as she'd feared. Older inmates explained that changes over the years had brought improvements to the institution. Although a dull, lifeless place, filled with hopeless and disheartening faces, the labor wasn't so different from the piece work she'd done so much of in the past, and the environment had given her stability of a sort, and a respite from the drama and apprehension of her life. Having had little to drink for several years, alcohol had little power over her, though the craving had not left her entirely. She missed Tom, her father, and her children. Telling herself that what she endured was worthwhile, Polly had stayed longer than she'd thought she would, perhaps out of a sense that she owed penance for having abandoned her children.

For all that, in early March of 1883, the relentless monotony of life in the workhouse seemed to catch up with her and the place felt increasingly like a prison. Despite the impression of being imprisoned, Polly knew she could leave at any time with reasonable notice to the staff. She knew she missed out on life every minute she remained, but at first she fought the desire to leave.

The mindless daily labor gave her too much time to think. Polly visited again the fantasies of reckless behavior she'd had in her youth, those of becoming a pickpocket, a palmer, or a highwayman, and her favorite fancy of becoming drunk and running naked through the streets. The appearance of Mr. Macklin chasing her in the daydream discouraged her little. Her urge for drink had risen up and quickly became insistent.

She couldn't help imagining a new life on the outside. Surely Papa did well enough again that he'd help her out until she found a way to earn her keep. Finding work would take time, and Polly knew she'd want to drink right away. Again, she considered prostitution. Her monthly curse had ceased to visit long ago, so she had little fear of pregnancy. She thought through imagined scenarios of her approach to men as clients, the sexual acts they might get up to, what might happen, and how she'd respond. Even those imagined transactions with abusive clients seemed life worth living compared to her current drab existence.

By the end of March, she'd made up her mind. She wrote to her father, and began the process of release from the Lambeth Workhouse.

* * *

Papa took her in.

Polly immediately set out to earn what she needed to have a drink. Having repaired her clothing as best she could, she looked for a good spot from which to solicit, one near Papa's room, yet not so close that he would likely happen by.

Polly took up a position out front of the Hour Glass pub at the corner of Queen's Row and Westmoreland Road. She feared that as soon as she felt vulnerable, the child within her would demand protection again. A man, on his way into the establishment, jeered at Polly and made obscene gestures. The girl did emerge within Polly's mind, but seemed to stand naked and unabashed, her dignity having withered away. The child had lost her innocence. What troubled Polly most about the loss was how quickly she turned her thoughts away from it.

The first man to respond readily to her overtures was a drunken fellow emerging from the pub. A laborer of some sort, he seemed even-tempered and relatively clean.

"You've little experience," he said. "I can tell. For what I want, I have a threpney bit."

Polly knew she could get a glass of gin, a full quartern, for three pence. "Yes," she said.

Her client took her to the small paved yard beside the pub and pushed her up against a stack of crates against one wall. He got her skirts up, began rubbing his penis in the cleft of her backside and quickly spilled his seed without penetration. Polly thought that easy money.

The next client took her while inside the busy Horsely Tavern at midday. He'd surprised and delighted her when he paid the fee for a drinking box. She thought he intended to feed her a meal or buy her drinks before they found a secluded spot elsewhere to complete their transaction. He reached under her skirts as soon as they sat down in the booth. With the opening to the drinking box two feet wide and the walls barely five feet tall, she feared they'd be seen. When he began choking her, she *hoped* the patrons saw and stopped them. Polly tried to cry out.

He applied enough pressure to prevent that, and let up periodically so she could catch a breath. He penetrated her vagina
while struggling to keep her on the bench-like seat.

Thankfully, he found release faster than her last client. When
done, he sat up, put his clothing back together, promptly paid
her, and left. Polly pushed her skirts back down and exited the
tavern. She'd got much worse violence from her own family
before. Still, the experience had upset her so much she immediately found a pub, and spent most of what she'd earned on
a glass of gin.

With time, she maintained her intoxication well enough that
she ceased to care what sort of man she found or what he did
to her.

* * *

"If you're going to drink like that," Papa said when she came
in late, stumbling drunk, "I needn't give up my bed for you.
Tonight you sleep in the army cot."

He'd borrowed the decrepit contraption from a neighbor
three weeks earlier when Polly had come to stay with him.
During the first week, she'd made an effort to sober up before
returning to Papa's room at night. Once she understood that
he knew she was drinking, she'd dropped all pretense.

"I can' sleep in 'at t'ing," she slurred.

"If it's good enough for a Royal Army officer, it's good
enough for you."

Polly grumbled, yet lay down on the thing. She wiggled rest-
lessly trying to get comfortable and the cot collapsed. She lay
in the wreckage, unwilling to get up. Papa made no move to
help her.

* * *

The following Sunday, while Polly nursed a bad hangover and Papa glowered and cursed her, she decided that if she offered him some of the money she'd earned to help pay for food and lodging, he might treat her better.

"I don't want your tarnished coin," he said. "I don't know where you're getting your money, and I suspect you wouldn't be proud for me to know."

"I'm working at the Ellis Shirt Manufacturers," she lied. "I've done piece work for them. Now I have a position."

"A flam not worth the breath it took," Papa said, giving her a look of disgust. "I don't believe you, girl. I know you *too* well."

"What have I ever done to you to deserve such mistrust?"

Papa merely shook his head.

Though she knew full well the answer, she preferred to play innocent. "You have no sympathy for me?" Polly cried. "I've worked hard all my life, and for what? I worked hard for you when I were young, and what did you give me for it? A beating if I complained. And what do I have now?"

"You have what your lies have got you. You have a demon after you."

Polly swung her fists at Papa. He dodged out of the way. She went at him again, and he shoved her. She fell into a heap on the floor.

"I'm sorry to say you're no good. I want you to find other lodgings right away," he said, "and be gone tomorrow."

"I will, and gladly!" Polly shouted.

She exited the room and walked along Maydwell Street toward the Surrey Canal, her anger slowly subsiding. Polly recognized her words to her father as a shameful sign of ingratitude. Thinking of the times Papa had saved her from Bill's abuse only made her feel worse. One more night with him, she decided, and then she'd find a room of her own and leave him in peace.

* * *

Stumbling home drunk late that night she fell by the side of Albany Road. At first, she wasn't willing to get up. Then she thought of the cot, which Papa had repaired, and how much more comfortable that would be than the gritty stone footway. She got to her feet and made her way home. As usual, she banged on the door for her father to let her in.

She'd become insensible on the doorstep by the time he opened the door. He grumbled several curses at her and got into his bed. She went in, and collapsed on the cot.

In the night, Polly awoke with a need to visit the privy. Locating the box of matches and the lamp on the bedside table, she lit the candle within, then moved out through the back door and into the facility.

Sometime later, she found herself asleep, still sitting on the pot, and didn't know how long she'd been there. The candle still burned in the lamp on the seat beside her.

She took up the lamp and made her way back inside. Lying down on the cot, she felt as if the life drained from her limbs by the moment. She reached out to set the lamp on the table and let go of it. A metal clang reached her ears, but curiosity didn't grip her. Her eyes had already closed. Blessed sleep waited just beyond.

* * *

Papa shrieked and began to wail. Polly opened her eyes to see bright flames licking at his bed clothes. She got up and threw her blanket onto the fire. Her father scrambled to escape on the other side of the bed.

Polly's blanket burned.

Papa got the padlock off the front door and they tumbled out into the street crying repeatedly, "Fire!" He ran back in, and Polly watched as he lifted first the ewer and then the basin on the cabinet beside the window and threw water from them onto the flames.

Neighbors on either side came out of their rooms. Some carried vessels that held water. They approached the doorway to Papa's room and handed the vessels to him one at a time. Within a few minutes the fire was out. Some of the neighbors began to retreat back into their homes, while others stood around watching and talking. They looked at Polly, who stood by, watching dully. Despite the thick cloud of her intoxication, the meaning of their stares got through to her, and the shame became all-consuming. Briefly, she thought she saw a set of glowing red eyes, watching her from the onlookers. When Polly tried to get a better look, they were gone. She crouched down on the pavement, her arms draped over her head, and watched for her father.

Blackened, he finally emerged from his room. The hair had burned off the left side of his head and left the skin an angry red. The damage made his expression all the more fierce as he walked straight to Polly, lifted her by the collar, and struck her in the face several times.

* * *

Polly awoke in a bed in a strange room, perhaps that of one of her father's neighbors. She discovered an aching new gap in her teeth.

She got up, looked around, and found no one in the chamber. Daylight came through the window. The door was unlocked, and Polly walked out.

Shame and grief snapping at her heels, Polly fled back to the Lambeth Workhouse.

33
Bargaining

Polly had been in the workhouse for less than a month when she received a post from Tom Dews.

Dear Polly,

Please forgive me. I left because I was harmful to you. I believed your father would take you in. After talking with him, I know I was wrong.

I drink in moderation now and am working every day at the Spratling Smithy in King and Queen Street. I have not been drunk in a year. I crave your company more than ever, whether you drink with me or not.

You cannot be happy in the workhouse. Please consider coming to me at your earliest convenience. I have a room at 22 Morecombe Street. If you will keep house for me, I will earn enough for us both and you will not need employment.

My neighbor, Mr. Frederick Barnes, has kindly written this for me to you.

Yours, with deep affection,
Tom Dews

Polly didn't know if she should trust Tom any more than she trusted herself, yet the workhouse had already worn her down again and she wanted out. Despite the shaming experience she'd recently had with her father, her desire for alcohol had not gone away and she knew that she would eventually drink again.

She remembered the times she and Tom had had on Jane Street, how he'd set the example in how much to drink and she'd not exceeded that standard. If he had returned to that discipline—if she could return with him to that discipline—Polly felt she might learn to live again.

Better to drink with one who cares for me than to do it alone.

* * *

Tom welcomed her to his room on Morecombe Street rather formally, his approach to the reunion sober and deliberate rather than jubilant. The room held the usual items: a rope bed with straw mattress, a wardrobe, a cabinet, with basin, ewer, and chamber pot, and a table and chairs. He had organized his possessions and cleaned the surfaces in his room, all of them swept and dusted. The effort won her heart.

For supper Tom had boiled a chicken and then reduced the liquid to a rich, concentrated broth. He toasted bread, and they dipped the slices into the chicken reduction.

Tom offered her a drink of whiskey which she declined. Although she knew she would drink again, Polly wasn't ready. With full stomachs they eventually found their way to his bed. His touch remained the same, warm and caring. Polly let go of her sordid past, at least for a time, and allowed herself to love and be loved.

* * *

After that first night, Polly took over the cooking and house-keeping.

She wasn't able to keep her past at arm's length for long. Certain incidents haunted her: having asked God to take the life of a child in her womb, abandoning her children, setting fire to her father's home, and her years-long dishonesty toward Bill. Burning guilt from all the wretched things she'd done while drunk kept her from wanting to drink again. Tom extended the invitation whenever he took a drink. True to his word, he drank in moderation, and never insisted that she join him. Still, believing her abstinence disappointed him, Polly kept a slight emotional distance between them.

"We aren't the same, Polly dear," he said one early spring evening in 1884, after they had been together for close to a year. "I long for a return to what we had on Jane Street."

"Yes," she said sadly.

"If you had a drink with me—a daffy would do it—I'm certain we'd find ourselves again."

"A daffy would just make me ill-tempered. I always want more."

"As do I, yet we have each other, and in the past that were enough to keep us on the straight and narrow."

She shook her head. "I'm afraid of drink. Give me more time."

Tom nodded, and dropped the subject.

* * *

In late summer of 1885, enough time had elapsed since Polly had set fire to her father's home that she was able to consider the incident without too much pain. Examining several more of her dishonorable acts, she discovered that the shame of them burned less acutely as well. With that realization, on August 27, the day following her true birthday, she knew her desire for drink wouldn't be held back much longer. Polly decided she'd wait to have a drink with Tom until the evening of August 31, the date her childhood friends, Martha Combs, Sarah Brown, and Bernice Godwin, had given her as a substitute birthday.

In her mind's eye, Mr. Macklin took a draft from the bottle chained around his neck to toast her decision to drink.

You'll have no cause to trouble me, she told him, *for I'll drink in moderation.*

On the evening of the 31st, she assured herself that she would go slowly as she had a small glass of gin with Tom. With the drink in her, she lost all reticence, and the distance between them melted away. They laughed and talked for a long while and then went to bed.

"You were right," she told Tom after they had made love. "I haven't felt so close to you since I came here."

* * *

As 1885 finished out and 1886 progressed, Polly's drinking increased steadily until her consumption matched Tom's.

In June, word came from her father that her brother, Eddie, had been involved in a paraffin lamp explosion. He had burned to death. Polly and Tom bought new clothes and attended the funeral. She spoke to her father graveside once most of the mourners had left.

"I'm sorry to say I hadn't seen Eddie in over twenty years," she said.

"He were happy, I think," Papa said.

Polly felt awkward. She wanted to tell her father how sorry she was for setting his home ablaze, yet couldn't think of a good way to broach the subject. Relief came as Tom approached.

"You've met Tom," she said.

"Yes, while you were away. Good evening, Mr. Dews."

"Good evening to you, sir."

Papa turned back to Polly. "I think he's done you some good. You look well."

She knew he meant that she didn't look and act like a drunk.

"Thank you," she said. "You do too." She was glad to see that the burn he'd received that terrible night hadn't left a permanent scar.

Papa gave her a kiss on the cheek before saying goodbye. For some reason, she couldn't feel it.

* * *

By 1887, Polly and Tom whiled away most nights drunkenly, and she would sleep late each day, neglecting the housekeeping.

Tom said little about her shirking for a long time, yet in the autumn, the problem began to come between them.

"You aren't doing your part," he said. "I work hard for us both, and you have little to do."

"I toil long hours," Polly said, putting on more outrage than she felt, "keeping our dunnage washed, the larder full, and preparing your meals."

"Yes, but you do not sweep. Slops are not cleared away completely. Pots and dishes are left crusted with spoiled food. The floor has not been scrubbed for months. The room reeks of the filth caught in the corners. My clothes fall apart and aren't mended."

"Perhaps you should buy *new* clothes."

"You do not earn a wage. You cannot tell me what I should buy."

"You aren't my husband! With our agreement, I'm not expected to earn a wage."

"Please," Tom said, lowering his voice, "we're talking about the housekeeping."

Polly didn't want to fight. She relaxed and let go of her anger. "I'll try harder."

* * *

With the drinking at night, Polly awoke late in the day, hungover and too tired to do her work. She found relief from hangover, as well as some extra vitality, in daytime drinking. Since Tom gave her money to do the shopping, which included buying alcohol, and he didn't ask for an accurate accounting of funds, Polly easily hid extra spending on gin. She kept a small supply on hand that Tom didn't know about, hidden in the new boots she'd bought to attend Eddie's funeral.

With a glass of gin in the morning, her pain went away, her spirits rose, and, with the short-term energy alcohol gave her, she became motivated to work. Knowing that inevitably her mood would drop quickly once the high began to fade, she hurried around, trying to get as much done as she could. Even on the way down, though, the residual effects of intoxication helped her to care less about not completing her housework.

In brief lucid moments, Polly felt deep shame, but horribly, her selfish, compelling need drove her like a taskmaster. She found the experience frightening, yet couldn't seem to turn from her course.

Polly ate less and drank more, remaining sodden with alcohol, day and night.

34
The Lush

Polly awakened to Tom's voice. He pulled his hammer from his belt and set the tool on the floor before crouching down beside her.

She'd become sore lying on the hard floorboards. How long had she been there?

"Polly, you're drinking away everything we have," Tom said.

She remained groggy and intoxicated from the gin she'd had earlier.

"I found the bottle of gin you hid in your gallies. I know you've been drinking in the daytime. I'd hoped if I treated you well and gave you time to do as you pleased, you'd get over whatever troubles you, and things would get better."

Polly didn't listen carefully. She needed another drink *right away* to soothe her aching head.

"I'm sorry I asked you to drink with me," Tom said, shaking his head. "Now I must take it away."

"No!" Alarmed, Polly had a burst of energy and sat bolt upright, then grabbed her head as if to hold her skull from breaking apart.

Tom got up slowly.

She had no time to reason with him. Polly picked his hammer up off the floor, and quickly found her feet. She caught up with him as he moved to the table where they left the bottle they shared. The threat was clear. Tom reached for the gin. She had to stop him.

Polly brought the hammer down on his fingers.

Tom cried out, cradling his hand. Blood ran from between his fingers as he toppled over onto the floor, howling in pain.

Polly stepped back, and dropped the hammer. Horrified and instantly sober, she hurried toward him.

"Get away," he cried and thrust out his left arm in defense, inadvertently striking her in the face. Polly shrieked as the blow bowled her over backwards.

She found her feet quickly and turned back to him. "I don't know what happened," she said.

"You broke my fingers!"

Polly tried to move toward him again. She stopped as he glared at her. Blood dripped from her nose onto her chemise.

"You've done me a great harm," he bellowed, his eyes bulging and his face red. "I cannot work with *this*." He held out his crippled hand, then thrashed in a paroxysm of frustration, accidentally striking his damaged digits against a leg of the table. Tom doubled up with the pain.

Despite fear that he'd strike her again, Polly hurried to him and held him. "I'm sorry," she said. "I don't know why—"

"It's the lush, and you know it," he gasped around the pain.

Yes, she did, and with the realization that there wasn't anything she was willing to do about it, her spirit collapsed. While Tom shook in her arms, she was lost to black despair. As he became calm, she returned to herself cautiously.

Polly touched his white, sweat-slicked face and he didn't flinch. She helped him get up and they sat at the table. He began to shake again, and she kept her arms around him.

"I don't know what should become of us," Tom said. "I

would leave you now, but I have no one else to help me."

Polly chose not to think about the future. Against her will, she glanced at the gin on the table to make sure the bottle hadn't been upset and spilled.

Satisfied, she turned her attention back to Tom. He'd gone slack. If not for her embrace, he'd have fallen out of his chair.

Polly heard a delighted humming, and could almost make out a tune. Her heart racing, she glanced about the room, thinking someone had come in while she attended Tom. No one appeared in the open. Then she heard, *The soul of you, a hole in you, as what your screams beseech…*, yet couldn't tell if the words came from within her head or without. She didn't want to believe that Mr. Macklin had come for her again.

"Tom," she whispered into her lover's ear. "Wake up. Help me."

He didn't respond. Polly clung to him, fearful that he had somehow died of his wounds, and left her alone with the intruder. She told herself that her imagination had got the better of her, even as she strained to see within the shadows of the open wardrobe, the darkness to the right of the door leading outside, and to the left of the bed.

Papa had been right when he'd said that Mr. Macklin haunted those who drank too much.

Misery craves companions in Hell. How many drunkard souls has Mr. Macklin delivered to the devil? How the drink must burn in Hell!

Tom inhaled sharply and coughed, startling Polly. She hugged him tighter, relieved to know he yet lived. Still glancing about warily, her fear continued to build. She was about to try again to awaken Tom when he groaned and sat up, shrugging her off angrily.

Polly got up, cautiously inspected the room, and found nothing unusual.

"Help me," Tom commanded, and she returned to the table. They inspected his damaged hand. His index and middle fingers were crooked, and each had a bloody cut. Polly fetched the ewer, the water-filled basin, and a flannel. She carefully cleaned the wounds.

Tom bent, and with his left hand, lifted from the floor a small crate in which Polly had carried vegetables back from market recently. "Hold it there, while I break off the side," he said.

Polly steadied the thing against the table top, and he snapped off a thin wooden slat. With her help, he shaped the piece of wood into a splint. Polly tore strips from an old chemise and used them to bind the splint onto Tom's hand so that his fingers wouldn't move.

"I'll pour the gin down the privy," she said, taking up the bottle. She intended to take the bottle out of his sight and drink the contents all at once.

"No," he said, wearily. "I need it for the pain, and I'll need more."

"I'll go get it," Polly said eagerly.

Tom gave her a long hard look before she went out. "Go also to the Spratling Smithy and tell Mr. Hooks I have an injury and won't be back for some time."

* * *

Indeed, Tom could not work. He drank heavily for the pain. Polly took advantage of the opportunity to drink heavily as well. Although he couldn't smell the alcohol on her, he knew she staggered about and slurred her words. She gave him bread to eat so she didn't have to cook. His anger toward Polly remained, but with his level of intoxication, he seemed unable to express his feelings in a meaningful way.

As he began to come out of his binge, Polly could see that his spirit had been broken. Tom didn't speak to her unless he had to. His movements were slow, yet not careful. His eyes held a frightening resignation.

Even when drunk in the past, he'd had a hopefulness; a strength about him that suggested he could get up and find his way in the world. His love for her had been his undoing.

"Go to the smithy, and tell Mr. Hooks I won't be back," he said.

Tom had given up on everything. Polly imagined him, head hung, entering the workhouse. Her heart turned over in her chest, her breath caught in her throat, and she turned away to hide her tears. She knew that to prevent that terrible vision from becoming a reality, she must speak to Mr. Hooks on Tom's behalf. Her effort might come to nothing, but she had to try.

"I'll go speak to him very soon," Polly said.

She spent two days sobering up, nursing from a bottle of gin only enough to keep her from trembling. On the third morning, while Tom still slept, she packed a change of clothes and a half loaf of bread into a carpet bag. She kissed Tom's cheek and left the room quietly.

Polly went to the Spratling Smithy in King and Queen Street, and approached the master blacksmith, shaking as she did so. He took her to the side, away from the work area.

"I've come to talk to you about Tom," she said.

He was a powerfully built fellow with a head of silver hair. "Yes, Mrs. Dews."

Polly didn't correct him. A week earlier, when she'd first met the man, she allowed Mr. Hooks to believe she was Tom's wife.

"Has he taken a turn for the worse?" he asked, with a look of concern.

"No," she said. "Well, yes, but it's my fault, and he shouldn't suffer for it."

His face became lined with concern, the black soot in the creases of his skin accentuating his expression. Polly saw that he struggled to understand.

"I drink…" she began, suddenly unsteady.

He reached out a hand to brace her.

Admitting her crime to a stranger would make the severity of her condition all too real. The prospect took her breath away. Still, gasping, she blurted, "In my drunkenness, I broke his hand."

He reached out with his other hand to hold her up as she began to sag. Tears streamed down her cheeks. "He's done his best for me, and I've brought him to ruin. Please don't give his position to another. He's a good man."

"Yes," Mr. Hooks said, "he is. He's one of the best I've had."

"I must leave him for his own good," she sobbed. "But he needs help. Is there anything you can do?"

He seemed to think for a moment. "I can take him in."

Polly gripped his hands. "Truly? Do you mean what you say?" She'd thought Mr. Hooks might hold Tom's position. Polly hadn't hoped for more.

"Why, yes. My eldest has left home. My wife, Alexandra, God bless her, fancies herself a Florence Nightingale after her experience helping in the workhouse infirmary for the church. She'll have him right in no time."

The man had a look of surprise as Polly pulled him close and hugged him. She released him and found that his look of concern had returned.

"You're in a bad way," he said.

Polly shook her head. "I'm well enough for what I deserve."

"Please allow me to help you."

"No one can help me. I've got a demon after me."

"You mustn't believe that."

"Yes, but I do." She handed Mr. Hooks her key to the lock on Tom's door. "His room is 22 Morecombe Street."

"Mrs. Dews, please," he said.

Polly turned away and made her way out of the smithy and onto the street. She would cross the river so that Tom might not find her easily if he should look.

To deaden her dreadful memories, and calm the storm of regret, grief, and shame that built inside her, Polly needed more drink.

35
Visitation

Polly stayed most nights at Gaskel's common lodging in Endell Street. She returned to prostitution. No emotional qualms stood in her way. On nights when she hadn't earn her doss or decided to drink away the funds instead, she slept in shrubs among the stands of trees in Saint James's Park.

When she'd arrived on the north side of the river in October, there had been hundreds of unemployed people sleeping rough in the park. In the middle of November there had been riots in Trafalgar Square over something concerning employment and Ireland. Afterward, the numbers of those staying in the park diminished, although not by much. If awake and aware enough when she arrived in the park at night, Polly heard many others moving about, also sheltering among the shrubs.

One night in late November, following three quarterns of extraordinarily cheap gin on an empty stomach, she was making her way along West Strand when she saw a heavy coat fly out of the window of a fine carriage traveling along the lane. As winter came on, she'd need a better coat. To her good fortune, none of the other pedestrians around her seemed to have noticed the fallen garment. Heedless of the manure piles, she hurried into the road, stumbled, and fell in the "mud."

Drivers leaned out to curse at Polly as they struggled to avoid hitting her. She got to her feet, and dodged her way drunkenly into the busier part of the road where the cobblestones were exposed. A hansom cab struck her as she bent to pick up the coat. As she flew backwards through the air, Polly knew she'd met her end, that the clattering hooves and wheels grinding along the road would make short work of her. That was, she decided, a fortunate turn of events.

Her head struck the hard granite surface of the road and all went black.

* * *

Polly found herself standing on the footway beside the road, watching the backside of the hansom cab moving away. A dread feeling accompanied the sight. She didn't understand how she'd got to safety, yet didn't have the presence of mind to think it through.

The black, fur-lined overcoat in her hands, made of fine cotton or linen, had clearly belonged to a gentleman. A smear of vile-smelling vomitus marred the fabric. She had a vague notion of cleaning that off in the pond in Saint James's Park.

With such a fine coat, she didn't have to spend four pence for doss—she'd be warm through the night, sleeping in the park.

As she staggered past Trafalgar Square, the dread feeling followed her. She saw a toff moving toward her, a white-whiskered gentleman all in black, wearing a square-crowned bowler and a short top coat or jacket, and no overcoat. He carried a cane. As she moved, so he seemed to move, perhaps a hundred yards away, pausing when she paused, hurrying forward when she did. Polly became certain that the coat she'd picked up belonged to him. Why, then, didn't he call out to her, approach, and ask her to return the garment? She saw no other reason a man of his obvious social status would take an interest in her. Polly had never had a client of his caliber.

She hastened west along Pall Mall East to Waterloo Place. Before turning south in the hopes of reaching the park and hiding herself among the trees, she glanced back and saw a glowing red about the head of the figure, a cigar possibly. As the red light brightened and became two embers, she recognized Mr. Macklin's glowing eyes.

Polly ran to the west side of Waterloo Place, and looked back. The figure came bounding over the two-story gentleman's club on the corner and landed with a light step in the road. He changed from the white-whiskered fellow into a thin man with dark hair, a cruel grin, and heavy black eyebrows. His short coat presently extended nearly to his feet. The cane had disappeared. Instead, he held a bottle connected to a chain around his neck. Polly turned away from his jeering face before his glowing eyes fixed upon her own. Her heart leapt up into her throat and escaped in the form of a shriek. The Bonehill Ghost had again stepped openly into her world or had somehow pulled her into another nightmare.

Running toward the park, she saw in her peripheral vision his inky black form giving chase with a blur of tiny, giddy footsteps. The sound of those steps had an odd mechanical rhythm, with a grating and snapping sound. Passing a columnar monument, she dashed down steps, and took another fall over the last few. The cushion of the coat helped break her fall, and she rolled onto the green, got up, and began dodging through the trees.

Polly felt the demon's fingertips reaching for her. She dropped the coat with the hope of tripping him up. Still, she heard the snap and grind of his rapid, mincing tread. The sound of sloshing, the rattle of chain, and a hollow thumping told her that his bottle banged against his empty chest as he ran. Shouting for help, she crashed through the shrubs where she and so many others slept at night. Figures rose up out of the greenery, shouting, flailing. Her knee struck a man in the head and he went down. Another man came toward her. She couldn't let him stop her or the demon would catch up. Polly struck the man in the face and kept moving. Two women grabbed for her. Polly twisted out of their grip.

The dark demon rose up in front of her. She turned sharply, tripped, and fell toward a tree trunk, striking the side of her head.

Then she found herself on the ground, the demon looming over her. He crouched, trying to catch her gaze. She kept her eyes averted. Raggedy men and women emerged from the shrubberies on all sides and held her down. Mr. Macklin took a drink from his bottle and blew his poisonous blue flame on her. She choked and gagged on the burning fumes and her belly began to convulse. Her gorge rose up and sprayed from her mouth. Her body caught the blue flame and she screamed with the pain as she burned.

This is a nightmare. None of it is truly happening! She wanted to awaken, but didn't know how.

Gleefully, the demon stabbed and gouged her gut with the metal claws on his hands. Then he pierced her chest several times, pried open her ribs, and sang as he peered inside.

"The soul of you, the whole of you, that's all what you can preach.

"The soul of you, a hole in you, as what your screams beseech,

"When darkness wants to sort you out, no more or less shall do.

"I take my time, and when I'm done, there's nothing left of you."

And with that, she knew he searched for her soul, that he

rummaged in her chest unable to find her spirit quickly without having first captured her gaze. Although his visits had always seemed like nightmares, Polly's world had been changed with each one. After his first, she'd known the demon's entire infernal song. With the second, he'd punished Polly by taking the soul of her unborn girl. This time, he'd have Polly's own soul if she didn't fight him. She writhed in agony, unable to escape, yet kept herself from looking Mr. Macklin in the eye.

Perhaps entertained by the song, the homeless had gathered. Sitting in a circle around Polly, they warmed themselves by her flames, as the demon continued his search. One man had a skewer. He pulled a half-eaten sausage from his pocket, stuck the meat on the skewer and began heating it above Polly's blackened, withering arm. She reached with the arm to grasp the skewer, and the man recoiled, but not fast enough. Polly had him by the arm. He cried out and dragged her away from the demon. Finally, he began beating on her with his free arm.

Another man, a constable, tried to pry her off. "Let go," he shouted.

Polly wouldn't as long as the homeless man carried her away from the Bonehill Ghost. Glancing back, she saw the demon rising to bound toward her.

The constable raised his truncheon. "You must give him what he wants," he said, and brought the club down on her head.

36
Many Need Help

Polly awoke slowly in a hospital ward, pushing through terrifying scraps of recent memory involving the demon. Her gut trembled in an agony of cramps. She found herself involuntarily quaking against leather straps that held her down against a bed. Her sweaty flesh had been rubbed raw where the skin came into direct contact with the leather. The room felt hot as an oven. The shrieks and moans of those in the other beds assailed her ears, contributing to the ache of her pounding head.

Polly couldn't stop her involuntary movements and tried to cry for help. Her voice came out a mere croaking, as if she'd gone hoarse from too much shouting.

A woman in her middle years, with hair graying at the temples, approached. Although she didn't wear a uniform, she looked clean and was moderately well-dressed. "Try to remain calm," she said in an even tone. "You've been here for several days. The symptoms will pass."

Polly decided the woman was a nurse.

"Will you let me up?" Polly rasped, her body still writhing against her will.

"I'm sorry. It isn't up to me. I'm told your body will flail uncontrollably without the restraints."

Polly hated the nurse. She tried to spit on her, but couldn't control her mouth well enough. Without choosing to do so, she began to pant. She felt the pulse of blood through the vessels of her neck distinctly as her heartbeat quickened.

The nurse sat in a chair outside of Polly's view and leaned away for a moment. "You'll be better soon," she said, straightening and placing a cool, damp flannel on Polly's forehead. "The doctor says you're suffering delirium tremens. The symptoms are slowly passing. I've been with you as much as I can since you were brought in."

Polly didn't recognize the name of the illness. The cool flannel felt good. The woman's soothing voice brought back vague memories of Polly's mother taking care of her in sickness. As quickly as she'd hated the nurse, Polly loved her. She moaned and strained against her bonds to turn toward the voice. The woman adjusted her chair so that Polly saw her more easily. Still, her eyes could not focus on the nurse's face.

"A hansom cab struck you in West Strand. A witness said you ran after a coat lying in the road."

While the coat was a distant memory, Polly recollected with clarity that Mr. Macklin had come for her, that he'd changed from a white-whiskered gentleman into a devilish black figure. If he could assume more than one form, he might be anyone, including, Polly realized, the woman caring for her at present.

She prepared herself to turn away quickly to avoid eye contact. Watching warily for a time, she decided that the nurse was indeed what she appeared to be.

"How long?" Polly asked.

"Five days. You're in the infirmary of Saint Giles's and Saint George's Workhouse."

The moist flannel lifted, and Polly moaned for its return. She heard the sound of the cloth dipping into water, and the liquid dripping off as the fabric was wrung out. Then she saw the flannel's blessed return, felt the cool cloth against her baking head.

"Thank you, Miss...?" Polly croaked.

"I'm Mrs. Hooks."

The master blacksmith's wife? If she knew Tom, she might tell him of Polly's presence in the workhouse infirmary.

"I'm Mary," Polly said, offering her given name instead of the nickname she'd used her entire life.

"Alexandra," Mrs. Hooks said.

She had the name of the master blacksmith's wife. She *was* his wife, a volunteer in the infirmary, not a nurse.

Mrs. Hooks dipped the flannel again and placed the cool, moist cloth back on Polly's hot forehead.

"Why?"

"They brought you here after you were struck down in the road. There weren't beds in any other hospital hereabouts. The doctors didn't know you'd suffer so without drink."

Clearly, knowing that Polly was a drunk didn't trouble Mrs. Hooks.

"Yes," Polly said, "but why do you do it?"

"Many need help," Mrs. Hooks said. "I'm sorry you've been so miserable." Genuine sympathy emerged with her voice.

How can it be as simple as that? Polly wondered.

She watched Mrs. Hooks. The woman didn't look for a reaction to her words.

Yes, for Mrs. Hooks, that is all there is to it. People needed help, never mind who they were or what they'd done in life.

Polly felt an odd pang of envy. She became curious about the source of the calm the woman possessed.

"I'm a volunteer here in the infirmary for a week at a time. They have a bed for me. Other times, I lend a hand in the workhouse proper. The work helps me feel grateful for what I have in life."

Despite the distraction of Polly's bodily torments, she'd heard Mrs. Hooks clearly. When the woman left in the evening, that was the last Polly saw of her. Mrs. Hooks's words stuck with Polly much longer.

She suffers this place of misery, and gains solace by helping the less fortunate.

The concept wasn't new to Polly. She'd seen in the woman's eyes that the endeavor appeared to have borne fruit—Mrs. Hooks seemed at peace with herself. Polly suspected that for the first time in a long while, God had sent her a message.

Several days later, she was transferred to the Strand Workhouse, Edmonton, where she remained for a little over a month, regaining her strength. She was given light sewing duties and slept in the infirm ward. Over that time, thinking about the message, a growing religious fervor turned her suspicion into conviction: Mrs. Hooks had brought her word from God.

The Bonehill Ghost didn't torment Polly just because she drank. He was after her soul. The Lord would not allow Mr. Macklin to pursue her if he favored Polly. He would protect her from the demon if not for her selfish ways. With sufficient selfless acts she might be redeemed in the eyes of the Lord, and perhaps in her own, as well.

* * *

As soon as she got back on her feet, Polly began looking for ways to make life easier for those suffering. She hoped that, as they were lifted up, so she would be. Her first success came when she found a pair of shoes for Mrs. Weir, a seventy-year-old woman who entered the Strand Workhouse barefoot on the same day as Polly. Mrs. Weir's twisted feet suffered a crippling arthritis. The best the infirmary had done for her was to wrap her feet in bandages. Polly found the shoes in a bin full of the clothing of those who passed away in the infirm ward. They had belonged to an unusually tall inmate. Because of their large size, they were adapted easily to fit Mrs. Weir's misshapen feet. The smile on her face when presented with the shoes was like sustenance to Polly after a long fast.

When Polly had regained much of her health, she was transferred to the Lambeth Workhouse since that had been the union where she first entered the relief system.

37
Paupers

Polly folded the letter from her father and put it away in a pocket of her uniform. The only important news the correspondence provided was that her eldest, John, lived with Papa again. She had not informed her father of her situation within the Lambeth Workhouse, but he'd known about her previous stay in the institution. That must have been the reason he'd thought to write to her there. Although he expressed concern for her well-being, she hadn't responded to him.

Sipping her broth and shuffling her feet to help wake them from a tingling slumber, Polly looked up at the overcast spring day outside the tall windows set too high on the brick walls to reveal more than sky. *Good morning,* she said silently toward the gray clouds. Then she glanced at the messages painted on the walls beneath the sashes in blue letters two feet high— "God is good. God is just."—and nodded in silent agreement.

Thank you, Almighty God, for this sanctuary, and for protecting me from the Bonehill Ghost. I know the dull life I endure here is fitting punishment for the selfishness of my past.

The high-ceilinged dining hall of the Lambeth Workhouse had the atmosphere of a house of worship. Since the saying of grace before the meal began, no one had said a word. They were all too intent on drinking their broth. Polly found the chamber peaceful in the morning, even with the strong odors of the infrequently washed bodies that filled it, the inarticulate moans of those among the gathering who suffered, and the murmur of their respiratory and gastric functions. She sat elbow to elbow with six other inmates, on a bench meant to provide seating for five, before a table wider than need be, considering the amount of food it was required to hold. Several rows of ten identical tables and their complement of benches filled the hall, and all seats were occupied by hungry souls.

Despite the ache in her hips and shoulders from sleeping on a straw mattress too thin to protect her forty-three-year-old body from a hard wooden bed, Polly smiled as best she could. The women facing her, young and old, some inexpressively sad, others resigned or despondent, avoided looking at her. Given their situation, she knew her smile made them uncomfortable. Still, she intended to provide others all she had that was uplifting.

The woman to her left, Laura Scorer, appeared to be under the weather. Since Polly would feel hunger pangs before the noon meal whether she finished her breakfast or not, she poured some of her own broth into the woman's cup. Laura smiled sadly and opened her mouth to say something. Instead, she eagerly downed the liquid food as if it might be taken away any moment.

The gift of broth was a small matter. Polly looked forward to a greater effort she made each evening; providing reading and writing lessons for the Dobson twins, young women too old to be included in the schooling provided for the children. Great or small efforts, all were good works that would see Polly through until God was ready for her.

May of 1888 had come, and Polly felt good about herself for

the first time in many years. She had returned to her habit of praying for others. Life in the workhouse became harder each day as her body slowly failed her, yet the institution provided protection from her own worst excesses, in part because alcohol, the poison which brought forth her self-serving, grasping nature, wasn't allowed inside the institution.

Clearly, her sins, especially those committed in her selfish pursuit of drink, had attracted the Bonehill Ghost to covet her soul. She believed that each of her selfless good deeds made her spirit less appealing to him. With patience and further sacrifices for others over time, she knew he would lose interest in her and she would be redeemed in God's eyes.

Chaplain Emes gave the after-breakfast devotion. While putting her hands together in prayer, Polly gently rubbed the aching joints of her digits, careful not to crack open the painful whitlows at her fingernails that came from endless hours of picking oakum.

At the end of the prayer, Polly added her voice to the others, "In the name of Christ. Amen." Then she rose and followed those moving between the tables to the women's stairs that led down to the women's yard, a paved rectangle under the open sky, bordered on two sides by blocks of the workhouse dormitories, and on the remaining two sides by high stone walls.

Dumps Alice waited as usual in the corner of the yard where the two blocks came together. Instead of the workhouse uniform worn by the inmates, the young woman wore a ragged gray-blue linsey skirt that had probably once been indigo, a stained brown woolen shawl, and a wilted gray bonnet. She seemed to move somewhat more freely in and out of the workhouse than did the other inmates, trading her wares: bits of mirror, candle ends, matches, and sundry dumps. When Polly had stayed in the Strand Workhouse, she'd seen Alice coming and going from there as well. She either had agreements with the matrons or masters of both institutions or with the governors of those poor law unions. Her trade wouldn't earn her enough for a significant bribe, however. Polly assumed that, like so many of the desperate scavengers of London, the woman barely eked out an existence.

While in the Strand Workhouse, Polly had asked another inmate, Grace Feldman, about the woman. "Don't talk about her," Grace had said. "She does nothing but good. She might be a *tramp major.*"

"A tramp major?" Polly said.

"Some vagrants are given shelter for a different service. I don't know what task she's given, but she doesn't have to labor as we do."

When Polly approached, Dumps Alice didn't look up. The woman kept her face always downcast, in angle as well as expression. She further hunched her already stooped shoulders. Locks of limp, oily brown hair, having escaped the confines of her bonnet and the tight bun at the back of her head, stuck to her forehead and neck.

"I have three buttons," Polly said. "I should like to trade for cigar or cigarette ends, if you have them?"

Without a word, Alice rifled through the dusty, stained sack which hung from her left shoulder.

Polly had plucked the buttons from garments in the laundry. She had worked many times in the laundry and noted that buttons frequently went missing. Even if she got caught, who would know she hadn't found the buttons lying on the floor somewhere? Still, her small theft, committed for the best of reasons, qualified as a refractory offense within the workhouse. Polly considered the possibility of punishment worth the risk to see Mary Ann Monk's craving for tobacco satisfied, if only for a short time.

Alice and Polly made their exchange simultaneously, palming their goods to one another. Polly received one cigar end and that of a cigarette. She turned away, satisfied that her day had begun with a good deed.

* * *

Following the afternoon work period, as Polly headed to the privy, the Porter, Mr. Overguard, approached. "Come with me," he commanded. Although startled and apprehensive, Polly had no thought to refuse him. A solid boulder of a fellow, he had a stout frame and slabs of hard muscle, black hair, heavy brow and deep-set eyes. She'd imagined that the reason his clothing always looked so threadbare was that it suffered from abrading against his skin. He conducted her to the office of Mrs. Fielder, the old, white-haired Matron. Seeing Dumps Alice seated within the chamber, Polly knew the young woman had told of their trade.

Mrs. Fielder rose from her desk and began a search through Polly's clothing. She found only loose strands of pitch-streaked oakum, leftover from the afternoon's labor. "Where is the tobacco?" Mrs. Fielder asked. Her brow arched high, stretching the translucent skin of her eyelids so thin that Polly seemed to see past the architecture of the eyes to the deep sockets of the old woman's skull. She shuddered to release the vision.

"I dropped it when I saw the Porter coming for me," she answered, then added quickly, "I'm certain someone else has found it by now."

Mr. Overguard shoved Polly into a chair beside Alice.

Mrs. Fielder stood over the two inmates and looked at Polly. "I should think you might find *one* or as many as *two* buttons of the same type, but *three?* There is no doubt in my mind as you took them from the laundry."

She turned to Dumps Alice. The young woman didn't look up. "Watching through a window of the women's dayroom," Mrs. Fielder said, "I *saw* the exchange."

The Matron had known of the trade, yet had waited until the end of the afternoon work period to administer discipline. At least Polly had been able to give the cigar and cigarette ends to Mary Ann Monk before the work period commenced.

Turning back to Polly, Mrs. Fielder said, "I could have charges brought for destruction or theft of workhouse property what could have you in prison."

Polly tried to imagine the suffering in prison. The punishment must be worse than what she experienced in the workhouse, but she couldn't quite imagine how. Still, there would be a lot of people there, some of them innocent, that she might help. Surely, they were in greater need of good deeds than those in the workhouse. Polly would deserve whatever she got, her suffering a worthwhile sacrifice for the help she'd given to Mary Ann.

"Since this is your first serious offense, however—" The Matron turned away, became silent for a time as she looked out the window into the Girl's Yard. "—each of you shall have two meals withheld and spend a day in a refractory cell."

She turned to Mr. Overguard. "Take them to the cellar and place them in the cells at opposite ends so they cannot speak to one another."

The Porter walked them out, through two halls, past the women's dayroom, and the kitchen to the gloomy stairs that led down into the damp darkness of the stone cellar. Mr. Overguard lit a lamp hung beside the door at the head of the stairs, took it in his left hand, and led the way, glancing back to make sure his charges followed. Polly had been in the cellar before on errands for the kitchen. She suffered no fear. Nor, apparently, did Dumps Alice.

At the bottom of the stairs, the Porter opened a stout wooden door. "In you go," he said to Alice. She entered without complaint and he shut the door and slid a bolt into place to lock her in.

Polly and Mr. Overguard walked on for some distance, making their way past the covered bins of vegetables for the kitchen, an area of discarded furniture and other household castoffs from the live-in staff, and shelves filled with dusty boxes of written records. A periodic sound of scurrying betrayed the presence of rodents. The Porter batted cobwebs out of their path. As they passed another cell, Polly heard a sound of movement coming from behind the stout wooden door.

She followed Mr. Overguard into a section of the cellar that she had never seen, where a part of the stone foundation had given way and allowed a small cascade of debris to enter the chamber. An open bin filled with mildewed gray rag, no doubt made from old workhouse uniforms, stood against the stone wall. Numerous buttons, like those she'd traded for tobacco ends, littered the floor around the bin.

Finally they came to another cell. The door stood open and Polly stepped around the Porter and entered. Mr. Overguard stared at her curiously, holding the light out to get a better look. She used the opportunity to look at the cell, knowing there would be no light once he left. Polly saw a worn wooden pallet against the sweaty stone wall and a stained bucket on the dirt floor.

"I'll bring water," the Porter said as he shut the door and slid the bolt into place.

She had never known such complete darkness. *I might just as well have been dropped into a giant pot of black ink.* Polly waved her hand before her eyes, but couldn't see it. She felt for the pallet and sat on its edge.

Still, she remained unafraid. Somehow, she'd got what she'd wanted.

What might Mrs. Hooks think if she could see me now?

Of all the sacrifices she'd made for others in the workhouse, her current punishment seemed most proper. To suffer for performing a good deed was what she'd needed all along, what she most deserved. If the situation felt so right, then surely God looked upon her favorably.

Feeling contented, Polly lay back on the hard wooden pallet and slept.

38

A Position

Upon her release the next day, Mr. Overguard took Polly to the Matron's office.

"I gave you the minimum punishment, Mrs. Nichols," the woman said, "because I know you've been a generous and helpful presence here. I now offer you an opportunity, and I hope you'll not make a fool of me."

"No, ma'am." Polly didn't want to be given anything. She didn't deserve a gift of any sort, but she kept that opinion to herself while she listened.

"The Clerk of Works for the police headquarters in Wandsworth, Mr. Cowdrey and his wife, Sarah, are looking for a domestic servant, and I've suggested they consider you for the position. You would have room and board. You'd cook and clean and do the shopping for wages of three and ten pence per week."

Polly frowned. She had no desire to help those who didn't truly need. That would do her soul no good.

"Don't you want the position?" Mrs. Fielder asked with a scowl. "You would turn your nose up at a warm bed and more than three shillings? When I suggested you might go to prison yesterday, you had a better response."

Polly did remember her desire to help those in prison, and

with the memory came an idea. If she took the position and then robbed Mr. Cowdrey, he'd surely have her arrested and sent to prison where she might do more good.

"Please, excuse me, Mrs. Fielder," she said. "If I have a sour look, it's because my stomach is unsettled. Yes, the position would be most welcome. I'm very grateful you thought of me."

The matron seemed satisfied. "They are well-respected members of their community, they are religious, and they are teetotalers, so there shall be no drinking in their home. Do you understand me?"

"Yes, Mrs. Fielder, I do." At least while with the Cowdreys, Polly would not be tempted with drink. Pleased with the turn of events and the plan she formed, Polly smile quietly to herself, careful not to allow the matron to see her eagerness.

* * *

The Cowdrey home, a modest brick building with gardens in front and back, looked cozy in its middle-class neighborhood of new homes. When Polly arrived in the early evening of May 12, 1888, both Samuel and Sarah Cowdrey answered her knock upon their door. They were a gray-haired couple maybe ten years older than she, Mrs. Cowdrey a little plump and Mr. Cowdrey thin and stoop-shouldered.

"Please come in, Mrs. Nichols," Mr. Cowdrey said. "Welcome to our home."

"Thank you," Polly said as she stepped inside, carrying a small travel bag with her few possessions. The interior, not the least bit fancy, had plain furnishings. Aromas of simple foods hung in the air. The walls and woodwork had a fresh coat of paint, and the floor shone with a fresh polish.

Mrs. Cowdrey must have seen Polly looking at the framed

tintype above the fireplace mantle of a group of constables. "We have no children," she said a bit sadly, "but Sam likes to think of the men he works with as family."

Mr. Cowdrey smiled and nodded.

Good, a man whose family is the law.

"We have a room prepared for you," Mrs. Cowdrey said. "Please come with me and I'll show you."

The room was about eight by ten feet, with a little window opposite the entryway. A small bed and a cabinet occupied most of the floor. Polly saw that she would be comfortable.

"It's lovely," she said.

"Have you eaten?" Mrs. Cowdrey asked.

"No, ma'am, but my understanding is that I'm to do the cooking."

"Not this evening. You'll start tomorrow. Tonight you'll dine with us."

Polly had not expected such generosity. She felt a tightening of her throat and a flash of shame.

Mr. Cowdrey seemed to notice her discomfort. "Well, I should think you'd want to get settled in, Mrs. Nichols. Come, Sarah, you can show her the kitchen after supper."

"Thank you," Polly said as they exited the room.

"I'll call you when supper is served," Mrs. Cowdrey said, shutting the door behind her.

Polly didn't feel good about what she would do to these fine people. Yet, they would recover easily, and her plan would send her where she'd do much more good.

Polly sat on the bed and closed her eyes. *Loving God, although Mr. and Mrs. Cowdrey have grown old, help them to have a family before it's too late. If she cannot become pregnant, please have some poor woman leave her bundling child on the doorstep.*

I might have left Alice for Mrs. Cowdrey, but not Eliza—the sweet child was too easily given to fright.

Polly felt a bit odd toying with such notions in the midst of prayer. Her weariness had caught up with her.

While most of the time Polly thought herself powerless to truly influence the resolve of the Lord, she also hated to think that her words might set him on a course that went against the desires of those for whom she prayed. Wondering whether Mrs. Cowdrey might not want a bastard, she quickly added to her prayer, *If Mrs. Cowdrey would find that desirable.*

She thought for a moment and concluded with, *Don't allow what I do here to harm them for long. Amen.*

As she waited to be called to supper, Polly found paper, a pen, and ink in a drawer of the cabinet and sat to write her father so he wouldn't continue to worry about her.

Dear Papa,

I write to say you will be glad to know that I am settled in a new position of employment, and all is going right up to now. My people have greeted me most warmly. It is a fine place, with trees and gardens back and front. All has been newly done up. They are teetotalers and religious so I ought to get on. They are very nice people, and I won't have too much to do. I hope you are all right and young John has work. So good bye for the present.

Answer soon, please, and let me know how you are.

From yours truly,

Polly

* * *

Polly had worked for the Cowdreys for a little over two months when she put her plan into action. She took from their wardrobes the best clothes the couple had, articles she hoped were worth ten pounds. She went to the area of commerce in Wandsworth along High Street, and visited the shops that bought and sold secondhand clothing and offered the garments she'd stolen for sale. Although of greater worth, the articles, including a fine top hat, fetched her three pounds, eight, and tuppence.

Once Polly had committed the crime, she couldn't help imagining that when caught she might hang for her offense. *If that's all it takes, half of London would be topped. No, they'll merely lock me away where I might do the most good.*

Instead of returning to the Cowdreys's home, Polly spent some of the wages she'd saved on a room in a doss house, and waited. When not sleeping, she spent time in the open about town, purchasing her meals from street vendors.

Two days went by before a constable approached her.

"Mrs. Polly Nichols?" he asked.

"Yes," she answered readily enough.

"Would you come with me to the police station?"

"Yes, I will."

As they proceeded to the station, she noted that the constable treated her as if he thought she was daft. He spoke slowly and loudly, the words he used particularly simple.

He can think what he wants. She smiled to think he helped her with her plan unknowingly.

* * *

Polly was held at the police station in a cell on her own, away from the other prisoners, all men.

"I'm sorry to say that the window leaked and has been boarded up until it can be repaired," the constable said, "and I'm not allowed to leave you with a flame of any sort, so the cell will be dark. There's water and a ladle in the bucket on the shelf, and…." He looked embarrassed as he gestured toward the tin pot on the floor in one corner.

Polly nodded.

"If you need help," he said, "pound on the door and someone will come."

Polly nodded. She entered and sat on a cot much like the one she'd broken when she'd last stayed with her father. The constable closed the door, leaving her in complete darkness.

As when she'd been locked in the cell beneath the workhouse, she remained unafraid. Polly had got what she'd wanted. Of all the sacrifices she'd made for others, going to prison would be the most meaningful. Again, her situation felt so right, she became certain God looked upon her favorably.

Her reaction, born of feeling instead of rational thought, left Polly elated for an indeterminate period. The delight slowly waned and was replaced with weariness, yet she could not find sleep. As time stretched on in the darkness, her thoughts began to unravel.

She had committed the serious crime of theft for monetary gain. *God might smile upon me when I get to prison, but He certainly won't approve of how I got there.*

And then a terrible question occurred to her: *Who am I to suggest what God should smile upon?*

The blackness surrounding her began to solidify.

"Such pride!" she said aloud. "I have nothing in the world but foolish pride!"

Again, Polly felt naked before God, her ugliness plain to see. She knew He found her wanting.

The darkness—or perhaps Mr. Macklin—reached out and touched her, and she screamed.

The smell of cheap gin filled the tiny room, an odor both

gut-wrenchingly noxious, and mouth-watering.

Polly's heart tumbled and banged around in her chest as she heard his song begin.

"The soul of you, a hole in you, as what your screams beseech,
"When darkness wants to sort you out—"

As before, she couldn't tell if the words came from within her head or without. Gasping loudly for breath to push the panic back down, she cut the verse off, rendering the words incomprehensible. Little good that did, since she knew them by heart.

The door opened and light streamed in, blinding Polly. Startled, she shrieked again.

"Are you hurt, ma'am?" the young constable asked.

Polly leaped toward the door. "You must let me out. I've suffered enough. I'm sorry for what I've done."

"No, ma'am," he said, pushing her back and trying to shut the door. "I cannot let you out."

The light fled as the door slammed shut. Polly returned to the cot, lay down, and hugged herself, making her body as small as possible so Mr. Macklin wouldn't find her easily. He'd never before made an appearance without her being deep in her cups.

Glorying in martyrdom is drunkenness of a sort.

Terrified to think the demon might turn up at any time now, whether she was drunk or sober, Polly squeezed her eyes shut tight, though she could not shut out her punishing thoughts. She faced a painful truth: Her "good works" in the workhouse had been an attempt to change God's opinion of her. Her reason for performing the good deeds wasn't truly to help those in need, but to redeem herself in His eyes and secure a place for herself in Heaven.

Mrs. Hooks would not be proud of me. Did she indeed deliver a message from God or was that my own cruel fancy?

Polly could not win for losing, and with that realization she began to fear going to prison.

Please, Almighty God, she began, intending to ask for help, then thought better of it, and stopped herself.

No, she would suffer the just punishment.

The hours of darkness stretched on interminably.

* * *

Finally the door to Polly's cell opened. She assumed her time had come to face a magistrate. As the young constable escorted her through the corridor that led to the front of the building, Polly kept her eyes down to hide her shame. When they reached the entrance to the police station, the constable turned to her. "Mr. Cowdrey will not bring charges against you. You are free to go, but he advises you to leave Wandsworth. Your position in his household is terminated."

Feeling the sudden relief that she would not go to prison, Polly staggered back against the threshold. The door gave some and she nearly tumbled over. The constable steadied her.

"Thank you," she said, tears brimming in her eyes.

Another constable approached and handed Polly her small travel bag, then opened the door for her.

Exiting into a light drizzle, Polly was glad to have the rain so she wouldn't have to feel the tears on her face. Despite her sense of relief, the shame of having distressed the Cowdreys darkened her thoughts. Her sins continued to pile up, creating a wall between Polly and her distant goal of redemption. Although she hadn't had a drink for some time, she knew that Mr. Macklin was not prepared to forget her.

She sat on the footway along High Street as the rain grew heavier.

Almighty God, please protect the constables here from the Bone-hill Ghost, who now knows something of the darkness of their gaol. Please allow Mr. and Mrs. Cowdrey to forget about me and what I've done, so they will trust others again. If Mrs. Cowdrey would truly like to have Eliza and you can find a way for that to come about, I would be happy for her to have the sweet girl. Thank you for the tears what fall from the sky today.

She ended with the penitent prayer.

Feeling foolish and small, defeated at every turn, she got up and wandered northeast.

39
A New Friend

Polly spent the rest of July, 1888, in Saint James's Park, sleeping rough and begging. On August 1, she'd had enough of sleeping in the open with the unusually chill nights and the rain. Wanting to avoid entering the workhouse, she moved east and made a compromise: she would stay in the Grays Inn Workhouse casual ward in Holborn. Although an outdoor facility, the ward had a roof to keep out the rain. Following two wet, chill nights, sleeping in a stall padded thinly with damp, loose hay, Polly told herself she'd had enough of the workhouse entirely. She removed to Wilmott's lodging house in Thrawl Street, Spitalfields.

The deputy of the common lodging, Mr. Bonfils, informed her that for the rate of four pence per night, Polly would share a bed with four other women. One of them, a woman about thirty-five years old, with dark, curly hair, busied herself scrubbing the floor with a wet coarse rag as Polly arrived in the room.

"Emily Hollund," the woman said, looking up from her work.

"Polly Nichols."

Raw-boned and pale, her hands red and her face splotched bright pink, Emily looked worn down, yet the face she presented was warm and friendly.

"I'll not keep others' pets for them, if I can help it," Emily said with mock outrage. Seeing the question in Polly's eyes, the woman added, "Chat, vermin, lice!"

Polly smiled and they both chuckled.

The bed had been stripped of its mattress and bedclothes, presumably by Emily. A bucket, containing water and another rag, rested on the floor beside her. Polly got down on her knees, took the wet rag from the bucket, and joined in.

"Thank you for your help."

"You're welcome."

Emily stopped scrubbing for a moment and said, "Perhaps we can help each other further. Are you looking for work?"

"Yes."

"We will go our separate ways, but if we should meet each day to have a meal and share what has happened, we'll feel better about our efforts."

Polly smiled. As she realized that she liked the woman, she became suspicious; was Emily in fact Mr. Macklin trying to lull her into a position of trust?

"Two o'clock in the afternoon in the kitchen downstairs?" the woman asked.

No, Polly told herself, *the demon would never be able to keep such a friendly face.*

"Yes," she said.

Emily smiled and returned to her scrubbing.

"Thank you," Polly said. She desperately needed a friend. She assumed that no one who knew her history cared about her, except, possibly, Papa. Scrubbing away at the corner of the floor, she thought about all that she'd done to hurt others. She remembered Papa saying that she'd got what she deserved. He was right, of course. Strangely, within the discouraging thoughts, she found encouragement: *Mr. Macklin would not still seek my soul if the Lord no longer valued my spirit. There must be some hope for me.*

* * *

Having met for midday meals over the course of three weeks, neither Polly nor Emily had had any good news about employment to share.

Sitting at the dining table in the kitchen of the common lodging, while the cook cleaned up around them, they talked quietly.

"Seems that getting a position is like wanting green eyes," Emily said, laughing. "There's no hope if you aren't born with them."

Polly smiled. Getting to know Emily had been a pleasure. She had an odd way of looking at the world that gave her words an unusual humor. Polly liked the idea of having a friend and confidante, and wanted to talk openly about her thoughts of resorting to prostitution, but she feared Emily might not receive them well.

"I'm thinking I should do well to take a room in the White House in Flower and Dean Street," Emily said. "As netherskens go, there is no worse, yet it costs little and there a woman might share a bed with a man."

Surprised, Polly hesitated, then asked, "Do you mean a client?"

"Yes." Emily chuckled.

Polly relaxed, and let go of her fear. "I thought I might turn to that too, since my funds are all but exhausted. What's the cost of the rooms?"

"A penny to hold the room, four pence for the night. The rooms have no window and hardly any door. The bedding is on the floor and wide enough for only one person. Of course, when there are two, one will be on top of the other." Emily laughed.

Surprised by the woman's enthusiasm, Polly decided that her friend looked for the best, even in the worst situations, an admirable trait.

She could not match Emily's good cheer. Prostitution was a last resort, and the White House didn't sound good. Still, the accommodations had to be better than sleeping rough.

Emily's eyes became wide and she smiled. "If we should meet nightly—"

Knowing what was coming, Polly interrupted. "As we've done in the day while looking for employment?"

Emily nodded and grinned. "—we will feel better about our efforts."

Polly nodded too. "Yes."

"We'll be out late," Emily said, "past when the pubs close."

"We want to give time for meeting and satisfying clients," Polly said, "so if we set a fixed hour to meet, one of us might miss it. I should worry if you didn't turn up."

"As I make rounds in search of clients," Emily said, "I always end up back at the grocer shop on the corner of Whitechapel Road and Osborn Street. You might do the same. If I saw you there at least once a night, I'd know you were safe, and that someone looked out for me."

"Still, I might worry if I didn't see you all night."

"If that happens, we meet at the latest time and walk back to the White House together."

"What should that time be?"

"Two o'clock in the morning."

Polly thought about that for a moment and nodded. She smiled to see Emily grin.

The woman clearly liked Polly.

She likes me because she doesn't know me.

Polly's craving for alcohol had returned and increased daily. Even though drinking would further tempt the Bonehill Ghost, she had assumed she'd take up the habit again so she could stomach the clients. Having divined Mr. Macklin's method for locating the soul, and surviving his worst attack so far, she tried to tell herself she could prevail again, but she had no idea what his next attempt might bring.

If she did drink, Emily might see the unlikable Polly.

If she knew me like my family does, like I do, she wouldn't care for me at all. She trusts I'm likable. She doesn't think I've done terrible things. As perhaps God does, she sees something good in my spirit.

Polly decided that enduring the clients sober might be a worthwhile sacrifice in order to have and keep a friend.

If that's all it takes, then why haven't I always done that? She didn't have to destroy Tom's love for her. Polly knew better than to drink with him, and did it anyway. Perhaps since she'd always eventually returned to drink, she'd thought there was no escape, and therefore no real purpose in prolonging the agony of unsatisfied need. Yes, and she'd been unable to see beyond that to believe she could change.

Yet things were *good when I wasn't drinking, and the need did lessen.* How could she prove to herself a willingness to avoid alcohol?

By staying away from it long enough that it's no longer a part of me. Yes, the only way was to see herself differently by becoming someone else, a person she might care enough about to treat well.

The solution came easily enough. *Just don't drink again—Ever!* She had some hope that continued abstinence might eventually ward off Mr. Macklin.

Despite that, Polly couldn't decide whether she'd commit to it. She wanted a drink even as she considered giving it up.

Emily brushed bread crumbs from the worn tabletop into her hands and ate them. Polly swallowed the last of her coffee, grounds and all.

O Lord, if Emily must suffer as I have, allow her to keep her humor. Amen.

40
Temperance

On Thursday, August 24, Polly hurried across Whitechapel Road to get out of the way of a temperance procession. She gained the footway on the opposite side of the road too late. The group of mostly women, several hundred of them, having entered the road at Osborne Street, blocked traffic and pedestrians alike. Men and women following along the footway on either side of the road shouted obscenities and insults at the procession. Within moments the lane was clogged.

Jostled along with the crowd, Polly watched the parade flow around a carriage stopped dead in the road. "Out of the way," shouted the coachman driving the vehicle. The lady seated calmly behind the coachman said something Polly couldn't hear. The coachman dropped the reins, folded his arms and sat silently, looking defeated.

Based on the quality of the clothing worn by many among the procession, Polly knew that some of the women came from a higher station. Rarely had she stood shoulder to shoulder with such finery. Distracted by the beautiful clothing, she stumbled along.

A woman clutching a Bible to her breast as she marched glared at Polly.

A banner, bearing the words, DRINKING LEADS TO NEGLECT OF DUTY AND MORAL DEGRADATION, flapped in the wind. The two women holding it aloft struggled to maintain their grip. The banner beyond that read, DRUNKARD, YOU ROB YOUR CHILDREN.

The slogans stung, as Polly thought both statements reflected her own failings.

Reading the next banner, Polly's heart thumped painfully in her chest. "DON'T LET THE DEMON RUIN YOUR LIFE."

He was here, she knew it. Mr. Macklin hid among the parade and would grab for her any moment. She had to get out of the crowd. Flailing, she pushed forward.

A plump woman in black silk satin spun on Polly with outrage. "Mind your elbows!" she said.

Startled, Polly took a step back and blundered into the person behind her. She heard a sharp cry of pain, and turned to see a woman bent over and straining to move forward. Polly tried to see the woman's face, but the brim of a straw bonnet obscured her view.

"My ankle," the woman said.

Hearing the female voice put away some of Polly's wariness, yet she feared that the turn of events was still somehow a ruse by the Bonehill Ghost.

Knowing she'd harmed the woman, Polly tried to lift her. "Take my arm," she said.

The woman grasped Polly's right hand and shoulder and leaned on her. Together they struggled to move through the marching bodies toward the edge of the procession. Gaining the footway, they pressed forward out of the gently buffeting current of humanity until they met the brick wall of a building. Polly leaned back against the hard, gritty bricks. As the woman stood upright her black straw bonnet tilted back and revealed the face of Mrs. Hooks.

"Mary!" she said.

The coincidence of meeting the master blacksmith's wife in the workhouse infirmary, compounded with the present encounter, brought Polly's suspicions to a boil. She glanced at the woman's warm expression without looking her directly in the eyes, yet saw Mr. Macklin in Mrs. Hooks's features no better than she had back at the infirmary. The immediate fear dropped off. Even so, Polly wanted to get away, and a moment passed before she recognize that shame drove the desire. Mrs. Hooks, a member of the Temperance Society, knew Polly to be a drunk!

"Thank you, love," Mrs. Hooks said, leaning back against the wall.

"A pleasure to see you, Mrs. Hooks. I'm so sorry I stepped on you. You'll be fine if you rest here a bit. I must leave you now. I-I have to, uh, find something to eat." She tried to pull away, but Mrs. Hooks held on.

"Please help me reach a quieter place to rest. I fear my ankle will turn again if I'm not careful. We could take luncheon together. Allow me to buy you a meal."

Although she had great respect for Mrs. Hook's generous nature, Polly didn't want to sit and talk with a Bible thumper. She felt hungry, though, and a meal paid for was as good as money in her hand.

She looked at the signage along the street and saw the Dolphin public house less than fifty paces away. She knew they had a luncheon bar in the lower class section. The thought of a cold chop made her mouth water. "I don't suppose a pub would do," she said.

"I'm no teetotaler," Mrs. Hooks said. She nodded with a grin.

Polly relaxed, and smiled. The procession had thinned, the

end of it in sight. Carefully, the two women made their way to the pub. By the time they entered and found seats, Mrs. Hooks seemed to walk much more comfortably.

The place had the stale, yeasty smell of alcohol that tickled at the edges of Polly's desire. She pushed the urge away and said, "You sit and rest while I get something for you at the luncheon bar. They have pork pies and plates of hot meat. They have chops, vegetables, and bread."

"A cold chop and bread, I think." Mrs. Hooks handed Polly a shilling, which she accepted with another flinch of shame. "A glass of water would be good too."

Polly got the same for herself. She paid the publican, and carried the meal to the table where Mrs. Hooks waited patiently, apparently content with her own company. Polly had two conflicting hopes as she handed over what remained of the shilling, a mere two pence: that Mrs. Hooks would tell her to keep the money and that the woman would accept the coins without any reaction. The latter being the case, Polly relaxed again and sat.

The two women occupied themselves with their meal for a time. Mrs. Hooks set down her utensils before she'd finished her plate. "You look like you're feeing much better than when last I saw you. I'm glad to see it."

Having abstained from drinking for a time, Polly knew she presented herself in a decent light. She also knew the image to be a sham. Just thinking about the woman assessing her brought back the throat-tightening shame. She set down her fork and knife as well, and lowered her gaze, her eyes lighting upon the ragged cuffs of her threadbare bodice with the stained undersleeves poking out from underneath. She knew the state of her clothing reflected that of her life.

"I am better," she said simply. Polly wanted to ask Mrs.

Hooks what she might know about Tom Dews, yet she still didn't want the man to find her. The memories of how Polly had harmed him remained painful. "But I've made a ruin of my life with drink." She'd said the words quietly, and Mrs. Hooks didn't respond immediately. As the moments passed, Polly began to hope that the woman might not have heard her. She glanced around the room at the other diners, men and women eating, drinking, talking, laughing. Seeing smiles, she had a sense that life went on without her, while she remained trapped within a cocoon of her shame and regret.

"Please don't think I wanted you here to talk about drinking," Mrs. Hooks said. "I am for the Temperance Society. I am not *with* them. I believe they mean well and will do some good, but many of the women are insufferable, haughty haybags who choose not to see how hard life is for those of a lower station, let alone the unfortunate."

She laughed, and Polly looked up. She felt a smile grow on her face, despite her embarrassment.

"I don't begrudge anyone a little comfort," Mrs. Hooks said. "My husband has a dram of whiskey every evening and no more. You don't have to explain yourself to me. I will listen, though, if you'd like to talk about it."

Again, Polly became aware that the woman gave with no anticipation of gain. Once more, she found herself speaking quietly. "I cannot have just one, and so I am better when I don't drink."

"I've known others who feel the same way. They say they are trapped. It must be a frightful way to feel. Can you do without?"

Polly realized she wasn't on the defense, and answered honestly, "For a time. The desire comes back."

Mrs. Hooks reached across the table to take Polly's hands.

"You are a beautiful woman with life ahead of you. You can choose your own path. We all despair of a better way to get by at times and do things we regret. That doesn't mean that's all we have to offer life or each other. After I lost my mum and dad, I had nothing in the world but my uncle Jack. He was a kidsman. I joined his street company of eight or ten children. We were all around ten years of age. He called us the Buzzing Mites. We fell upon the old, robbed them, and took what we stole to Uncle Jack. He fed us, and we moved around, to keep clear of the constables."

Polly knew she gaped at the woman, and smoothed her features so as to not offend. She would never have believed Mrs. Hooks had such a background if the words hadn't just spilled from the woman's mouth.

"After we grievously harmed an old man and he died shortly thereafter, I left Uncle Jack behind. I thought the shame of what I had done would destroy everything good in my life. I was wrong. Once I tried to do what I saw as good, my days got better. I have had my share of suffering, and even with that, life has been good. We can start again, anytime, and be who we wish to be. It's not easy, yet it's easier if you're not bullied by the drink."

Although Polly wanted to accept what the woman said, she had difficulty believing that change could come so easily. Surely, after all she'd done, God would not allow the good in Polly's life until she had paid for her sins with sufficient suffering. Just how much she must endure, Polly didn't know.

With all that, she could see that Mrs. Hooks, a good woman with a troubled past, clearly didn't feel superior to anyone. Polly found herself looking upon her as an equal, and that provided a sense of hope. She didn't know what to say but, "Thank you."

Mrs. Hooks squeezed Polly's hands, released them, and stood. She tested her ankle. "It's not bad," she said. "I must go, or my husband will worry."

Out front of the pub, as they parted company, Polly gave Mrs. Hooks a fragile, uncertain smile. With a slight limp, the woman crossed Whitechapel Road and continued south. Again, she'd left a strong impression, just like she'd done in the workhouse infirmary. This time, though, Polly would think long and hard about the conversation before deciding what Mrs. Hooks meant. Something about her words tugged at Polly's notion of being cocooned within her own remorse. If she encouraged that tugging, a tear might form in the cocoon itself. Then, like a moth, Polly might emerge a changed being.

41
The Price of Solace

On Sunday, August 26, Polly and Emily each paid a penny to hold a room at the White House. Polly looked in on her room. A rancid smell of rubbish allowed to ferment greeted her when she opened the small door. Although not quite as tight as she'd pictured from Emily's description, the room would easily provoke claustrophobia. Stains of various kinds streaked and mottled the walls. The bedding, coarse gray-striped ticking filled loosely with straw and stiffened with mildew and old sweat, lay in a jumble on the floor.

The two women left the White House, and sat together in a tavern for a light meal of bread and cheese. Emily had a glass of bitter. Polly abstained in the face of powerful craving.

Once they'd finished most of their meal, Emily looked at Polly earnestly. "For some time now, I've needed someone to look after, someone who would also help look after me. I lost my husband, Devin, to drink. He stays at another doss house in Flower and Dean Street. He's of little help to me—a shilling from his army pension at the end of each month, is all—and I am tired of being alone."

Polly noted that Emily had only the one glass of bitter.

She isn't against drink. Still, I shall not feel good allowing her to see me drink.

"Most everyone I know looks out for themselves alone," Emily said. "I'm glad we found each other, and that you're willing to help and be helped. The world has grown so much more dangerous than when I was a child."

Emily looked upon her with such trust and spoke to her so warmly, that Polly felt as if she'd gained a sister. The woman clearly felt they had much in common. Emily needed Polly to be her friend, confidante, and protector, and offered the same in return. Polly knew that two women against the dangers of London didn't amount to much, but their combined strength had to be better than what she'd had. As alone as she'd been for so long, strangely even while with those she loved, Polly valued the offer highly and wanted to be worthy of it.

She resolved that she would indeed give up drink. That had to be done if she wanted to break from her cocoon and have a good life. She'd gone long periods without alcohol before, and knew that she could give it up for good. Polly would prove her worth to Emily, and therefore to herself. She imagined that with the confidence that would give her, she might also then prove herself to Papa, and eventually to her children. She might even become worthy of all that the Heryfords did to protect her. Somehow, she would find a way to gain her family's trust and to make up for all the ways she'd wronged them. These thoughts came on with such clarity and purpose, and contrasted so greatly with the odd thinking and poor decision-making of her time with the Cowdreys, that Polly looked back over the summer in wonder at her bizarre behavior. Even so, something stood in her way.

I must not only quit drinking, I must also find a way to better myself so that I will not go back to it.

Yes, something within Polly stood in her way. She became determined to ferret it out and be done with it.

She grasped Emily's hands across the table. "We *will* help each other," she said.

Emily squeezed Polly's hands. "We can but try."

They left the tavern, and set out in opposite directions along Osborn Street to secure clients.

* * *

Keeping in mind that the Bonehill Ghost could change form, and had turned up even when Polly was sober, she reminded herself to avoid looking her clients in the eye as she resumed soliciting.

On Thursday, August 30, Polly went to her room at the White House about four o'clock in the afternoon with a young Irish client. The room was paid up until five o'clock, after which she'd have to pay a penny to hold the room for the night or get out.

While thrusting himself into her, the Irishman explored her torso and head with his mouth, nuzzling and licking her face and breasts. When he pulled back a bit to look her in the face, she immediately looked away. He seemed to think little of her avoidance and went back to working on her breasts. Moments later, he pulled back again to look at her and she responded the same as before.

Defiantly, he twisted about, trying to catch her gaze, yet she kept her eyes turned away.

"Why won't you look at me?" he asked, his face red with outrage.

"I'm sorry, sir," Polly said, "I can't."

"Do I offend you?" He seemed to have forgotten they engaged in an intimate act.

"*My* shame," Polly said, thinking the simple response would suffice.

"I require you should look at me," he said, his spittle peppering her face. "I cannot find release without it."

Polly feared the worst: She'd become trapped in the tight space with the demon. Mr. Macklin was Irish! How had she forgotten that? He'd finally found a way to pin her with his gaze, but she would not give up her soul without a fight.

"No!" Polly shouted and tried to push back. Although flimsy, the wall behind her held firm. She had no way to escape from the angry monster.

He reared back and boxed her right ear, as Bill had done to her left ear on two occasions. Polly cried out with the pain and looked up. The eyes appeared blue, not red. She squinted against the agony in her head.

"Open them wider if you don't want more."

Preferring the risk of looking the Irishman in the eye to prolonging the man's abuse, Polly opened her eyes wider and softened her expression.

Within moments, the man writhed in an ecstasy of release.

She'd been fortunate; he was merely an angry man, not the demon. He paid her, backed out of the room and left.

Polly couldn't hear with her right ear. Experience told her that the hearing would eventually return.

As she lay in the fetid bedclothes, giving time for the agony in her head to subside, an uncharacteristic thought occurred to her: *I punish myself.*

For most of her life, Polly had believed that all her suffering, mild or harsh, had been in some way retribution for her sins. She'd thought that if God were not doling out her punishments, He certainly allowed for them by demonic forces. Since Mr. Macklin had not shown up to deliver each blow, the Lord must have also permitted the natural misfortunes of circumstance to find her easily. Yet when she'd sought His grace, she'd never seen any indication that He welcomed her efforts. Never had there been any respite from hardship or trouble.

Not all suffering is punishment, and most of the misfortune I brought upon myself. If the Lord values my soul, it could be He has forgiven me. Perhaps I have His grace already, and the change Mrs. Hooks spoke of is indeed possible.

The card from which Polly had read the penitent prayer had rotted away long ago, but she still carried the words in her head and heart. If God had indeed forgiven Polly, her torments were punishments of her own choosing. Her inability to forgive herself, and nothing more, was what encouraged the Bonehill Ghost. Within that notion, she felt a kernel of truth wriggling to break out.

Polly knew that seeing herself in a better light was the key to improving her life. To gain that brighter view, she'd have to be forgiven for many things.

Her need for an escape from the troubles and pains of life had led her to alcohol. She'd been dishonest and scheming, not to hurt anyone, but to maintain an avenue to alcohol as her means of flight. Even as a healthy young woman, doing piece work, she'd needed that escape—possibly more so then.

My means of escape trapped me long ago.

At present, what led her to drink as much as anything else was the forgetfulness intoxication provided; a much-needed respite from a memory overflowing with her failures to herself and her wrongdoing to others.

Yes, she'd have to be forgiven for many things, but perhaps most importantly, she'd have to find a way to pardon herself.

How can I, after all my grasping, greedy, uncaring deeds?

Others had been forgiving. Mrs. Hooks could easily see what Polly had done to herself. Surely the Heryfords knew she'd had a hand in creating the strife in her home, yet they defended her because what Bill had done to her was wrong. Mrs. Hooks and the Heryfords seemed to believe Polly capable of goodness, whatever her past—a past they never even paused to consider. Their unquestioning acceptance of her spoke of a greater forgiveness.

The more she thought about the idea that God had forgiven her, the more excited she became, until, quite unexpectedly, notion became conviction.

My torments are my own, and that means I can do away with them. I must begin to expect the best from myself as Mrs. Hooks and the Heryfords did.

How?

Again, the matter came to how she saw herself.

Alcohol is not the problem. The need to be comforted is the heart of my troubles.

She wondered if the solace she'd sought for so long in the bottle might be had from another source, one without a corrupting influence.

She'd got something like that in her relationship with Tom, some hope for the future perhaps.

When she'd begun her marriage, Polly had hope. In her experience with Bill, she hadn't set out with dishonest intent. When their union began, she'd believed herself capable of good. The grind of life, including the unexpected cruelty of her husband, and the need for escape had taken the hope away.

In a moment of wanting more than anything to have that hopefulness back, she realized the solace she'd always craved *was* hope. Yet she knew that what had allowed for such optimism was a dangerous naivety. Could one be had without the other?

Yes, if I choose to see the good and don't allow myself to be driven by dread. She thought of Emily's desire to find the good, even in the worst situations.

Polly knew that to prove herself capable of that, she must embrace what small gains she could to improve her life and her nature. *I can build hope by holding to the goodness of life whatever the hardships, just as Mrs. Hooks said she'd done. Time will give me what I need, if I persist.*

Eventually, I'll find a way to forgive myself.

Despite the ache in her ear, Polly found her hopeful thoughts exhilarating, and she became determined to find a way out of the life she'd created. Even so, a surge of pain in her ear hampered her ability to focus on the matter.

She writhed in the filthy bedding, trying to rub off her agony.

Further questions and answers would have to wait. Polly needed distraction. She got up and paid the Indian deputy of the lodging house a penny to hold her room, then left the White House with the goal of meeting up with Emily at the corner of Whitechapel Road and Osborn Street.

Even with her new pledge of abstinence, as she waited on the corner, trying to stay out of the rain under the overhanging upper floor of a building, Polly did little but think about having a drink for the pain in her ear. While she did her best to resist the idea, she was glad she'd said nothing about her drinking or her decision to quit to Emily. The woman had no expectations in that regard.

42
Storm

Lightning flashed and thunder boomed in the distance. The rain came down in sheets, thinned to a drizzle, and then became heavy again. Miserable, Polly waited for Emily on the corner at dusk. The pain in her right ear sharpened each time the wind blew across the opening. She cringed with the deep ache, and dissuaded herself from going for a drink twice. If she did have a drink for the pain, she decided, that wouldn't be the same as seeking comfort from intoxication. Still, she'd resist the urge as long as possible.

A horse-drawn vehicle, perhaps an omnibus, approached the intersection, moving along Osborn Street at a fast clip. The driver seemed to have little control of his team of horses. Likely, they were spooked by the thunder and lightning. Polly checked to see if anything came toward the crossing along Whitechapel Road. Although relieved to find she wasn't in the line of oncoming disaster, she backed up against the nearest building to avoid getting splashed as the massive carriage drew near.

The passengers on the vehicle's roof looked to be miserable in the rain, their heads down and shoulders hunched. One among them, a woman, cried out and stood as her bonnet was caught by the wind and thrown down at Polly's feet. The woman seemed to argue with the driver as the vehicle passed through the intersection and kept going.

Polly bent to pick up the bonnet. All black and made of straw, with trimmings of velvet, the stylish little cap seemed none the worse for exposure to the weather. As the pretty thing reminded her of the one she'd seen Mrs. Hooks wearing just a few days ago, she realized that her new sense of hope had begun during her conversation with the woman.

Mrs. Hooks has sent me this hat, she thought. Despite her pain, she smiled as she took the foolish notion even further. *It's a sign of the good that will come into my life now that I am changing.*

She removed her threadbare and hopelessly stained cloth bonnet, then shook the water off the straw one and placed it on her head.

Finally, about eight o'clock in the evening, Polly's head and heart lifted to see her friend appear among the foot traffic along the street.

Emily seemed happy to see her as well. "What a pretty new bonnet."

"Thank you."

"Have you done well?"

"Yes," Polly said. "I've held my room, but no more. I do have my night's doss." She had indeed earned her four pence along with the damage to her ear, and currently had seven pence in her pocket. She wouldn't trouble her friend with a full re-counting of events.

"You can earn it again before bedtime. Let's have a drink at the Frying Pan."

Polly instantly weighed the risk of another visit from the Bone-hill Ghost against the need for relief from her pain. After all, Mr. Macklin didn't show up every time she drank. Emily's suggestion had quickly become permission. "Yes, I'll have a drink."

Troubled to have so easily dropped her commitment to abstinence, Polly told herself that if she expected to quit drinking, she'd need a good night's sleep, something that would be impossible while enduring the pain in her ear.

"Tomorrow is the last day of the month," Emily said. "I'll meet with Devin and he'll give me a shilling of his pension. I'll take you to the Beehive and we'll have a good meal."

Polly nodded at the invitation. She remembered that August 31 was the birthday given her by Martha Combs, Sarah Brown, and Bernice Godwin, so long ago.

Yes, tomorrow I'll be reborn. I'll be able to commit to abstinence then.

She almost expressed her thoughts to Emily, then decided against bringing attention to the anniversary since the date wasn't her real birthday.

The two women set out during a lull in the rainstorm to walk to the Frying Pan pub.

* * *

The going rate for a quartern of gin was three pence. Polly quaffed the four ounces in one draft.

"Careful," Emily said, "you don't want to find yourself foolish. You ate your supper?"

"Yes," Polly lied.

"Let me get you another," Emily said, "and then I'm off to make my rounds." She fetched two more quarterns.

Polly paced herself while she talked with her friend.

Finally, about half-past ten o'clock, Emily got up to leave. "Shall I see you in a few hours?"

"Yes, about two in the morning at our usual spot."

Emily ran out into the rain and disappeared in the gloom. A flash of lightning illuminated her briefly as she moved south along Brick Lane.

Polly quaffed her gin, and got up to fetch another. The pain in her ear had diminished with each glass, but not by much. She sat for a long while, nursing her drink, taking little notice of the activity within the pub as she looked out the window, watching the discouraging rain. By midnight she'd finished her glass of gin and knew that if she didn't buy another drink, the management would eventually ask her to leave. As the rain lightened to a drizzle, she saw a black man standing in the wetness out front of the Frying Pan.

Polly got up, exited the establishment, and approached the man. She avoided looking him directly in the eyes. "Will you take four pence?" he asked with a West Indian accent.

"Yes," Polly said. "Shall we go to my room?"

The man pointed across the street to a small tool house beside an entrance to a back court. The structure had a broad eave and a roof of tin. Rain water poured off the metal in a sheet that provided a thin curtain of privacy. "Few will be out in this weather." He gestured up and down the empty, rain-soaked street.

"What if the rain slackens?" Polly asked.

"I like the risk."

Polly and the man slipped beneath the curtain of water. He turned her to the wall.

Good, she thought, *he won't expect me to look him in the eyes.*

He opened his trousers, lifted her skirt and satisfied himself. Giving her a kiss on the cheek, he pressed four coins into her hand and walked away, adjusting his clothing.

The transaction had been so painless and quick, Polly had confidence she could readily repeat the process. She walked back into the Frying Pan for another quartern of gin, and sat drinking the sharp liquid until the management of the pub began to give her the evil eye.

Exiting the establishment during a lull in the rain, she noted an orange glow in the sky to the southeast. Some part of the city burned.

The downpour increased and Polly became chilled to the bone. Hoping for a warm, dry place to wait out the storm without having to return to the White House, Polly walked west along Thrawl Street to Wilmott's lodging house, and knocked on the kitchen door.

Mr. Bonfils answered. He looked her up and down, asked, "Do you have your doss?"

"Yes," Polly said. The lie didn't sit well with her. She had only one penny in her pocket. Having paid for the room to be held at the White House, she had no intention of staying the night at Wilmott's.

Although drunk, she knew that if she had any hope of expecting the best from herself, as Mrs. Hooks and the Heryfords had, she'd have to become honest with herself and others. That sort of integrity would be required to reach the life she imagined. Yes, she must stop lying, but as with the drink, she would begin her abstinence tomorrow.

As soon as Polly entered, Mr. Bonfils held out his hand to receive payment.

"I hoped you'd allow me to stay and warm myself till the rain is past." She saw two raggedy women and an old man seated at one of the tables within.

"I cannot allow that," Mr. Bonfils said, folding his arms.

Polly gave a false smile and touched her head. "I'll earn my doss soon enough, now as I have such a jolly bonnet."

Mr. Bonfils scowled at her.

Realizing that the alcohol had loosened her tongue and that she'd as much as admitted that she was soliciting, Polly turned away and exited, ashamed.

She heard a church bell strike half past one o'clock in the morning as she headed south along Brick Lane to where the thoroughfare became Osborn Street and intersected with Old Montague Street. She found another client, a short, dark-haired fellow in a naval uniform, outside the Bell pub on the corner.

She avoided looking him in the eyes as she said, "Miss Laycock, four pence."

He looked her up and down as Polly stood with as much grace as her intoxication allowed.

"Perhaps," he said.

"My room?"

"So your toughs can roll me? No crinkum crankum is worth that. You come with me or there's no deal."

Polly agreed with some trepidation, and he led her east along Old Montague Street. *If he is Mr. Macklin come for another try, I'll—*

Polly had rarely allowed herself to dwell on what life would be like without a soul, yet a distracting question had formed unbidden. *Would I feel any different beyond relief that the fight was over?*

She remembered Sarah Godwin's description of one of the girls whose soul Mr. Macklin had taken. *She can no longer speak, and does nothing but stare into the distance all day.*

Yes, I would be different; I'd have no hope of reward after death. Somehow, the notion that she'd no longer need to redeem herself was a far worse immediate concern than the loss of reward.

With nothing to lose, my selfishness might lead me to terrible criminal acts. The daydreams she'd had as a young woman of becoming a palmer and a dragsman were tame compared to what she saw as possible in a future with no soul. Without constraint, she might murder to gain money or something as simple, though necessary, as food and shelter. Polly turned quickly away from the thoughts.

When the Bonehill Ghost came for Polly again, she could only hope he had no new tricks. If she survived and continued over the next few years to change for the better, she was confident that he'd lose interest in her soul.

Until then, I must face whatever he brings to the fight.

The sailor gripped her hand at the entrance to Green Dragon Place—a thin back lane she knew ran south to Whitechapel Road—and led her into the alley. The lane narrowed and became a passage underneath the second floor of a brick building. With the late hour, no one was about. The sailor took Polly quietly from the rear, while standing in the low passage. Upon his release, his muffled cries echoed eerily along the brick tunnel.

He paid Polly and she headed for the Bell and spent another three pence on a quartern of gin. The Bell's gin seemed stronger.

Three pence remained in her pocket. One more client and she would have her doss and enough remaining to buy one more drink for the pain.

The last drink I'll ever have, she told herself. Despite her drunken state, she remained committed to quitting forever and cleaning up her life. She felt the hope stirring within her, waiting for the pain in her ear to subside before helping her to move from the destruction of her old life into the new.

Even with all her hopeful thoughts, she knew that after each client, she'd had her doss and could have returned to the White House and slept. The pain in her head notwithstanding, Polly knew she'd prolonged her last night of drinking because she wanted more alcohol. Still, she would not allow that knowledge to dampen her enthusiasm for tomorrow.

43
One Last Client

S taggering drunk, Polly made her way along Osborn Street to Whitechapel Road to meet Emily. Thankfully, the rain had died down. She hugged herself against the chill in the air, thinking the night unusually cold for August. Much of the summer had been unseasonably cool.

Emily waited for her, a concerned look on her face. "You're in a bad way," she said, moving to help support her. "We must get you to your room right away."

Polly pulled back and leaned against the wall of the nearest building. "I don' have my doss. I've got it three times already and spent it."

"I would offer you help, but I've had little luck tonight. You must have got all the clients there are. The deputy at the White House knows us too well or we could double up in my room. You know he won't allow it."

"Won' be long before I have my doss again," Polly said.

"Were you here earlier?"

"No."

"I were afraid I'd missed you. I went to see the dry docks fire." Emily pointed southeast and her face forgot her concern for Polly for a time. "I've seen blazes before, but I never knew fire could become so big, so alive. It flew high into the sky. The rigging of a ship were caught up in it, and sparkled like a spider web dripping with dew at sunrise. And, oh, the frenzy of firemen and their equipment as they hurried to put it out. You should have seen."

If Polly hadn't had her mind on finding her last client and earning her doss, she might have found the description fascinating.

A church bell began to strike, and the sound seemed to draw Emily back to the here and now. "That's the bell for half-past two," she said. "Let me help you."

"No, I'll do for myself. I mus' take greater pride in my own efforts if I e'spect to get on in life."

"But you can hardly stand."

"Tired is all." Polly succeeded in straightening and standing properly on her feet. Willing herself to become steady so Emily would not worry, Polly looked her friend in the eye and said carefully, "I will suffer through this night on my own. Tomorrow is the beginning of a new day for me." She wanted to say that her birthday, August 31, had come. Then, concerned her friend might make a fuss about it, she thought better of the idea. "I must be allowed to get there on my own."

Emily looked at her doubtfully, but finally nodded her head.

Polly turned and walked away along Whitechapel Road toward the northeast, doing her best to move steadily for Emily.

* * *

Polly spoke to three men as she made her way along Whitechapel Road. None were interested in visiting with Miss Laycock.

She continued along the footway, moving in the direction

of the London Hospital. Although she continued the search for a client, her thoughts returned to considering her future: *How do I forgive myself?* Somehow, she knew that to be the hardest part of the change to come. Indeed, the change could not come without it. *How can I expect the best from Polly Nichols, as Mrs. Hooks and the Heryfords did?*

What if I'm sober, and still find no work?

Can I forgive myself if I'm still a whore? Can I forgive myself while living in the misery of the workhouse?

She tried to shake off the worry. *I mustn't let the questions discourage.*

Still, her mood darkened as she considered the depth of her drunkenness. With the excuse of the pain in her ear, she had returned so quickly, so readily to what she recognized as a wretched view of herself; one in which seriously weakening her senses and then wandering the dangerous streets had become reasonable. One or two drinks might have been prudent enough, but having become truly sodden, she knew, spoke of a desire for her own destruction. The inability to forgive herself drove the desire.

If I cannot forgive myself, my need to escape, to be comforted, will always damn me.

Polly knew she must find her own, personal absolution, but how?

On the south side of the road, the London Hospital loomed, dimly backlit by the orange glow of the two fires at the docks. As Polly approached the imposing structure, she imagined going in and finding help for her ear, but she hadn't the funds to pay a doctor. The clock above the building's entrance showed the time as ten minutes past three o'clock.

Polly turned her head quickly toward the sound of a door opening on the darkened western side of the building, and saw warm light emerge briefly from within. Moments later, she saw a dark figure walking toward Whitechapel Road along Turner Street.

Polly saw no one else. She crossed to the north side of the road. Something about the way the figure moved, with rapid, short steps, reminded Polly of Mr. Macklin's mechanical, mincing gait.

He would not catch her so easily. As she turned north into Thomas Street, the wind blew painfully across the opening of her right ear. She wrenched her head quickly out of the wind, then cringed and stumbled, experiencing severe vertigo. Dizzied and nauseated, she staggered toward the building on her right, holding out her hands to prevent running headlong into the structure. She heard footsteps approaching rapidly. Her vision spun and she couldn't see clearly.

"Let me help you," said a male voice.

She flinched violently when she felt the touch of hands upon her upper arms. "No!" she cried.

The hands let go, and she slumped against the brick wall of the building. She tried to make out the figure, but her vision twisted and turned. Polly couldn't make sense of what she saw.

"You can't see properly," he said, his accent strange. "I'll take you to hospital. It's just there. You'll see a doctor."

Polly turned her head away from the sound of his voice and shut her eyes. Even with them closed, she experienced the sickening dizziness and fought to keep the contents of her stomach.

The man didn't act like the drunken ghost, having none of the giddiness she'd previously seen in Mr. Macklin. Powerless to get away, she allowed him to take her by the arms and lift her to stand erect. He smelled of sulfur and soap.

If he is the demon, she thought, *he'll have a fight on his hands.*

Supporting her around the waist, he helped her to move along the pavement.

If he's a good Samaritan, perhaps he'll pay a doctor to heal my ear. A hospital bed would be better than the one at the White House.

She opened her eyes briefly several times as they moved. The glimpses she got of their surroundings were darker each time. "I don't see the gas lamps of Whitechapel Road."

"The front of the hospital building is closed at this hour," he said. "We must go 'round to the back entrance."

Polly's vision began to clear by degrees as she took frequent quick glances. Each time, her surroundings made more sense. They moved along a brick wall toward a gate. She thought they might have reached the back entrance to the hospital building.

At the gate, they stopped. She remained crouched, ready to flatten herself on the pavement should the vertigo return. Her vision had finally cleared. She saw nothing unusual: a back lane lined with brick structures choked with deep shadow.

"You'll feel much better once the doctor has seen you," he said, drawing Polly up to stand straighter.

He turned toward her, and she looked away just in case he was Mr. Macklin.

Then his hands took her neck in a hard, tightening grip.

He is the demon!

Keeping her eyes averted, Polly clawed at his hands, but gloves protected them. She kicked at his shins, and raised her knees violently toward his crotch, yet couldn't land a solid blow.

Pray for yourself!

She struggled against panic to find the words.

At long last, pray for yourself. Only God can save you now!

Polly couldn't muster the thoughts to form even a quick prayer.

If she caught his eye briefly, he might become distracted and let up on her neck. She opened her eyes and looked the man in the face.

His eyes *did not* glow red!

He's just a man!

Pray for him!

Still, she couldn't put together the words. Meaningless, they tumbled about in her head, and in that moment, she knew that words were all the prayers had ever been.

A scar on his forehead caught her eye, a flaw nearly identical to her own. The shiny oblong with a slight lip on one side gleamed in the wan light. He'd been damaged much the way she had.

Her throat spasmed in an agonizing effort to find air. She looked to the man with a pleading in her gaze, and saw deep into his eyes. The emotion within them was clearly born of great need. Desperation of some sort drove him to commit the hateful act.

His hands slipped briefly, allowing her a short breath of air. Frustration flashed in his features and his hands became tighter still.

Indeed, he *was* but a man, with all the emotion of a human being. Unstoppable desire forced him to act, much as her all-consuming needs had driven her.

She couldn't feel her body. Her thoughts became simple and elegant, as the darkness closed around her.

She *became* the man strangling Polly Nichols. She knew him as she knew herself.

Yes, he did a terrible thing, as she'd done terrible things.

We commit a dread, wicked deed.

Again, the question: *How can I forgive myself?*

No. How do we *forgive ourselves?*

The answer opened a door upon a moment of undiscovered peace.

By forgiving him.

Acknowledgments

This is a work of fiction. Although the novel is inspired by real historical events and actual human lives, the characters have been created for the sake of this story and are either products of the author's imagination or are used fictitiously. Any resemblance to actual events or locales or persons, living or dead, is entirely coincidental.

Thanks to Cameron Pierce, Kirsten Alene, Melody Kees Clark, Eric M. Witchey, Jill Bauman, Mark Edwards, Elizabeth Engstrom, Mark Roland, Frank Freemon, Simon Clark, David Nicholls, Garrett Cook, Pigg, Michael Green, and Matt Hayward.

About the Author

Author and illustrator, Alan M. Clark grew up in Tennessee in a house full of bones and old medical books. He is the author of seventeen published books, including ten novels, a lavishly illustrated novella, four collections of fiction, and a nonfiction full-color book of his artwork. As a visual artist, he has created illustrations for hundreds of books, including works of fiction of various genres, nonfiction, textbooks, young adult fiction, and children's books. Awards for his work include the World Fantasy Award and four Chesley Awards. Alan M. Clark and his wife, Melody, live in Oregon. www.alanmclark.com